McCAULEY'S WAR

CHARLIE HERRON

GUILDHALL PRESS

Published in July 2010

GUILDHALL PRESS
Unit 15, Ráth Mór Business Park
Bligh's Lane
Creggan
Derry
Ireland
BT48 0LZ

T: 00 44 28 7136 4413
E: info@ghpress.com
W: www.ghpress.com

The author asserts his moral rights in this work in accordance
with the Copyright, Designs and Patents Act 1998.

Designed by Kevin Hippsley/Guildhall Press
Copyright © Charlie Herron/Guildhall Press
Illustrations by Katie and Jamie Herron
Back cover image courtesy of Phil Cunningham

ISBN: 978 1 906271 31 2

This publication is available in various e-book formats
from www.ghpress.com.

A CIP record for this book is available from the British Library.

Guildhall Press gratefully acknowledges the
financial support of the Arts Council of Northern
Ireland as a principal funder under its Annual
Support for Organisations Programme.

About the Author

Born in Derry in 1935, with strong Donegal connections, Charlie Herron grew up in the Marlborough area of the city. Charlie was a keen footballer in his youth and his claim to fame remains his time with Derry City FC reserves in the mid-1950s. For many years principal of Foyle View School, in his retirement Charlie's love of spinning tall tales has stood him in good stead as a stalwart of the Colmcille Debating Society and as a four-time winner of the 'prestigious' Baron Von Munchausen competition. More recently known for his story-telling on local radio, Charlie continues to write with storylines never far removed from his native Derry and Donegal.

ACKNOWLEDGEMENTS

I would like to acknowledge with sincerest thanks all those who helped me get this novel into the light of day: my wife, Margaret, whose constant encouragement and support gave me the inspiration to stick with it; my daughters, Mary and Ciara, for their assistance with typing and editing the manuscript; my brother, Hugh, who read the first draft and gave me invaluable advice; and the rest of my family for their continued support of my writing efforts. Special thanks also to my granddaughters, Katie and Jamie, for their contribution to the novel's artwork.

Thanks also to Kate O'Halloran, Susan McReynolds and Colm Arbuckle, members of the BBC Radio Foyle team, past and present, who encouraged me to write and present my short stories on air, and gave me the idea of publishing my work; to Inishowen Community Radio and Highland Radio for allowing my stories to reach a wider audience; and to the dedicated staff of Guildhall Press for their professional and constructive advice and assistance.

Without everyone mentioned, this book would never have been published.

To Margaret,
With love and thanks

PROLOGUE

'He's all right, Kitty, look – he's coming round. His eyes are open.'

'God Almighty, what happened him, Barney?'

'He just fainted, Kitty, but he's all right now.'

'Dickie, Dickie.'

I could see my da staring down at me, calling my name. I couldn't say anything. I was paralysed. I couldn't talk. My lips wouldn't move. My mind could hear the bangs in the plots and see the flashes in the dark and the silhouettes running across the lane. And the dead B-man, lying on the turnips with a spade in his hand. And blood all over him.

CHAPTER 1

If Hitler Doesn't Do It, We'll Do It

'Dickie, Dickie McCauley, will ye stop swinging on that glass door this minute! Or you're in for it!'

Our Liam laughed when he heard my ma shouting from the kitchen at me. Actually, it was maybe more of a snigger. He was sitting on the bottom stair waiting on his turn to swing. I didn't stop right away because my ma always shouts when she's in a bad temper. She's called Kathleen, but everybody calls her Kitty. She even shouts at me when I'm not doing any swinging, or doing anything wrong at all, and I can't understand why. I mean, I could be sitting in the corner of the same room as her, reading the *Beano* or something, and she wouldn't even know I was there, and she'd still roar out as if I was still swinging on the glass door.

My ma is a lot like that these days and I blame it on my da, because Uncle Jimmy told me that my da is as thick as two planks. That's what Mr Philson says to us in school sometimes when we get things wrong. He says we're as thick as poundies as well. Uncle Jimmy said that thick as two planks was the same as thick as poundies. But I didn't think that was right because anybody should know that planks can be thin as well, even if there's two together, and poundies can be thin if you put milk and butter on them and squash them on your plate.

Mr Philson also called us Ballybunkumskites. I know how to spell Ballybunkumskites because Philson wrote it on the blackboard one day and we all had to write it out ten times – 'I am a Ballybunkumskite.' The Stupids in the back didn't have to write it out because they can't write. They just draw lines and make marks on pages and they never have to do any homework because they're stupid and Philson never says anything to them about it.

Uncle Jimmy is my ma's brother and he's not married or anything. He has a house in Donegal but when he's working in Derry he stays in our attic bedroom in Rosemount Terrace. He has a job buying and selling clothes round the houses in his blue van. I like Uncle Jimmy because he gives me a shilling sometimes and he gives me old books because he knows I like to read.

Uncle Jimmy bought my ma and da a big wooden wireless that lights up at the front and you can get all the different stations on it from all over the world. But I like to listen to the BBC and Radio Athlone because they play great music. My da's always listening to the news on it about the war. It began in 1939 when Adolf Hitler invaded Poland and has been going on for two years now to this very month, September.

I like my da most of the time because he never shouts at me like my ma does, even when he's drunk. It was him who showed me years ago how to hold the two handles of the glass door and wrap my legs round it and then push myself back and forward. My ma never shouts at our Liam, even when he's swinging on the handles, and she never shouts at my two big sisters, but she shouts at my da a lot when he's looking for money for drink. Things like: 'Barney, Barney, Barney, what am I going to do with you anyway? Ye have me heart broke, so ye have.'

The whole street must know by now that she never has enough money to pay the rent man and the milk man and the bread man. It really is very embarrassing sometimes.

My da's a docker, but he doesn't get work every day. He says it's because of the war. My ma says that the twins earn more in the shirt factory than he does and that isn't much. They're called Kate and Laura, and they've been making shirts since they left school two years ago. Kate and Laura are always shouting and arguing about something. One day when they were having a row, Kate threw a shoe at Laura. It missed but hit the glass door and cracked it and the crack is still there, but that was years ago.

I've been swinging on the glass door nearly all my life, but all the fuss from my ma lately is putting me off the notion anymore, and there's no fun in it if people are getting on to you all the time so I told Liam he could have his go now. He wasn't long in jumping up from the bottom stair and heading for the handles. I'm nine and Liam's only six. I taught him how to swing about three years ago and he does it more than me now.

I was halfway up the stairs when I heard my ma shouting again, 'Will ye get off that bloody door, Dickie! I'm warning ye for the last time. Oh! It's you, Liam. That's okay, Son, don't heed me, I thought it was that big brother of yours.'

And that's the way of it, so I just headed into the bedroom to read some comics that my pal Billy Burnside gave me. Billy gets a whole lot of comics from his ma and da and he gives them to me when he's finished with them.

Billy Burnside is a Protestant, but he's my best friend, even if he doesn't go to the same school as me. I go to St Eugene's Boys' School and he goes to the Model School. Billy lives four doors up from us and he invites me into his house sometimes. His ma is very nice. He calls her Mum and she gives me biscuits and cake and glasses of milk.

Billy's house is always very clean and tidy and there's a lovely smell of polish and perfume in it. Our house is just ordinary, with stuff all over the place. They have a tiled bathroom and real toilet paper and great towels. We only get toilet paper at Christmas and when Aunt Minnie is coming to visit us.

Aunt Minnie lives in the Free State and she's my ma's sister. She smuggles stuff across the border on the train from Donegal.

You can't get sugar and jam and things in the Six Counties because of the rationing. She was bringing up a turkey before last Christmas but the customs man spotted that she was very fat looking from the last time he had seen her. She had the turkey tied round her waist under her skirt. He took the turkey off her but the man didn't notice the two chickens up her blouse. My ma and da were laughing about it all, especially when Auntie Minnie said that she hoped the customs man choked on a turkey bone. I didn't understand why they were laughing. Big people are strange like that.

Billy Burnside's da is a sergeant in the RUC. That means he's a policeman and he gets well paid and he wears a gun in his holster. If I was a Protestant, I'd be a policeman when I grew up, but Catholics don't join the RUC because that's only for the Prods so they can defend their country.

But my da says that Ireland's not their country because they came over from England and Scotland hundreds of years ago and took over our houses and our land and everything. And they got all the best jobs so that they could afford to buy anything they wanted – like toilet rolls and biscuits and cakes and things – and the Catholics got nothing.

That's what my da told me when he came home drunk one night. He came into the house singing a song called *Kevin Barry*. It was about a boy from Dublin who was hanged by the British over twenty years ago because he shot a soldier. He was hanged on a Monday morning in a place called Mountjoy Jail and my da said he was proud of him because he didn't cry or anything before they killed him and he was only eighteen years old. And the gang Kevin Barry was in fought the British after that and chased them out of Ireland. But they didn't chase them out of the *whole* country, just the part across the border called the Free State.

So my da said there was still work to be done to get the rest of them out and if Hitler didn't do it, he would do it. Then he put his two fingers to his lips for me to be quiet, even though I

12

hadn't said anything, and he took me by the arm and pushed me up the stairs in front of him and into the bathroom. When he knelt down on the floor, I knelt down, too, thinking he might be starting the Rosary or something, but he reached under the bath and lifted the loose floorboard. I knew about the loose floorboard because I'd discovered it last year and that's where I hide my marbles and chestnuts in a jam jar in case my ma would find them in my bedroom and throw them out.

When my da put his hand under the bath, my heart was racing in case he would find the jam jar and give it to my ma because she would dump it, the mood she was in. But he lifted something else out wrapped in a brown oily cloth. He put it on the floor between us and began to open it.

Before I could see what was in it, he stopped and put his two fingers to his lips again. I knew this to be a secret kind of sign so I nodded and he bent forward towards the parcel again. I could smell the Guinness coming from his mouth and his hands were shaking; a big smile crossed his face as he lifted a gun from the dirty cloth. I stared at it and I felt a bit afraid.

'This is what's going to free Ireland,' he said, holding the gun towards me. 'Touch it, it won't bite now – but it soon will.'

I didn't know what he meant and I didn't know what to say.

'Touch it,' he said again. 'Isn't it a beauty?'

It was dark and shiny, a bit like the guns the cowboys had in the pictures. And it had a bigger handle than the police one in Billy's father's holster. I touched it with my finger.

'This'll make them shift,' he whispered to me, 'when the time's right; say nothing about it, Son. Don't tell anybody I showed it to you. Say nothing to your ma or the twins or to Uncle Jimmy; and nothing to Liam, do you hear me? It's *our* secret.' Before wrapping it up again in the brown cloth, he rubbed his fingers across the barrel of the gun.

After he had put it back in the space under the floorboard, he gave the wood a hard tap with the palm of his hand and turned

13

round to me. We were still on our knees, but he reached out his hand and shook mine the way big people do when they meet.

'Don't forget, Dickie, this is *our* secret,' he said again, and he tightened his grip on my hand. It was sore, but I didn't say anything. I was more afraid than sore because I knew that it was only supposed to be police and soldiers who had guns and they didn't hide theirs under floorboards. I knew my da wanted me to say something.

'If Hitler doesn't free Ireland, Da, you'll do it,' I said, and he tightened his grip even more. 'You'll soon shift them, Da.'

A smile crossed his face as we rose from the bathroom floor.

'Aye, you've got it, Dickie; if Hitler doesn't do it, we'll do it. We'll soon shift them, Son.' And the two fingers went to his lips again.

***

I read one of Billy's comics and did my homework. Liam was still swinging on the glass door downstairs: you could hear the hinges creaking. My da was always to put oil on them but he never did. Maybe if he oiled them my ma wouldn't hear me swinging. But I liked the creak so I was glad he didn't, and I was getting used to my ma shouting at me anyway. Besides that, I wouldn't have to listen to her for most of tomorrow, because Saturday's the day when our gang heads to Killea Reservoir. At least when the weather's good we do, and nobody knows that we go there. We're all sworn to secrecy.

I put the exercise book back in my schoolbag and the comics under the pillow on my side of the bed. Before going downstairs I looked out the window at the yard of the police barracks, just across the street. A policeman was putting some rubbish into a dustbin and I could see the gun in his holster. I thought of the one hidden under the bath; and I thought about Hitler and what he was going to do to help my da to shift the cops and all the British out of the Six Counties. And I thought about Billy. If his da was shifted, his ma would have to go, too, and so would

14

Billy. He was my best friend. Who would I get any comics from if Billy left?

I went downstairs: our Liam was still in the hall. My ma shouted, 'Dickie, Liam, your tea's ready!' We always got tea and a piece of bread and jam after school. 'And you'll have to hurry, Dickie, or you'll be late for Confession.'

Our class always went to Confession every Friday. You got rid of all your sins that way. I just had a few to tell this week, a couple of bad words and spitting on four people's faces. Liam didn't have to go to Confession yet. He'd be making his first Confession next year. He could curse as much as he wanted and spit on as many faces as he wanted, and it wouldn't be a sin for him. Liam hadn't reached the age of reason. He was too young. That's why as well he wouldn't go to the reservoir with us tomorrow. You had to be eight before you could go to the reservoir. That was the rule, and it was me that made the rule.

I still had bread in my hand as I opened the glass door.

'I'm away, Ma,' I shouted before I left. 'I'll see you in a wee while.'

She didn't answer. Maybe she didn't hear me. I headed down to Helen Street to line up with the rest. Mr Philson would count heads before we marched down to the chapel. If someone was missing, he would have to know the reason why.

I liked going to Confession because then you could go to Holy Communion on Sunday at Mass and then your soul would be as white as the driven snow. That's what Father Mooney had told us. If you committed a venial sin between Confession on Friday and Communion on Sunday you could say a special Act of Contrition and that would be okay. But if you committed a mortal sin, you couldn't go to Communion and then everybody would know because they would spot you not going up to the rails. And if you went to Holy Communion with a mortal sin on your soul, you would go to Hell if you died. And that's for certain.

CHAPTER 2

The Opposite Of Gravitational Pull

Killea Reservoir is like a big lake. It's in the Free State, just across the border from Derry. You can walk to it from our house in Rosemount in about an hour, along the back road. There's no customs post there, but you sometimes see the customs men's cars coming and you can hide in the ditch if you're smuggling anything. We don't smuggle, but we still hide anyway as if we had stuff. We hide as well if we see a police car. There's loads of ditches.

The reservoir has hills all around it and it can be dangerous swimming there because the water gets deeper the further out you go. If it's raining for a long time, it fills up to the brim, but if it's sunny for long, like in the summer, the water's lower. It's still warm enough in September for a swim.

We always took a piece of bread and jam each to the reservoir for whenever we got hungry. We made the pieces ourselves because we didn't want anybody to know. I told our Liam if he didn't blab on us, I'd take him when he was older. He hasn't blabbed yet and we've been going now for nearly a year. My ma asks him sometimes where I am and he always tells her I'm away playing football. When he makes his First Confession, he mightn't want to tell lies for me, but I'll think of something else when that time comes.

Before we left, Kevin Doherty said, 'Say a wee prayer the reservoir's full.'

Kevin always said that – 'say a wee prayer' – in case of this or that or if something might go wrong. He learned it from his ma. Kevin's ma goes to Mass every morning and twice on Sundays. She says about a hundred Rosaries every day for people she knows and everybody who is killed in the war, and for all our deceased relatives and for all the souls in Purgatory. Kevin always has his Rosary beads with him in a wee leather purse with Lourdes written on it. Kevin told us that Lourdes is a place in France where Our Lady appeared to a bunch of children. Lourdes water cures people of diseases and things. Before the war, people brought it home in bottles to put on sick people's heads, but you can't go there now to get any because the French are fighting the Germans and you could get killed if you went. Kevin knows everything about it because his ma told him. That's why he's always praying and blessing himself.

Kevin wears jam-jar glasses so his eyeballs look bigger than they really are, and when he looks up to Heaven, his eyeballs seem to disappear into his forehead. All you can see are two round whites like big clay marbles. Strange looking. And that's why we say bad words and stupid things to him, just so that we can see the two big whites. Kevin is the spitting image of his da, glasses and all.

Our friend Danny Doherty says the worst things to Kevin and I sometimes have to tell him to shut up when I'm fed up listening to him. He's not related to Kevin, even though he has the same name. There are lots of Dohertys round our way. Danny goes to the reservoir with us as well. He hasn't missed since we started. Danny Doherty farts a lot. We think it's because he's so fat. His ma's fat, too. We never met his father because he's dead. Danny told us that he was killed by a cow that kicked him in the head in the slaughterhouse. Danny never met him, either, for he died before Danny was born.

We think it's great, somebody's da being killed by a cow, because a whole lot of das just died of ordinary things like TB. Kevin told Danny that he prays for his da's soul every night in case he's in Purgatory, but Danny told him to shove off because his da was in Heaven. We asked Kevin once if he ever prayed for the cow that killed Danny's da. He didn't say anything.

'Is Cecil coming with us?' asked Billy. 'He's late.'

'He'll be here in a minute,' I said. Cecil Colhoun was always late going anywhere; it took him that long to get dressed. His ma always wanted him to look nice when he went out anywhere, even to play football. He was stupid like that because he always got messed up the same as the rest of us after a while. We saw him coming down the street; he was so tall and thin you couldn't mistake him. I knew he had his piece in his pocket because I could see the bulge. Cecil is a Protestant, too, but he isn't the same kind of Protestant as Billy. He's a Presbyterian and Billy is Church of Ireland.

Cecil's da has no job; well, not a real one anyway. He's a B-Special and he goes out four nights a week to catch IRA men. That's not what you would call a real job. During the day, he works in the plot down below our school and he grows vegetables and things. Cecil told me he never caught any IRA men. He wears a dark uniform when he's working and he has a rifle, but he has no gun in a holster like Big Burnside's. B-Specials aren't real policemen like the RUC and their uniform is different.

My ma told me one time that Protestants were all mixed up, not like the Catholics. They had a whole lot of different churches and we just had the one. She said that they were all Catholics hundreds of years ago, but the Pope and King Henry of England had a bust-up over Henry wanting to marry a whole lot of different women and the Pope wouldn't allow it so Henry just left and started up his own church in protest. That's why they're called Protestants. Danny asked Billy and Cecil about this one time, but they said they didn't know anything about it. My da

18

told me as well that it was because King Henry liked women so much. He called it fascination. And that's why there was all this bother in Ireland now between the Protestants and the Catholics. I couldn't understand it because there was never any bother between Billy and Cecil and us.

I looked up the word 'fascination' in the dictionary that Uncle Jimmy gave me, so I knew what it meant when I heard my da talking to my ma one night in the living room. I was out swinging on the door and Liam was up in bed sleeping and the twins and Uncle Jimmy were out.

I heard them laughing and giggling and my da told my ma that he was fascinated by her and she laughed even more and told him he was drunk. Then they went quiet and I went to bed. If Philson ever asked me in school what 'fascination' meant, I'd be able to tell him that it was 'to cast a spell over or to bewitch'.

'You're late as usual, Colhoun,' shouted Danny when Cecil got nearer.

'Shut up, Danny,' I told him. He was annoying me and we hadn't even started for the reservoir yet.

'Shut up, yourself,' he said, so I punched him to make him shut up. But he farted.

'Right, let's go,' I said, laughing.

Halfway there, we sat on the side of the road on the grass and ate some of our bread. It tasted nicer than the stuff at home, but I knew it was really the same.

'Let's go to where you can stand in two different countries at the same time,' said Cecil and he led the way, running.

I'd been there before but some of us hadn't. We followed him anyway, Danny at the back, panting and wheezing. Cecil waited until we all arrived.

'Where is it?' shouted Kevin.

'There,' said Cecil, pointing down to the road, 'where the tar road stops and meets the stony road, that's where the border is between Ulster and the Free State.'

19

'Where?' shouted Kevin. He hadn't been before and couldn't see it because his jam jars were all steamed up.

'Here,' said Cecil again as he put one foot on the tar part and the other on the stone part. Then we all did it, jumping back and forward from one part to the other, shouting and roaring.

'I'm in the Free State!'

'I'm in Ulster!'

'I'm in the Free State!'

'I'm in Ulster!'

Danny stopped after a minute. He didn't want to do any more. He was sweating. 'This is stupid,' he said, and I agreed with him.

'Let's go!' I shouted, and as we walked in silence I began to think back about what my da had told me about Kevin Barry's gang chasing the British out of the Free State, and about the tar road and the stony road and the line between them and us jumping from one country into the other. But it was all the same country, except that I knew it wasn't. The trees and the ditches and the houses and everything looked just the same. But I knew by the way my da talked that it was different, and I knew from what I had read in one of the books Uncle Jimmy gave me that there was a lot more to the whole thing than a tar road and a stony road.

'Right, boys,' I shouted to them before we reached the reservoir, 'there's something up here that I want to show ye all.'

'What is it?' Billy shouted back.

'A tree house,' I said – as if I were some sort of expert! It was Aunt Minnie who had told me about it and the road it was on – one of the four roads that led to Killea Reservoir. That's why I had picked on this one. I couldn't wait to tell them. At the top of the slope around the corner, it was as Auntie Minnie had described it.

'There it is,' I said as we turned the corner, 'a real tree house.' I said it as if I had seen it before. We all stared in amazement. It was high up in the tree and it was made of wood and it had a door and two windows and curtains. It was as big as a garden shed, but it looked like a small house. There was a long rope hanging from it with knots in it. It was fantastic.

'My God, bloody Hell,' said Danny. Kevin fingered his beads and I could see his eyes going up into his skull at Danny's curse. It wasn't the time to laugh – even though I felt like it. I had more to tell them.

'A man with no legs lives up there,' I said.

'Don't be stupid,' blurted Danny, 'how could a man with no legs climb up there? And there's no such thing as a man with no legs. You can't live without legs. You're making it up.'

The rest of them just kept looking up at the tree house. They didn't say anything, just kept staring. It was great.

'He doesn't climb up,' I said, 'he clambers up.' I'd looked that word up in Uncle Jimmy's dictionary after Aunt Minnie told me the story. They didn't know what 'clamber' meant.

'He drags himself up with the knots quickly,' I said. 'Aunt Minnie told me.'

'Your aunt's a chancer,' shouted Danny, 'and she always gets caught smuggling by the customs!'

'She does not!' I shouted back. I was getting angry with Danny. He was always arguing with me.

'And your uncle's a crook and your da's a wastrel as well, and your two sisters are keeping bad company.'

'If you say that again, I'll hit ye.'

'Try it,' he said.

I pushed him back and put my fists up to fight him.

'Nobody talks about Aunt Minnie like that, or my da or Uncle Jimmy or the twins!' I shouted at him as the rest of them watched us. 'Don't ever say that again or I'll knock ye down!'

'Your uncle's a crook, your aunt's a dope and your da's a wastrel,' he shouted, 'and your two big sisters are tarts!'

It was on the tip of my tongue to tell Danny that my da had a gun and he would sort all his relatives out, but I didn't. I just knocked him down with a push. Fatso Danny was lucky. I could have punched him on the nose or split his big lip or put his eye out with a spit. The rest watched but they didn't say anything. Kevin still had the Rosary beads out, but his eyes were back to normal. He wasn't praying or anything, just watching like the rest of them.

**

I'd been spitting on people for years and it had got me into trouble a couple of times. I just did it on anybody who annoyed me or if I didn't like them for some reason.

The first time I did it to Danny there was Hell to pay. It was more than two years ago and I'd spat on his First Communion suit when he'd told me it was new and that mine was only second-hand. He called it an Uncle Jimmy suit. He was raging, but so was I. He went home to blab to his ma without wiping the spittle off.

I was sitting on the hall floor shortly after that, playing Snakes and Ladders with our Liam, when I heard a noise in our porch. I looked up and saw the shape of Mrs Doherty through the glass door. She had big fat legs and no teeth and she had hairs growing above her lip like a moustache, only it wasn't. Women don't grow moustaches. She knocked hard on the glass and it rattled. I told Liam to answer the door and say that I was out. As I headed for the coalhouse in the yard, I could hear shouting in the living room; a big row. I was in for it.

Liam came out to the yard and told me that my ma wanted me. I hated him for blabbing. He was laughing and said Mrs Doherty had spilled the beans to my ma.

'And to think,' my ma shouted at me when I went in, 'that only last week, that suit was worn by somebody who went up to the altar to receive the body of Our Lord Jesus Christ.' She had me by the ear. 'And wasn't it the very same Lord who was spat on before He was crucified? You've brought shame on this house and on all the McCauleys, ye brat.'

I tried to explain that Danny Doherty had said things about *my* suit, but she wasn't having it.

'Now get down on your knees, Dickie McCauley, in front of that Sacred Heart picture and ask God for forgiveness for the terrible thing ye did.'

She pushed me down on the floor and pulled my head up to face the picture. I looked up. Our Lord's eyes were blazing down at me. I swore I'd never spit on a First Communion suit again.

A while after the row, I spat on Liam's face and warned him never to blab on me again. But I gave him a gobstopper as well and promised him a future supply as a piece of insurance. I'd get my own back on Danny Doherty.

The next time I spat on somebody that got me into bother was during a science class with Mr Philson. It wasn't the same kind of bother you get into with your ma because you couldn't fool her. But you could fool Philson if you were smart enough and you could get out of trouble if you used your head.

Philson was explaining the law of gravity to about forty of us and none of us was really listening to him because everybody except the Stupids knew that everything, except clouds and aeroplanes, falls down to earth, unless aeroplanes are hit by shells. He opened his lunch box and took out a sandwich that was probably made for him by Mrs Philson. He pointed to me.

'Come up here, McCauley. I want to demonstrate that in certain circumstances things can go up instead of down, even with the strong gravitational pull of the earth.' I swaggered to the front of the class, proud that I had been picked for the experiment even though I hated Philson. The three Smarts at the front looked jealous. I could see it in their faces. They were just a couple of feet away from me. The whole class was hushed. They had never seen a real scientific experiment before.

Mr Philson broke a large piece off the sandwich and handed it to me. He told me to put it in my mouth and chew it. I was feeling cock-a-hoop. You'd have thought I'd won a prize.

I popped it in and grinned at everybody. They all stared at me as if a miracle was about to happen. At the first taste of the sandwich, I stopped grinning. It was cheese and some sort of pickle. I hated cheese and I hated pickle. It made me feel sick.

'Now, McCauley, chew what you have in your mouth, but don't swallow it yet.' My stomach was churning. 'This experiment,' continued Philson, 'is about the opposite of gravitational pull.'

I felt like vomiting. Mr Philson reached for me and as the whole class gasped and then laughed, he turned me upside down. Before I knew it, my head was touching the floor and Philson had his hands round my ankles.

'Now, McCauley, swallow the sandwich and, when it has left your mouth, put your two arms out to indicate that the food has begun to journey upwards instead of downwards – the opposite of gravitational pull.'

As sick as I was, a plan was forming in my mind. And the plan included Philson and the three Smarts. I didn't hate the three Smarts – they couldn't help being what they were – but I hated Philson for always talking about them to the rest us, about how goody-goody they were and everything. The plan was great. I quickly divided the mix of cheese, bread and pickle, half to each side of my mouth, and gave a loud gulp without swallowing. That's when I put my two arms out.

'Now,' said Philson, 'the food is passing up McCauley's throat, up into his oesophagus and shortly it will go up into his stomach. You will notice that I say *up*, for this is the basis of the experiment: that the gravitational pull can be reversed by a force which can be even greater – that of the human being, which McCauley is, or we hope he is.'

Some of the class laughed at that. Most of them didn't. Even from upside down, I could see who was laughing: I took a mental note of their names.

Philson turned me right way up. I felt dizzy. He was finished with his experiment, but I wasn't finished with mine. Saliva

24

poured into my mouth at the thought. It mixed quickly with the bread, cheese and pickle, and before I had moved half a step back to my seat, out it all came in the form of a vomit. It had only taken me a few seconds to mix the whole lot to the centre of my mouth. I tried to divide it evenly. Mr Philson got the first vomity spit, right in the middle of his trousers. Then the three Smarts got a jet each. It was the best I'd ever done: four in one. It was terrific, and I got off with it. I fell in a mock faint to the floor and moaned. It was all Philson's fault; at least, that's what he thought. I felt a bit sorry for the three Smarts. Well, just a wee bit.

***

I lifted Danny up from the ground. It wasn't worth fighting with him, even if he did say bad things about my family. He was probably jealous because he had a big fat ma, but I gave him one last poke with my finger as a final warning. He didn't reply, just shouted, 'Look!' as he pointed down the road. We all turned and stared.

'It's a dwarf,' he hissed, 'coming up the road.' We all jumped into the ditch.

'It's no dwarf,' I told them. 'It's the man with no legs.' Brilliant. I just loved Aunt Minnie. The man was smaller than a dwarf.

'How does he walk if he has no legs?' whispered Danny. I told him to shut up and he would soon see. I didn't know, either, but I didn't tell Danny that.

'May the Holy Mother of God help us and protect us!' wailed Kevin. 'May God Almighty look down on us and take pity on our plight!' His beads were rattling.

'Shut up,' I whispered, 'or he'll hear ye!'

The man with no legs was getting closer. Kevin's eyes had gone up into his skull. Cecil and Billy were staring down the road, saying nothing, but their faces had gone white. Danny was sweating like a pig.

'Heads down,' I whispered as the wee man got nearer. 'Keep down or he'll see youse.'

Everybody put their heads down except me. The wee man was moving fast. He was only yards away; we could hear him. He had a sort of trolley attached to him, like a sleigh with wheels. He had big pads on his hands and he was pushing himself along. I pulled Danny's head up by his hair so he could see him. The rest didn't look. They were scared. Kevin wailed again, 'May the saints in Heaven preserve us!'

'Ssssh,' I whispered, but the wee man must have heard us.

Danny put his head down. I put mine over the ditch a wee bit. We'd been spotted. I stared at the man with no legs. He stared back at me and grinned. He turned, reached for the rope and clambered up in a flash, trolley wheels and everything.

'Did ye see that, boys?' I said.

'See what?' asked Danny as he and the rest of them raised their heads.

'He climbed up that rope like a flash, trolley and all stuck to him, and then he went into the tree house and his wife came out to meet him. She had no legs, either,' I lied.

'Aye, right,' said Danny with a sneer. But he looked impressed.

CHAPTER 3

The Bogside Dohertys

We ran the rest of the way from the tree house to the reservoir. You could hear Danny Doherty wheezing and panting behind us. The sun was belting down from the sky. Cecil Colhoun and me were away ahead. We were the best runners. We climbed over the gate and waited on the others to catch up before we stripped.

Everybody piled their clothes in a bundle, all mixed up. We were in our pelts. We headed towards the water, whooping and shouting like cowboys and Indians. It was great. We went in up to our waists, splashing away at each other. Kevin's glasses were soaked, but you could see the big eyeballs behind the jam jars. Danny was the only one who could swim. It was because he was so fat. He just floated on top of the water and moved his arms like Tarzan. We tried it, but we just sank. That's when the shout came.

'Out! Out now! Come out of there this minute!'

We all stopped and turned round to the shore. An official-looking man was standing there. He had a stick in his hand and he was waving it above his head. He had one foot planted on the pile of clothes. He kept roaring at us to come out. We were caught. We were in big trouble. We had no defence. The notice board at the gate said that trespassers would be prosecuted.

'Let's make a run for it,' whispered Danny.

'Don't be stupid,' I told him, even though it was the first thing I felt like doing. But he had our clothes so I knew we had nowhere to go. You don't run anywhere if you're starkers.

I hated being caught in the pelt. I had dreams about that a whole lot of times, like sleepwalking down the stairs with my wee short vest on. I would always open the glass door and then the front door and for some reason I went out and down Creggan Hill. The dream was always the same. I never knew why, but people coming up from Mass would be looking at me, and me trying to pull the wee vest down between my legs. It was always too short and I would cry and wake up, still crying.

I closed my eyes, hoping, but this was no dream. And I hadn't even a short vest on me. We were all in the same boat. In the pelt. Maybe we could rush him and push him over and grab our clothes and then run for it. Naw, he was too big for that. It wouldn't work.

'Let's rush him,' said Danny.

'Shut up,' I told him. 'I'm thinking.'

'May the Sacred Heart of Jesus have mercy on us,' hissed Kevin, 'and may the Blessed Mother protect us.'

'Shut up and listen,' I whispered. 'We're all called Doherty.'

'We are not,' said Kevin. 'Just me and Danny are.'

'Tell him we're called Doherty, stupid. We're all first cousins and we're from the Bogside. Do you hear me? And try and look innocent; it's our way out.'

Nobody else said anything. The man was still roaring at us to move. I started to walk towards him. The others followed. Kevin was whimpering. His lips were moving. Trembling like. We lined up in front of him, our hands between our legs. He took a notebook and pencil out of his pocket and licked the end of the pencil. He had a big red face and a massive nose with dimples on it. He looked angry.

'Right, Big Ears, I'll start with you. Name?'

Doherty, Big Fat Dimple Nose. I thought it but didn't say it.

'Doherty, Sir.'

'First name?'

'John.'

'Where do you live?'

'Bogside, Sir.'

'Number?'

'Six, Sir.'

'Next.'

'Doherty, Sir, Danny, number eight, Bogside.'

'Next.' Cecil was next.

'Doherty, Sir, Jonathan, number fourteen, Bogside.'

Dimple Nose was about to say next. He didn't.

'Do youse take me for a fool? You can't all be Doherty.' He turned to Kevin. 'You!' he shouted.

'We're all cousins, Sir,' I told him innocently. 'We're all first cousins.'

'I'm not talking to you, Big Ears,' he shouted. I could see the spit on his big fat lips. 'Right, you, Specky.' Kevin was murmuring a decade of the Rosary. I could see his fingers counting the Hail Marys. His beads were in his coat pocket under Big Fat Face's foot.

'Kevin Doherty, Sir, and may God strike me dead if I'm lying to you. Honest to God, Sir, my name's Kevin Doherty.' Kevin's eyes were halfway up into his skull.

Big Face wrote it down in his notebook. He forgot to ask him his address. Lucky. Kevin didn't have to lie. He turned to Billy, pointing the pencil at him.

'Name?'

'Billy Doherty, Sir, number twenty-seven, Bogside.'

He licked the lead again before writing it in his notebook. Then came the lecture about the reservoir and the dangers of swimming in it. 'And another thing,' he roared as he put the notebook and pencil back into his pocket, 'did you not see the warning at the gate, "Trespassers Will Be Prosecuted"?'

'No, Sir,' I told him, 'we didn't see it, but we can't read any-way. What does "Trespassers Will Be Prosecuted" mean, Sir?'

Big Thickie Nose grunted something about education and took his boot off the clothes. We all scrambled forward. He put the foot back on the pile.

'And another thing,' he said again, 'your mas and das will be hearing from me. Youse are all in big trouble. Don't ever come back here again. I'll be watching out for the lot of ye, and I know every last one of youse now.'

You know nothing, you big fat-faced, dimple-nose lip-spitter, and if I had my da's gun, I'd shoot the big dimple nose off your face and I'd get Hitler as well to drop a bomb on your baldy head.

'Right, Sir. Sorry, Sir,' I mumbled as I fumbled for my clothes with the rest of them.

CHAPTER 4

Bringing Bloody Policemen To The Door

It was Sunday. My ma was working in the kitchen. I could smell the dinner cooking. It was a chicken that Uncle Jimmy had brought home the night before in the van. I liked the smell of it cooking but I hated the smell of it when he had plucked the feathers off it in the basin of boiling water. It was rotten. You had to open the windows and the front and back doors to let the fresh air in. The smell lasted for hours. It made Liam and me feel sick.

Later, Liam and me were out in the hall playing marbles. Liam had only four marbles and he always loaned me two so that we could play. I just did it to please my ma. It was silly, winning his two off him all the time and then giving him back the four at the end. My ma must have liked me playing with him because she didn't shout at me then.

Billy never came out to play on a Sunday because his ma and da didn't allow him, and Cecil would be over at the plots sometimes, helping his da to weed turnips or something. Cecil's da loved working on his plot every day, including Sundays, because of having no real job. You could hire a plot for five shillings a year from the Corporation, but my da didn't bother because he said he had no time to spare.

Mr Colhoun sent Cecil down to us sometimes with a cabbage or a turnip or a lettuce and scallions. My ma always gave him a penny when he brought anything. My da said he would never eat any of the stuff. He said it would make him choke, eating anything that came from a B-man. It didn't make *us* choke and it didn't make my ma or the twins or Uncle Jimmy choke. I saw my da one day eating Mr Colhoun's potatoes and turnips, but I didn't see him choking. Uncle Jimmy said you should take everything you can off them because it's all ours anyway.

I kept playing stupid marbles with Liam in the hall, because after the dinner I was going to the park to play with Danny and Kevin, and maybe Cecil as well, if he wasn't at the plot. The twins were out somewhere. Probably seeing boys. I saw them with two boys in the park last week.

My da and Uncle Jimmy were in the living room reading the Sunday papers. You could hear them talking sometimes about Hitler and the Germans, and about London being bombed. I heard my da saying something about going down to Minnie's in the Free State if the Germans came back with their bombs. My ma heard him, too, from the kitchen. She shouted in, 'Minnie's got enough on her plate with six wains without all of us trooping in on top of her.'

'I'm only saying,' shouted my da, 'that if the bombing gets serious, you and Dickie and Liam could go.'

'And what about the twins, and you, for that matter, and you, Jimmy? Can a bomb not hit youse, too?'

'The twins'll be okay and Jimmy and me can look after ourselves. Don't you worry about us.' My ma was shouting again. She left the kitchen and went into the living room. She was still shouting at my da and Uncle Jimmy. Uncle Jimmy tried to shush her, but she shouted even more.

'Don't you shush me, Jimmy Breslin. I'm going nowhere, Hitler or no Hitler.'

I put my hands up to my ears and laughed. Liam did the same. He always copied me. The arguing went on. We went back to the marbles. But I was wondering about Hitler and the

Germans, about them killing all those people in Pennyburn in April of this year and about my da wanting us to go to the Free State. He'd told me in the bathroom that he was waiting on Hitler to come to help him get rid of the British out of Ireland. And I was thinking as well that if Hitler did come, he wouldn't know my da anyway and he wouldn't know where we lived and he might bomb us before my da got word to him. The whole thing was stupid because Hitler could just as easily bomb Minnie's house as ours.

There was a knock on the glass door. I looked up. Liam didn't. It was Big Burnside, the cop. I knew his silhouette. For a second, I froze. He must have found out about the gun under the floorboards. Somebody had blabbed. My da was in big trouble. They would put him in jail in Bishop Street or shoot him, or maybe hang him like Kevin Barry. They were all still arguing in the living room. Liam spoke: 'I beat you,' and he scooped up the four marbles.

'Liam,' I whispered, 'I've got something to do; tell my da that Big Burnside's here.'

There was another knock on the glass door. This time louder. The glass rattled. Liam put the marbles in his pocket and headed for the living room. I flew up the stairs to the bathroom. My hands were shaking as I reached under the bath and lifted the floorboard. I wanted to get the gun and put it somewhere else. Cops were bound to see the loose floorboard under the bath. The best place was under the water tank through the wee door in the attic. It was dark in there and dusty and dirty. Nobody would look.

I could feel nothing. I pushed my hand in further. Nothing there except the chestnut and marble jam jar. The gun was gone. My da must've shifted it. He was smart. He must've known the cops would be calling. I went downstairs slowly. Not the whole way, just to the first landing. I could see into the hall. The glass door was wide open. My da was talking to Big Burnside and I could see the gun in his holster. His face was stern.

'It's very dangerous, Mr McCauley, and a grave offence. I'm just warning ye about it anyway. They don't want a repeat of it. It's very dangerous, ye know. Anything could have happened.'

He didn't take my da away, arrest him or anything. They must've come in the middle of the night and found the gun. Burnside was just warning my da not to let it happen again. It was because Billy was my friend that he didn't arrest him.

'Right,' I heard my da say. 'Right, right, I'll see to it,' and he closed the glass door.

'Dickie, come down here. I want ye,' my da shouted. It wasn't the kind of shout that was pleased. It wasn't the voice, either, that was about to tell me that he was glad that I was Billy Burnside's friend. It was rough. It was an order, a command. I went down to the hall. Liam was grinning. I didn't know why. I hated that grin.

My da caught me by the ear and pulled me into the living room. Something was up. I didn't know what. Maybe he thought I'd blabbed about the gun. The twins came in and Laura said, 'What's up?' The living room was packed. A big scene.

'We just saw that bastard Burnside leaving the house,' said Kate. 'What did ye do, Da, rob a bank or something?'

'It's not your concern,' replied my da.

'Only asking,' laughed Kate. 'Can ye not ask a civil question in this house anymore?'

My da still had me by the ear; it would be red for a month. Liam was still grinning. My ma was sitting there waiting. Uncle Jimmy was listening to the wireless. The one o'clock news was on about the war.

My da pushed me onto the floor and kicked my backside, not very hard, it was a show-kick. My da was like that.

'Bringing a bloody policeman to our door,' he said. He wasn't angry, just annoyed. I knew what was coming next. It had to be.

'What happened?' my ma asked.

'He got caught at the bloody reservoir, that's what happened. Him and the rest of them. They should know not to get caught.' My da left the living room. I was relieved and annoyed at the same time. Relieved that my da hadn't got caught with the gun; annoyed at Billy Burnside – he must've told his da. Billy Burnside was in trouble. Big time. Billy Burnside was a blabber.

My ma rushed over to me from the couch. I was still on the floor. More trouble for me.

'Get up!' she shouted. Kate and Laura were laughing.

'Our Dickie was caught at the reservoir,' sneered Kate.

'Aye, and I bet ye were in the pelt,' laughed Laura, 'Dickie's dickie spotted in the reservoir.'

'It's not funny!' I shouted.

'Naw, it's *not* funny,' shouted my ma as she dragged me up from the floor, 'not a bit funny at all. Youse could've been drowned, the whole lot of ye. How many times have I told youse not to go near the reservoir?'

'I dunno, Ma.'

'Hundreds,' said my ma. 'Now, get down there on your knees in front of that Sacred Heart picture and say you're sorry for all the trouble you're causing.'

I knelt down. The twins were still sniggering and even Liam was giggling. I looked up at the holy picture and mumbled a few things under my breath. One of them was that I'd get back at Billy Burnside before the day was over, even if he didn't come out on a Sunday. I bet *he* didn't have to kneel down and promise not to do things; and anyway *he* didn't have a Sacred Heart picture in *his* house. Protestants only had pictures of the king and queen and soldiers and sailors hanging on their walls.

I left the house when the fuss was over. Kevin and Danny Doherty were standing at the lamppost.

'Your left ear's red,' said Danny.

'Shut up,' I said. 'Get Burnside for me.'

'He doesn't come out to play on a Sunday,' replied Danny.

'Just get him,' I snarled. Danny knew I meant business. He walked up to Billy's house and knocked.

A minute later Billy and Danny came walking down the street. Everybody knew something was up. I pushed Billy back. He just looked at me. Innocent Billy.

'You blabbed to your da about us at the reservoir.'

'I did not,' said Billy.

'You did.'

'I didn't.'

'You did so.'

'I didn't.'

I slapped his face. Twice. Billy stepped back. He had nothing more to say. There were tears in his eyes, but I didn't care. He looked sad. Guilty as well. He just walked home without saying anything. I was thinking there'd be no more comics after this. I didn't care. I hated Billy Burnside. I hated blabbers.

CHAPTER 5

Trespassers Will Be Prosecuted

Me and Danny and Kevin were the first in to school on Monday morning. Philson was standing up at the blackboard in class with a stick in his hand.

'Come up here, McCauley,' he said quietly.

I knew by the sound of his voice something was up. He was too smooth and he had a smirk on his face. He was confident. I didn't like it. I could hear Kevin's beads rattling in his pocket. Danny's breathing was heavy. They knew something was up, too. It was torture-chamber time.

'Me, Sir?' I asked.

'Oh yes, you, McCauley. Unless you know another McCauley in this room?' His voice was rising.

I looked round with a bad feeling about Killea Reservoir.

'No, Sir, there's no more McCauleys.'

'Come up here when I tell you, you impertinent brat!'

I rose from my desk and walked to the front. The others were filing in, some of them smiling. They must have thought this was going to be another scientific experiment. They would have liked that. They enjoyed the last one. This was going to be even better for them. But not for me.

'Now, boys,' said Philson when everyone was in, 'this morning we're going to have four lessons in one, and the champion

swimmer from Rosemount, one by the name of Richard Mc-
Cauley, is going to help us.'

Some of the class sniggered. I noted their faces.

'The four lessons,' Philson continued, 'are drawing, reading,
local geography and the consequences of breaking the law of the
land.'

I was right, it was Killea. The bastard knew. The class hushed.
The rack was ready for Dickie McCauley. Philson turned round
to the blackboard and drew a large square on it.

'Now, McCauley,' he said, 'tell everybody what that is. What
have I drawn on the board?'

I looked at it, puzzled like.

'It's a square, Sir.' I noticed that the three Smarts had their
hands up to answer. Philson didn't heed them.

'Right, McCauley, now tell me what this is.' He drew a thick
line downwards from the bottom of the square. 'Speak up, Mc-
Cauley, we can't hear you.'

I knew it was a notice board.

'I don't know, Sir. Is it a bat, Sir?'

'No, McCauley, it is *not* a bat.'

He turned to the class. The three Smarts still had their hands
up. I looked down at Danny and Kevin. They knew what it was,
too. Kevin's eyes were halfway up behind the jam jars. Danny
was sweating.

Philson turned to Frankie Smart. 'Francis?'

'It's a notice board, Sir.'

'Well done, Francis.' Then he turned to the class. 'So, there
we have it, boys, our drawing lesson for the day – a notice board
– and I want all of you to draw a notice board on your jotters, a
large one.'

Philson's torture chamber was warming up. I began to walk
towards my seat.

'Where do you think you're going, McCauley?'

'To draw a notice board in my jotter, Sir.'

He pulled me back roughly. 'Not so fast, McCauley. We've some more work to do here yet.' Philson turned back to the board and wrote TRESPASSERS WILL BE PROSECUTED inside the square. He turned to me. 'Read that out, McCauley.' The three Smarts' hands were up.

'Trespassers will be prosecuted,' I read.

'Correct,' he said, but I didn't feel pleased. It was only the beginning. I had a lot of thinking to do to get out of this one. Philson turned to the class.

'I'd like someone to tell me what "trespassers" means.'

A lot of hands went up: the three Smarts and about eight boys from the Marlborough area. Even one of the Stupids' hands was up. Philson noticed. 'Ah,' he shouted, 'even our good friend Duffy at the back knows. Do you see that, McCauley? Duffy knows what "trespassers" means. Right, Duffy, speak up.'

This should be good. Duffy had a stutter. It normally took him three days to get a sentence out. It would give me time to think. I needed a plan. Duffy saves the day: three cheers for Duffy.

'It's,' started Duffy, 'it's a . . . it's a . . . it's a . . .'

Uncle Jimmy had told me how to beat bastards like Philson. Be smarter than they are. Beat them at their own game. A plan was forming.

'It's a . . . it's a . . . it's a . . . it's a . . .'

The class was sniggering. Not at me this time.

'Right, sit down, Duffy. Well done, Duffy.' Duffy sat down, spit running down his chin. A lot of hands were still up.

Philson pointed to the second Smart. 'Yes, John?' he asked.

'Trespassers means going into somebody's property without their permission, Sir.'

'Well done, John,' said Philson. 'And now,' he continued, 'can anyone tell me what "prosecuted" means?'

Another ten hands went up, including the three Smarts.

Philson looked at the third Smart. 'Yes, Timothy?' he said.

'It means brought to court, Sir.'

'Correct, Timothy. Good boy, well done, well done.' Philson put his hand on his shoulder, patting him with praise. He always did that with the three Smarts. He did it with the Stupids as well, but for a different reason – patting them on the back, getting rid of his snots. Every day he did it, down the back, on the coats of the Stupids. He thought we didn't know, but everybody knew, except the Stupids.

Philson rambled on. I didn't care anymore. My plan was completed: action shortly. The rack was tightening in the torture chamber.

'And, Timothy, would you now inform McCauley what a court is?'

'It's a legal place, Sir, a courthouse. Where criminals are brought to be fined or sent to jail, Sir.'

'A place where criminals go. Did you know that, McCauley?'

'Yes, Sir.'

'Did you, now? In that case, if you're so clever, maybe you could answer the geography questions.' Philson turned to the board again and drew a rough circle and wrote ROSEMOUNT inside it. Below that he drew another circle and wrote BOG-SIDE in it.

'Now, McCauley, which is which?'

I pointed over. 'The top one's Rosemount, Sir, and the bottom is Bogside.'

'So, you know the difference, McCauley? You can actually read, McCauley?'

'Yes, Sir, sure you know I can read, Sir.'

Philson then banged the blackboard with his cane. He looked angry. Everybody jumped with the shock.

'So, there we have it, boys,' said Philson, pointing to the board. 'A large notice which states clearly that one shouldn't enter without permission or one will be brought to a place of justice and sentenced accordingly.'

Philson·raised his cane and whacked my backside. I winced a little but didn't flinch. I didn't want anybody to see I was afraid.

'Where *one* shouldn't enter,' continued Philson, 'but there was more than one, wasn't there, McCauley, in Killea Reservoir?'

'Yes, Sir,' I answered. I looked down at Danny and Kevin. They had both turned white and Kevin's eyes were gone.

'Names, McCauley, I want names.'

I looked at him blankly.

'I asked you a question!' shouted Philson. 'There were others with you at the reservoir. Speak to me, boy. Who were they?'

'I don't know, Sir,' I whispered.

'What did you say, boy? Speak out.'

'I don't know them, Sir. They were just boys who were dipping when I was there. Honest, Sir, I don't know them. They were all called Doherty, Sir. That's what they told the man. They were all from the Bogside.'

The rack was so tight it could snap at any time. That's when I looked up at Philson. He'd had long enough, it was now my turn. My time had come. I sensed it. My own torture chamber suddenly opened for business. *Tighten the rack now on Philson,* I thought, *full stretch.*

'Sir,' I said, innocent like.

'Yes, McCauley?' he said gruffly.

'Sir,' I said again, 'is it true that Our Lord said that we should forgive everybody who trespasses against us?'

Philson glared at me. The class hushed. They knew Dickie McCauley, they knew it was McCauley versus Philson. I stared back into his eyes.

'Only if they repent, McCauley, only if they repent.'

'I repented, Sir, in front of the Sacred Heart picture on my knees and I promised I wouldn't trespass in the reservoir again.'

Philson went quiet. His face scrunched up. Puzzled.

'Did you, now?'

'And I'm going to repent again on Friday evening in Confession, Sir. My ma says I have to.'

'Did she, McCauley?'

'Yes, Sir, because it's a sin to trespass, Sir. It's the same as stealing or shouting at people or hitting people, no matter what they have done. Or being sarcastic with people or bullying people in school or in the street. That's what my ma told me.' *Tighter now,* I thought.

Philson said nothing. Just looked at me. Tortured like. The class was waiting. It was time to tighten the rack to full stretch.

'And, Sir,' I went on, 'trespassing is like putting snots on people's backs or farting up their noses or scratching our arses in front of people. That's trespassing, too, Sir, isn't it? Maybe worse than trespassing in a reservoir, Sir? And I've done all those things before and I've told them to the priest in Confession, Sir.'

Philson's fingers tightened on the stick. He looked a bit pale. The class was still quiet. I was winning.

'Sit down, McCauley. I hope you've learned your lesson. And remember, I'll have my eye on you from now on, you can be sure of that. Yes, McCauley, you can be sure of that.'

Victory to McCauley. My thoughts raced. *And you can be sure, big nose-picker and arse-scratcher, that I'll have my eye on you, too. I hope you've learned a lesson or two as well.*

But all I said was, 'Yes, Sir.'

I went back to my seat. I'd live to fight another day. But how did Philson know about the reservoir? There were too many blabbers in this world, that's how.

CHAPTER 6

Fifth, Thou Shalt Not Kill

I ran home after school because I didn't have to wait for Liam. My ma got him out early for some reason. I was praying that there would be nobody in the house because I wanted to see if the gun was back under the bath. My ma was out and the twins were working. Uncle Jimmy was in the kitchen making a piece. He said my da was in bed. 'Second home to him,' he laughed. 'And how was school today? Philson still giving you a hard time?'

I laughed but I never said anything about the torture chamber. I just wanted to go upstairs to check on the gun. It wasn't a good time. I'd have to wait a while because I knew Uncle Jimmy wanted to talk. He was like that sometimes when he had nothing else to do.

'Do you do history in school, Dickie?'

'No, Uncle Jimmy, just geography and sums and reading and writing and science and stuff like that.'

'That's good,' he replied, 'but ye should be learning a bit about the history of your own country. It's only through history that you learn how to deal with the future.'

I didn't know what he was talking about. It didn't make sense.

'I've bought ye another book,' he said. 'It's on the sofa in the living room. It's all about the English and the Scots invading

Ireland and ransacking the country and outlawing priests and religion and taking our land and our houses and starving people to death. And we weren't allowed to have schools, either; they didn't want us to be educated. They wanted to keep us ignorant. But our day's coming, Dickie.'

'Aye,' I said as I walked into the living room to look at the book, 'my da told me something about that, Uncle Jimmy.'

He laughed, 'Aye, he would know all about it, Dickie.'

I knew by the way he laughed that he didn't mean what he said about my da. But he was wrong. It was my da who owned the gun. It was my da who had plans to get rid of the British, and it was my da who would sort everything out. Uncle Jimmy just bought and sold old clothes so what would he know except the things he read in books? My da was a smart man and he knew how to deal with the likes of Big Burnside and he knew that Hitler was coming soon. That's why I wanted to check if the gun was back under the floorboards . . . or maybe if somebody had taken it . . . or maybe if my da had hidden it under the mattress or someplace like that. I just wanted to protect my da and I just wanted to make sure that the gun was in a safe place. I just wanted to go upstairs to check the bathroom, and now Uncle Jimmy was holding me back.

I flicked through the pages of the thick history book. The writing was small and I couldn't understand a lot of the longer words – not like our reading books in school. I'd need Uncle Jimmy's dictionary to understand it. I knew I'd never read it.

'Thanks for the book, Uncle Jimmy,' I said to him as he came into the living room with his piece and cup of tea. 'I'll take it upstairs to the bedroom.'

'Do you want some tea, Son?' he asked me.

'Naw, it's okay, I'll get some later when Liam comes in.'

He sat there eating while I pretended to read the book.

'Liam's a good lad,' he said, 'and it's great the way you and him play together, especially the way your ma is at the minute.'

44

Uncle Jimmy was smarter than I thought because he knew that I was playing more with Liam now to keep my ma from shouting at me. He supped his tea. I knew I couldn't leave yet to check on the gun and I knew by the way he was looking at me that he wanted me to say something else.

'Is it a sin to kill somebody, Uncle Jimmy?' It just came out. I don't know why I said it.

He didn't answer at first as he had a load of bread and jam in his mouth. He took another drink of tea before he spoke. 'It is and it isn't, Dickie. It depends.'

I didn't know what he meant, and I still didn't know why I asked him because I knew from the Ten Commandments that it was a sin to kill somebody.

'Fifth, thou shalt not kill,' I said, because that's what was in the Catechism. So how could he say 'it depends' as if it wasn't a sin?

Uncle Jimmy took another bite of his bread and jam. He looked at me for a good while before he spoke.

'What age are ye, Dickie? Eight, is it?'

'Nine, Uncle Jimmy. I'll be ten in December.'

'That's right, that's right,' he said. 'You're growing up fast.'

Shut up, I thought. *Stop talking, will ye? Ye could be up in the bathroom by now checking on the gun situation instead of talking rubbish.* My brain was putting words into my mouth and I couldn't stop.

'It's even a sin to *think* about killing somebody, Uncle Jimmy; the priest told us that,' I went on.

'Aye, you're right, Dickie, and the priest's right, too. But the sort of thing he's talking about is murder. Now that's a sin. But what you've got to understand, Dickie, is this. If you're at war with another country that is your enemy, it's not a sin to kill them because if you don't kill them, they'll kill you.'

What he was saying made sense because I knew that in school if somebody was going to hit me, I'd hit them first. I could kill with a good spit; well, nearly, and if we heard that the Marlborough crowd was going to attack us, we'd get in there first. Pick them off before they could group. Because they were the enemy, even if they weren't from another country.

'Like the Germans, Uncle Jimmy?' I asked him. 'Killing Germans is okay?'

'Aye, something like that, Son, except we're not at war with the Germans. It's the British and a whole lot of other countries that are against the Germans. Ireland's not in the war so the Germans aren't our enemy. The British are the enemy: it was the British who invaded Ireland.'

I was a wee bit confused but I didn't tell Uncle Jimmy that in case he thought I was stupid. But I knew he was telling me the same kind of thing my da had told me the night he was drunk in the bathroom. And I wondered if maybe Uncle Jimmy knew about the gun, too, and wasn't letting on. If he *did* know about the gun, then him and my da must be in cahoots. I knew that much.

'Here's sixpence, Dickie. Go on to the shop and get yourself some sweets.'

'Thanks, Uncle Jimmy,' I said as I pocketed the money. 'I'll go later, after I do my homework.'

'Good boy,' he said. 'Studying's a great thing – you'll do well if you study.'

Uncle Jimmy lifted the newspaper and began to read. The chat was over. I lifted my schoolbag from the couch and went up the stairs to the bathroom. I did a pee and pulled the chain, and while the noise of the flushing water was still loud, I got down on my knees and put my hand under the bath to lift the floorboard. I would soon find out if the gun was there. There was a knock on the door. 'Are ye finished in there?'

'Right, Da,' I shouted. 'I'll be out in a minute.'

There was no way I could lift the floorboard now. My da knew I had flushed the toilet so he would wonder why I wasn't coming out. I slid the bolt.

'Good boy,' he said as he roughed my hair. 'Did you have a good day at school?'

'Aye, great, Da, great.'

'Good, Son, good. I'll be down in a wee while to make you some tea. Is Uncle Jimmy still there?'

'Aye, Da.'

'Your ma's at the doctor's. She'll be home soon. She took Liam with her for company.'

'I didn't know my ma was sick, Da.'

'She's not sick,' he said, 'she's just down for a check-up.'

'Oh, that's okay,' I replied. But it wasn't okay, because why would my ma go to the doctor's for a check-up if she wasn't sick? I'd ask Liam later or maybe listen to what was said when they came home. Liam was probably too young to know anything, but he might know something. And if I didn't find out that way, I'd ask the twins when they came home from the factory. They're bound to know if my ma's sick. They always know everything that goes on in the house. Except for the gun under the floor-board or wherever my da had hidden it now. It was only me and my da, and maybe Uncle Jimmy, who knew about that. If my ma had known about it there would be ructions. She was bad-tempered enough these days without having to worry about a gun in the house and about what would happen to my da if the cops found it.

And on top of all that, Billy Burnside was a blabber and I'd have to buy my own comics from now on.

I went into the bedroom and did my homework. Sums. A composition. Spelling. They were easy. When I finished, I tore out a page of my jotter and started writing down all the sins I'd committed since last Friday. I'd never remember them all unless I put them on a list. I was cursing more and hitting more people. The priest wouldn't be pleased. Neither would anybody else if they found the list, except for Liam – he couldn't read very much. I put the page under the lino for safety. It was only

Monday. The way I was feeling, there'd be a lot more sins before next Friday.

My da had gone downstairs to make a cup of tea and a piece for me. I didn't want to go down yet because they would just start talking to me about school and all and I hated that. School was bad enough without talking about it afterwards. I walked over to the bedroom window and looked into the barracks yard. Four policemen were playing football in their shirtsleeves. Their coats and belts were lying on the ground as goalposts. I could see their guns in the holsters.

Before going into the bathroom again, I listened from the landing. I could hear my da in the kitchen and Uncle Jimmy had the wireless on. It was safe. I bolted the door behind me and got down on my knees and lifted the floorboard. The gun was back.

'Dickie!' shouted my da from the hall. I jumped, scared. 'Your tea's ready.'

'Right, Da, I'm coming.'

I forced the floorboard back in place. Happier now, I went down for my tea.

When I had eaten, I stayed in the living room for a while with my da and Uncle Jimmy. They didn't talk to me about anything, just to each other about the war. I got fed up listening so I told my da I was going out to play. He didn't say anything. My ma and Liam weren't back from the doctor's yet and the twins wouldn't be back until after six. I wouldn't find out anything about my ma until then.

Danny and Kevin were playing marbles in the street. It wasn't the marble season, not for another month. They stopped playing when they saw me. They knew I was laughing at them, but they didn't put the marbles away. They looked back at me – smiling, like – pleased with themselves for some reason. I'd soon know why. Danny put his hand in his pocket and took out a shilling. He handed it to me.

'That's for you, Dickie,' he said.

I took it. I knew why he'd given it to me. He was paying for a favour. I never paid anybody for a favour except maybe our Liam to keep his mouth shut. I didn't say thanks because I didn't need to.

Kevin then handed me a bag of marbles and a pair of Rosary beads in a leather purse with Fatima written on it. Fatima is a place in Portugal where Our Lady appeared to another bunch of people. I knew that because my ma told me the whole story about it. I'd give my ma the beads as a present. They might make her better. I still didn't say anything. I wanted them to speak first.

'You didn't blab on us,' said Kevin, 'in school the day, I mean, to farty-arse snot-nose, about us being at the reservoir.'

I stared at him. The jam jars were steamed up a bit. I'd never heard Kevin saying words like that before and his eyeballs stayed normal behind the glasses. There'd be a lot of Rosaries to say after this. I spoke.

'I don't blab on anybody.'

'The three Smarts were looking for ye after school.' Kevin went on, 'They said they hated big Philson and they want to talk to you.'

I said nothing, but I was lapping up the praise without showing it. I didn't feel tough at this time, but I loved the adulation. Adulation is praise. I knew that because I had looked it up in the dictionary after Philson made me write out 'I must treat life with adulation and not with scorn' twenty times in my jotter. That was after he caught me squaring up to three of the Marlborough boys in the playground. They were slagging me because the backside was out of my trousers. I had torn them climbing over a fence behind Helen Street to prog apples. I hated the Marlborough crowd. They were snobs. It must've shown on my face. Scorn, Philson called it, a face full of scorn for others. He didn't give *them* any lines to write out. I felt scorn for Philson, too.

'Billy Burnside's not guilty,' said Kevin.

I put the shilling and the marbles and the Fatima Rosary purse in my pocket before I replied.

'What are ye talking about?'

'Burnside's innocent,' replied Danny.

My heart sank. I knew immediately what they were talking about. I had made a bad mistake. Somewhere along the line I had messed up and immediately began to feel rotten.

Danny continued. 'He's not to blame for Big Burnside going to your house. He didn't blab on us to his da. It was the reservoir man. He went to all the Bogside door numbers we gave him and when he couldn't find us he was raging. Bap Kelly told us. The man came to his door and said he was looking for a boy called Doherty with big ears.'

Bap Kelly was a boy in our class who lived in the Bogside.

'Bap knew everything that went on. He knew it was us but he didn't blab. The reservoir man then went to the Strand Road barracks and told them about us,' said Danny. 'The sergeant there must've told Burnside in Rosemount barracks, and that's what gave the game away – your big ears!'

Danny Doherty knew that his shilling would save him from a back-of-the-throat job to his face – for now. I'd get him later, the time wasn't right. Nobody got off with calling me Big Ears.

'Burnside went to your house and must have told Philson as well,' Danny added, 'and we all know what happened then.'

'Shut up!' I shouted. 'You don't have to tell me what happened. I already know what happened, so why are youse keeping on about it?'

Kevin and Danny wanted me to say something else, but I didn't. Instead I just turned my back and walked into the house; I had some thinking to do.

It wasn't the first time my big ears had got me into trouble. I hated them. I hated my da, too. My big ears were the same as his. Everything was my da's fault. Everybody said I even looked like him and I didn't want to look like him, with his big belly and the smell of Guinness off him. Even though I had no big belly and no Guinness smell, I'd rather look like Ma or the twins, or even Liam. They had normal ears. But, for now, I had to think. Billy Burnside was innocent and my ma was sick. That's what I had to think about. And I was annoyed. And it's hard to think things out when you're annoyed.

CHAPTER 7

Aunt Minnie's Ex-Boyfriend

By lunchtime the next day, I still hadn't worked out what I would do about Billy. I was slowing up. Probably because I had too much on my mind.

The three Smarts came over to me and Danny and Kevin in the playground. The Smarts were clean and tidy. They always looked like that. They were rich; they couldn't help it. They talked posh as well; they couldn't help that, either. They looked like Protestants. I could speak posh if I wanted to but I didn't. Billy didn't speak posh and Cecil didn't speak posh, and they were Protestants! It was Uncle Jimmy who told me that Protestants speak posh because they're trying to imitate the English. But he was wrong because Billy and Cecil were just ordinary like us, except for Billy dressing up in his best clothes all the time. Cecil didn't, and neither did his da.

Frankie Posh spoke first. 'Hello, Dickie,' he said. 'Would you like to come to my birthday party in December?'

'Okay,' I said. 'Can Liam come, too?'

'Yes.'

'And Danny and Kevin and Billy and Cecil?'

'Yeah, surely. And, Dickie . . .'

'What?'

'Philson's a bastard.'

'Yeah, and he's nothing but a big, smelly bully,' Timothy said.

'He's more than that,' snorted John. 'He's nothing but a rotten, filthy nose-picker!'

Danny laughed when they spoke. I looked at Kevin out of the side of my eye. He was just staring at the three Smarts. His eyes were normal and his beads were quiet. I tried to look hard; it was difficult, but I had to do it.

'What's up?' I said, wondering at the same time if it was a sin to enjoy listening to bad words as well as saying them. Maybe I'd ask the priest next time I was in Confession.

'We just wanted to give you this,' said Frankie. He handed me the *Film Fun Annual*. I'd never seen one before but I'd heard about it. I didn't say thanks.

They were paying a debt or something, but I had never done anything for them. Not that I knew of anyway. Not for the Smarts. Maybe it was because they admired me more now for the way I'd handled Philson over the reservoir carry-on. They walked away without saying anything else. I looked at Kevin and Danny. Kevin's eyes were now nearly halfway up into his skull because of the Smarts' bad language.

'May the Lord have mercy on their souls,' prayed Kevin.

Danny told him to shut up.

'May their guardian angels protect them from evil.'

'Shut up!' Danny shouted again.

'May the Holy Mother of God look down on them with compassion.'

'Shut up!'

'May the Good God in Heaven keep them safe from harm.'

I turned on the two of them. They were annoying me.

'Fuck up, the two of youse,' I said to them and walked away, putting the *Annual* up my coat in case Philson would see it and take it from me. But I was thinking at the same time that there would have to be a lot of sins told to the priest at the end of the week, and not just from me.

After school, I ran home. Liam was in the hall, playing Ludo by himself. The glass door hit him in the back when I opened it. The glass rattled because of the crack. 'Stupid,' I said, but he didn't heed me; he just kept playing. Uncle Jimmy was in the front room packing clothes into cardboard boxes for selling round the houses. The clothes came in big bags from the Free State. They weren't new so my ma always washed and ironed them so that Uncle Jimmy could get more money.

'Where's my ma, Uncle Jimmy?'

'She's upstairs, Son.' I had the *Film Fun Annual* in my hand.

'Where'd you get the book, Son?'

'It's Billy Burnside's,' I lied.

Another sin for the list. Uncle Jimmy just grunted when I told him and didn't look pleased. I went upstairs. My ma was in the bedroom tidying up. I hoped she hadn't found my sin list under the lino. She was singing *Danny Boy* and that made me feel good. If she was singing, she couldn't be dying and if she was tidying up, she couldn't be dying. You couldn't sing and tidy up if you were really sick.

'Hello, Ma,' I smiled, but I felt guilty about my sin list under the lino and about the new ones I had to add to it.

'Hello, Son,' she lilted, as she took me by the hand and shoulder and danced me round the room, still singing '. . . *the pipes, the pipes are calling, from glen to glen, and down the mountainside . . .*'

When we finished dancing, she hugged me and I could feel her big belly against my chest. I felt sad that she still had the sickness, but I didn't say anything about it. The doctor must've given her medicine, so maybe it was going away.

'And where did you get the lovely book, Dickie?' she asked me.

'That's Billy Burnside's,' I told her, and this time it was no lie because before I spoke, my mind must have worked out that it would be a good idea to give it to him instead of having to say sorry. Things were working out okay, but I'd still have to find out more about my ma.

'That's lovely, Son,' she said. 'Now, I'll be down in a few minutes to make youse all some tea.'

As I walked down the stairs, I could hear her singing another song. '*If you ever go across the sea to Ireland, it may be at the closing of your days . . .*' It made me feel good listening to her.

I went into the sitting room. Liam was still playing in the hall. I sat down to read the *Film Fun Annual* before I gave it to Billy. There was no point in missing out on it. But I just looked at some of it. I had something to ask Uncle Jimmy.

'Uncle Jimmy?'

'Yes, Dickie?'

'The man with no legs – the man that lives in the tree house beside the reservoir – how did Aunt Minnie know about him?'

Uncle Jimmy laughed. 'That's a story and a half, Dickie. Aye, a story and a half.'

He laughed again, but I couldn't see what was funny about it.

'His name's Harry Burke and it was his foolishness and stupidity that lost him his legs.'

Uncle Jimmy wasn't making sense, but I said nothing because I knew he was going to tell me more.

'It all started, ye see, Dickie, when him and Minnie were going out together. Minnie worked in a shirt factory then and had lodgings in William Street. He was a nice fella, and Minnie was very fond of him. This was long before she got married to Johnny O'Donnell in Donegal. Oh, aye, long before that.'

My mouth was wide open. I couldn't believe what Uncle Jimmy was telling me. That's because my mind was picturing Aunt Minnie walking down William Street hand-in-hand with a two-foot-high man on a trolley. Uncle Jimmy looked at me and laughed when he saw my face. He burst into laughter again before he spoke.

'No, no, Dickie, he had legs then; but the problem was that he had no job, and Minnie told him that she wouldn't marry him if he didn't get a job.'

'Phew,' I said.

'Ye see, Dickie, it was very hard for a man to get a job in Derry in those days, especially if you were a Catholic. And what did the bold Harry do? Well, I'll tell you what he did. He did the stupidest thing in the world. Unbeknownst to Minnie, he joined the British Army. And he stupidly turned up in broad daylight at Minnie's lodgings in William Street, uniform and all, showing off. When Minnie saw him, she couldn't believe what she was looking at. She pulled him into the hallway before you could say Jack Robinson and banged the door behind them.'

Uncle Jimmy started laughing again. Grown-ups were strange like that – laughing at things that weren't funny at all.

'He wasn't in the house more than fifteen minutes, Dickie, when the front door was burst open and four fellas rushed in and dragged him out to a waiting lorry. It was the IRA, Dickie, and they took him away and shot his legs clean off before dumping him outside that very barracks across the street from this house. After that, the stupid man went a bit mental and that's why he lives in a tree house now. Minnie never saw him again, but she knew where he was living.'

I didn't really know what to say, though I had a lot of questions I could've asked, so I let it go for now.

'Tea's ready, boys,' my ma shouted from the kitchen. I had nearly finished the *Film Fun* book. I'd seen enough of it.

'Isn't that grand?' said Jimmy. 'All the work done and now time for a nice cuppa tea and a wee biscuit.' He rubbed my head as we walked out of the room. Liam followed us in.

'Uncle Jimmy's brought some nice pork sausages and bacon for later,' said my ma as we sat around the table, 'and your da got three days' work, so things are looking up, boys, in the Mc-Cauley house.'

I love pork sausages and bacon. You couldn't get much of them in the shops in Derry because of the rationing, but Uncle Jimmy knew where to get anything like that he wanted. He was a businessman.

My da wouldn't have known where to get meat or anything. He never went into shops, just pubs. But he knew where to get a gun. And that made him smart. I was proud that I had a smart da, but I wouldn't talk to anybody about that. It was dangerous. And I wouldn't tell anybody, either, that the man with no legs could have been my uncle if Aunt Minnie had married him. It would be stupid even to mention it to anybody because they would just laugh. And I didn't want people laughing at him because he had enough problems. Or laughing at me, either.

After the tea, I told my ma and Uncle Jimmy that I was going to Billy Burnside's house to give him back his book. My ma told me to take Liam with me, to get him out of the house for a while because he was bored. I didn't really want Liam to come with me because he would be cute enough to know that I was lying about the *Film Fun* book when I gave it to Billy Burnside. But I couldn't say no to my ma, now that she was back in good form and not shouting at me.

Before I closed the front door behind me, I heard Uncle Jimmy saying to my ma that I shouldn't be going to that cop's house or playing with his son because things could get hot soon. I didn't know what he meant about things getting hot, but it made me a bit sad, Uncle Jimmy talking like that, because Billy Burnside was *my* friend and not his. And it wasn't his business anyway who my friends were. I mean, I didn't talk to anybody about who *his* friends were and I wouldn't anyway, even if I knew them, because it was none of my business.

Liam wanted to stay and swing on the glass door, but I pulled him away from it because I was annoyed. Annoyed at having to take him with me and annoyed at closing the kitchen door too early before I could hear what my ma's answer to Uncle Jimmy was about Billy Burnside. I cursed at him.

'But I want to swing,' cried Liam as I dragged him out of the house. 'I'll tell my ma you were cursing,' he said, 'if you don't buy me a gobstopper.'

'I wasn't cursing,' I told him, and I let him go back to have a couple of swings, hoping he would forget that I'd said a bad word. But I knew he wouldn't forget because I had given him a gobstopper recently to shut him up about something else and he kept asking for more. If I wasn't careful, I'd be feeding him gobstoppers for the rest of my life.

'You said a bad word,' he went on as we headed up the street, 'and I still want another gobstopper.'

'What bad word did I say?'

'You said fuck.'

'I did not.'

'You did. I heard you.'

'How do you know that's a bad word?' I asked him.

'Because it is.'

'Aye, but how do *you* know?'

'Because I know. I heard somebody saying it.'

'You said it, too,' I told him, 'the bad word.'

'I did not.'

'You did.'

'I did not.'

'You said fuck when I asked you what bad word I had said.'

'I did, but it's not a bad word if you tell somebody else what the word was.'

'You'll have to tell it to the priest when you make your First Confession.'

'I will not.'

'Yes, you will.'

'No, I won't.'

'Why?'

'Because when I make my First Confession, I won't remember that I said it.'

'So you *did* say it!'

He didn't reply and I knew he was smarter than I was at his age. I bought him a gobstopper anyway, just in case he would blab. It only cost a penny so it was worth it, but I was thinking that I would have to find out sometime who taught him the bad word. I'd sort them out in my own way and in my own time. I'd have to think of ways of getting more money, too. Buying a lot of gobstoppers could be expensive.

Before knocking on Billy's door, I told Liam to stay down the street a bit. I didn't want him to know what was going on. It was Big Burnside who answered.

'What do you want?' Gruff-like.

'Is Billy in? I just want to talk to him.'

Burnside looked different. He hadn't his cop uniform on and he just looked ordinary. I wondered where his gun was. Probably on top of the wardrobe.

'I don't think he should be talking to the likes of you, McCauley. You're the sort of boy that would get him into trouble, trespassing in reservoirs and what have you. The next thing is you'll be breaking into shops and houses, and then I'll have you, boy. Mark my words, I'll have you.'

He turned his back on me and shouted for Billy. I said 'fuck you' under my breath and it made me feel good, as if I'd really said it to him. Maybe I would say it to him out loud when Hitler and my da were tying him up and getting rid of him. He wouldn't be so chirpy and bossy then about slagging me.

'Hello, Billy,' I said when he came to the door, 'look what I've got you,' and I handed him the *Film Fun Annual*.

'Gee, thanks, Dickie, that's smashing. I haven't seen that one before.'

'You can keep it, Billy, for good.'

I knew by looking at him that I didn't have to say sorry for blaming him in the wrong. Billy was like that. He was my best friend, better than Danny or Kevin or Cecil; and he didn't say anything now about me slapping his face or pushing him. But I was thinking at the same time that I might tell the priest about what happened in case it was a sin. It would be easier to say sorry to the priest instead of to Billy, because I was never used to saying sorry to anybody except my ma and to priests in Confession.

Our Liam was behind me and he had heard everything. Now he would know that I wasn't returning the *Annual* to Billy, but giving it to him, that I hadn't borrowed it from Billy at all. And he'd be cute enough to find out from Danny and Kevin where I'd really got it. And then the blabbing could start to my ma, and to Uncle Jimmy, and the whole thing might come out about the Smarts, and about why they gave it to me; about the way they liked how I stood up to Philson about the reservoir thing and all.

Uncle Jimmy would probably say, 'Well done, Dickie. That'll rub it up Philson.' But my ma would batter me and make me kneel down once more in front of the Sacred Heart picture, and the twins would be laughing at me again. I knew by the look on Liam's face that he wanted me to buy him another gobstopper. I gave him a penny and told him to go to the shop.

Before leaving Billy, I asked him if he wanted to come down to the chapel with us on Friday evening. He said okay. Billy and Cecil nearly always came with us when we were marching down the hill to Confession. They stayed behind us a good bit in case Philson would see them, but they never came into the chapel because it would be a sin for a Protestant, the same way it would be a sin for a Catholic if he went into a Protestant church. I told Billy and Cecil one time that they would be struck dead if they put a foot inside the door. That's why they always waited in the porch after we went in.

Uncle Jimmy told me that Protestants didn't go to Confession like us. They had no Confession boxes. If they did anything wrong – if they cursed or anything – they just asked God to forgive them and He did, and I thought that wasn't fair because why should there be one rule for Protestants and a different rule for Catholics? And Protestants just went to church on Sundays and we could go every day if we wanted to. Danny's ma went to Mass every day and twice on Sundays. Everybody knew that.

CHAPTER 8

God Works In Mysterious Ways

When Liam and me got home later, we could smell the pork sausages and bacon cooking. I was starving with hunger. Liam was still sucking his gobstopper but he put it into his pocket when he smelt the fry. Uncle Jimmy and the twins were sitting at the table in the kitchen.

'Right, boys, sit down,' my ma called to us. 'Your da's not in yet so we'll start without him.' She began to dish everything out. It looked great.

'Bless us, O Lord, for these Thy gifts which of Thy bounty we are about to receive through Christ Our Lord, Amen.' My ma always said Grace before meals and then there would be quiet for a wee minute. Then she would sometimes say, 'Thank God for another meal on the table, what with the war on and all; and thank Uncle Jimmy for getting this nice food for us.'

And Uncle Jimmy would always give a big smile and say, 'Sure isn't that what I'm here for?' I hated him saying that.

Kevin Doherty's ma and Kevin always said Grace before, and even after, meals as well. I was in their house one evening when they were having their tea. I was waiting on Kevin to come out to play. After they said the last Grace and cleared the dishes away, Kevin's ma and him knelt down and started the Rosary. I couldn't just leave, so I had to kneel down with them. It seemed to last for hours because Kevin's ma prayed for everybody and they said a whole pile of novenas as well, and when I stood up, I was stiff and numb. The Rosary in our house only lasted fifteen minutes.

The sausages and bacon were lovely. Uncle Jimmy and the twins had a fried egg as well. Liam said out loud that it wasn't fair; he wanted an egg, too. My ma clipped him around the ear, but not hard. She told him to have manners and to be grateful about getting anything to eat at all because there were people in Europe and Africa starving and the black babies were dying of hunger every day. I knew that because Mr Philson had a charity collection box in the classroom and there was a photograph of a black baby on it.

Sometimes I was sent round the school with it on Monday mornings and children in different classes put money into it. I never put anything in. Liam didn't, either, because he never had any money. When the box was full, Mr Philson took it down to the chapel and the priest counted it. The money was sent to Africa and the box came back up to the school for more collections. Just before Christmas last year, Father Mooney came to the school and read a letter out from another priest in Africa to thank everybody for the money. He said a penny could feed a black baby for a whole day. My ma said it took about twenty pennies to feed me and Liam for a day.

Father Mooney gave out raffle tickets for a draw and Liam won first prize. He got a wooden duck on wheels with a handle attached to it and the duck's wings flapped when you pushed it along the ground. The priest congratulated Liam and said that this was God's way of thanking him for helping to feed the black babies. Liam just smiled up at him. But a whole lot of boys laughed because they knew that Liam never put any money into the charity box. I didn't laugh because I remembered a priest telling us one time that God works in mysterious ways. I knew he was right because that was the first new toy that our Liam ever got. But I took a mental note of who was laughing at our Liam.

Uncle Jimmy left soon after eating, as he said he had some business to do. When the dishes were cleared away, my ma told us all to kneel down for the Rosary. Halfway through the third decade, there was a terrible noise in the hall. We heard the glass door banging. I thought the glass was going to break, but it didn't. It was my da. He was singing *Kevin Barry* very loud and staggering when he came into the living room.

Liam and me started to laugh. My ma and the twins rushed towards him to stop him falling. Without saying anything, the twins turned him right round, pushing him out the door and up the stairs. My ma started to cry, so Liam and me stopped laughing. It was just that we thought it was funnier than a fart during the Rosary, but it wasn't funny if your ma was crying.

You could still hear him singing *Kevin Barry* when he reached the landing. My ma went up after them. Me and Liam were still on our knees when she came down again. She was still crying and then Liam started to cry. He jumped up and ran over to her and she hugged him. But she didn't hug me when I went over to them.

'Youse two go up to your bedroom for a while,' sobbed my ma. 'Everything will be all right. Off youse go now.'

Liam walked over to me and took my hand. He was still crying and everything was annoying me again. That's when it crossed my mind that it wasn't right that my da had a gun. And I was going to do something about it. I didn't know what yet, but I knew a gun was dangerous, especially if you were drunk. You could shoot somebody you didn't mean to shoot. Even somebody in your own family.

'You can read my comics if you like,' I said to Liam when we went upstairs. His eyes were still a bit red.

'Thanks, Dickie. I never read comics before. Do you mean I can read them all the time, not just tonight?' Liam couldn't really read, but he could look at the pictures.

'All the time, you can read them all the time.'

'Wow! Thanks, Dickie.'

'I'm going for a pee,' I told him.

'Okay, Dickie, I'll see you in a wee minute.'

I went out of the bedroom and listened from the landing. I could hear my ma and the twins talking downstairs. The living-room door was closed, so I didn't know what they were saying. My ma was probably still crying. I hated my da for annoying her, especially if she was sick. I could hear him snoring in the other bedroom. That meant he wasn't dead. You could die from too much drink – Uncle Jimmy told me that. I was glad he wasn't dead because everybody would know that it was the drink that killed him. It would be far better if he died after being hit by a crane or something at the docks or if he was drowned trying to save somebody who fell into the Foyle. You could talk about that to everybody, but not the drink part.

And anyway, he could go to Hell if he died when he was drunk because it's a mortal sin to get drunk and he wouldn't be able to get to Confession. And you can't go to Confession any-how if you're drunk because you would be singing and shouting at the priest and he would throw you out of the box. It would be like mocking God. And mocking God is the worst thing you can do.

Mocking people is the second worst thing you can do and you could end up with the same thing as the person you mocked. Kevin Doherty told me that. That's why Kevin always said 'God bless the mark' when we saw somebody who was a cripple or something, or if they had a club foot and a big heel on their shoe to stay level. We saw a boy one time that had polio. He needed crutches to walk. When he passed us in the street, Kevin knelt down on the footpath. His eyes went into his head when he said 'God bless the mark'. I prayed every night afterwards that I wouldn't get polio. Danny Doherty told me you could catch it if somebody threw a bucket of cold water over your head. I believed him at the time.

But my da would be back at the docks in the morning and my ma wouldn't talk about him being drunk tonight. My ma never said any bad things about anybody, especially about my da. But Uncle Jimmy did, and if he said things in front of my ma, she always shushed him and told him that Barney was a good man but he had his weaknesses.

I went downstairs and into the living room. My ma and the twins were just sitting there as if nothing had happened. Kate said, 'What do you want?' I said nothing because it was none of her business. Laura didn't say anything. She was working at the Singer sewing machine, making something. It looked like work that she brought home from Ritchie's factory sometimes, cuffs and things, maybe. Nearly everybody called it Ritchie's. One of the Smarts overheard me one day in the playground calling it Ritchie's and he told me it was called Richards. He said that the man who owned it was called Mr Richards. I thumped him hard and he never mentioned it again. But that was before the Smarts gave me the *Film Fun Annual.*

If the twins hadn't been in the living room, and if it had just been my ma, I would have gone over to her because I think she would have taken me on her knee and hugged me and rocked me and told me that I was her big son. That's what I thought anyhow.

'Can I have a drink of hot milk, Ma?' I said. 'And one for Liam?'

'Ye can surely, Son.' She got up and went out to the kitchen. Her face was very pale. I went over to Laura at the sewing machine. I liked watching its wheels going round and the sounds they made.

'What are ye making?' I asked.

'A patchwork quilt,' she said. She had a big bag of cloth pieces at her feet, different shapes and colours. I knew she got them from the factory scraps.

'Who is it for?'

'It's for whoever needs it.'

Me and Liam had a patchwork quilt on our bed. My ma had made it when I was wee. 'Did you make our quilt?' I asked her, even though I knew she hadn't.

'Naw, your ma made that years ago, when I was your age.'

'It's lovely,' I said.

'Do you mean this one or the one on your bed?'

'The one you're making,' I lied. My ma's was better, but I thought I'd be nice to her. This was me sucking up because I needed money now and again and it was time I started on the twins. Starting now was a case of better late than never.

Kate was listening to a song on the wireless. I didn't like it. It was somebody called Vera Lynn singing *The White Cliffs of Dover*. I liked music without the singing. Orchestra stuff. But I didn't say that; I just smiled at her and said, 'Nice music.' She didn't speak. Kate never said much to me except to slag me about a dirty nose or smelly socks. They both talked to Liam and played with him sometimes, and took him to the park. I didn't care. I had plenty of friends. They were just my twin big sisters, but they could be good for money at a later date.

My ma came in carrying two cups of milk and handed them to me. I told her they were too hot to drink yet so she said I could wait there for a while. The milk wasn't really hot. I just said it so that I could stay downstairs for another few minutes. Another lie. A small one. It was nice being there with my ma, but I didn't like being with the twins, not much anyhow.

'How's Liam?' my ma asked.

'He's great; he's reading my comics.'

'Good boy,' she said. 'You're good to Liam.'

I could hear Kate sniggering. But it made me feel good when my ma said that. It would take me longer than I thought to get round Kate. But get round her I would. It was only a matter of time. I smiled at Kate before I left the living room with the milk. A made-up smile, for I was still sad to see my ma's big belly and her white face. My ma closed the living-room door behind me.

I walked up the stairs slowly so as not to spill the milk on the lino in case somebody slipped on it. I left the two cups on the landing floor and went into the bathroom. I locked the door and knelt down beside the bath. I put my hand underneath it and lifted the floorboard. All I could feel was the jam jar. I searched further, as far as I could reach in all directions. The gun was gone again. The only thing I could think of was that my da had taken it. He probably had it under his mattress. I felt afraid, not for me but for my ma and the twins and for Liam. I didn't know what to do. I really was afraid, and I was stumped.

I went out to the landing, lifted the two cups of milk and headed for our bedroom. I heard the glass door opening and then the living-room door. Uncle Jimmy was back. Maybe I should go down and tell him about the gun. But then I thought about the promise that I had made to my da. *It's a secret, Son, tell nobody about it.* I was in a real dilemma.

I walked into the bedroom with the milk. Liam was sitting up in the bed. He was sleeping, his head down on his chest. The comic was on the quilt in front of him. I looked at him while drinking my milk at the same time. Then I drank his. I would tell my ma in the morning, if she asked me, that he enjoyed it. He wouldn't remember, and even if he did, he wouldn't say anything. I was beginning to trust Liam more that way, mostly because of the gobstopper arrangement.

Before I got into bed, I took the exercise book with the sin list inside it from underneath the lino. I decided to write down the latest sins in case I would forget them on Friday. The list read:

✓ Cursed eight times
✓ Lied fourteen times to my friends
✓ Spat on people seven times
✓ Pushed people ten times

I took the pencil out of my schoolbag and began to write more:

✓ Said bad words sixteen times
✓ Had bad thoughts about other people five times
✓ Lied by omission to the twins four times
✓ Lied to others six times

That was all the sins I could think of. I was tired and wanted to go to sleep. But I wasn't too tired to know that it would be stupid to put the sin list under the lino again. My ma might find it when I was at school and she would go mad if she saw it. She had enough to worry about. I took the exercise book from my schoolbag and put the list inside it. I put the book into the bag with the rest of my stuff. It would be safe there. I promised myself that I wouldn't commit any more sins before Friday. This was the longest list I ever had. The priest would go mad with me.

I was too tired to read a comic, like I always did before I went to sleep. And my mind was thinking all the time about my sick ma and my drunken da and the gun he might have in his pocket or under the mattress and about Hitler coming. And about the money I might get from the twins if I kept playing my cards right.

It must have been hours later that the nightmare came. It didn't waken me. You don't waken during a nightmare, only after. It was the worst nightmare you could imagine. I heard my da going mad in the landing and my ma squealing at him to get back to bed. Then I heard him in the bathroom pulling up all the floorboards and shouting out loud about the gun. I saw him, too, in my room looking for it. I heard Uncle Jimmy arguing with the twins downstairs, and them crying. And for a second or two, I saw our Liam standing in the corner of the landing, watching everything.

I don't often have nightmares. But I can say now for certain that this was definitely one of the worst. It was weird.

CHAPTER 9

The Sin List Exposure

When I woke on Wednesday morning, Liam was sitting up in bed, staring out at the landing. I thought that was strange because before this, I was always the one who wakened Liam.

'Come on,' I shouted to him as I pulled on my clothes, 'we're going to be late for school.'

'I'm not going,' he said.

'Ye have to go to school,' I told him.

'I don't care. I'm not going. I want to stay with my ma.'

'Ye can't, ye have to go.' I tried to pull him out of the bed but he spat at me. He'd never done that before. My bad example. Bad example was another sin I'd have to add to the list. Liam must be sick. I'd tell my ma when I went downstairs.

I went into the bathroom. Most of the floorboards were pulled up. I was shocked. The gun? The police? A raid? I didn't know what. I'd soon find out. The jam jar was lying there, too. Marbles and chestnuts lying all over the place.

'What happened in the bathroom, Ma?' I said to her when I went into the living room. She was there herself. My da and the twins and Uncle Jimmy were all at work. She was sitting in the armchair beside the fire, her face white with black rings around her eyes. Her belly looked bigger. She must be really sick.

'Come over here, Dickie,' she said, pointing to the side of the

69

seat. I sat down beside her. She was quiet, but I knew by the sound of her voice that it was interrogation time. Interrogation is quizzing to find out if you're lying. And you don't lie to your ma. Well, not really. Not about serious stuff anyhow. She would know right away if you weren't telling the truth. She had the knack.

She put her arm around my shoulder before she spoke. I liked that and snuggled in closer to her. I was nervous. I could feel her big belly on my side.

'Is everything all right, Dickie?'

'Liam must be sick, Ma, he won't get up for school.'

'That's all right, Dickie, I'll see to him. I'll bring him down myself and make sure he goes into the classroom.'

She didn't speak for another wee minute; she just took a few big breaths. That's when I saw my schoolbag sitting near the hearth. I felt sick. She must've seen the sin list. She'd kill me. I'd be in front of the Sacred Heart picture all day, maybe even all week. My world was over.

'Tell me this, Dickie,' she said quietly. 'Did you take anything from the bathroom?'

'No, Ma, I didn't. What would I take?'

'It's just that your da was looking for something in there in the middle of the night. You know he was drunk and he was very annoyed.'

I knew right away that she was talking about the gun. I was off the hook. She couldn't have seen the sin list.

'Yes, Ma, I saw him drunk, and you and the twins had to put him to bed.'

She took another few big breaths.

'Ye see, Dickie, I was thinking that when you were sometimes getting your marbles and chestnuts, ye might have seen something else that was in there.' My ma was smart; she knew about the jam jar so she must know about the gun as well.

'Naw, Ma, I didn't see anything else, and I didn't take anything out of the bathroom.' I was lying, but she believed me.

'That's all, Son. You're a good boy, Dickie. Now let me get you something to eat.'

She went into the kitchen and I could hear her pouring water into the kettle. I looked again at the schoolbag. I didn't know how it had got downstairs. It was a big mystery, but I knew I'd get the answers soon.

After breakfast, I lifted my bag and headed out through the glass doorway. I closed it quietly behind me, not wanting it to rattle, but the hinges creaked. On the way down the hill to school, I was thinking about my so-called nightmare. It was real, the nightmare that never was: my da looking for the gun when he was drunk; my ma knowing about the gun; the twins and Uncle Jimmy knowing about the gun; and all the shouting and squealing and everything.

I was one of the last getting into the class. Philson was standing at the front. He had a cane in his hand and a smirk on his face. Somebody was in trouble, surely it couldn't be me. Not this time. I hadn't done anything wrong since yesterday. There was a hush when we all sat down.

'Richard McCauley,' shouted Philson. My heart sank. Not another Philson versus McCauley thing. What had I done now? Nothing. It must be a mistake.

'Stand up, McCauley.'

I stood up. He lifted a book off the desk in front of him. An exercise book. I relaxed. I heard somebody sniggering. I didn't know who, I was too busy watching Philson's face.

'Bring up your exercise book, McCauley.' I opened my bag and searched inside, but it wasn't there.

'Is this what you're looking for, McCauley?'

'I dunno, Sir.'

'You don't know, eh? So, if it's not in your schoolbag, and the one I have in my hand has your name on it, then this must be it.'

'I suppose so, Sir.'

'You suppose so, McCauley? Either it is, or it isn't. Which do you think, McCauley?'

'It must be it, Sir.'

I walked up towards him with my hand outstretched, hoping he would give it to me. I just had to get the exercise book before he saw the sin list inside. How he'd got his hands on it wasn't important yet. The important thing was what was inside it, and me getting my hands on it before he did.

'Stop right there, McCauley!' he shouted as he banged the cane down on the front desk. The three Smarts jumped. I stayed calm.

'Did you do your homework last night, McCauley?'

'Yes, Sir, I always do my homework.'

'You do more than your homework, McCauley.'

He opened the book, took out the list and held it up. He knew about it. Big snotty-nose Philson had seen my sin list. Big hypocrite Philson knew all my Friday-night sins for Confession. I would have to think fast. Faster than I'd ever thought before. A plan was coming. The biggest plan ever. A special.

'Is this your list, McCauley, written out on a jotter page inside your exercise book?'

'Yes, Sir,' I replied, 'that's mine.'

'And did you write it, McCauley?'

'Yes, Sir.'

Five or six of the class were now sniggering. The Smarts weren't.

'Silence!' shouted Philson as he whacked the desk again with the cane. Everybody went quiet. I could see the veins standing out on the side of his head.

'And is there a purpose in you writing this filthy list, McCauley?'

'Yes, Sir.'

'And what might that purpose be?'

The class was very quiet. They knew a crucial point had been reached.

'For Confession, Sir.'

'And is this the type of language and behaviour you get up to every day? This disgraceful, dirty language? Is this the life you're leading, McCauley?'

'No, Sir,' I lied.

'What do you mean, no?'

'Not me, Sir,' I lied again.

'Not you?'

'No, Sir.'

'Let me get this clear, McCauley. You admit that you wrote out this filthy list and you admit it's a list for Confession. And yet you're telling me now that it's somebody else's list, even though it's in *your* exercise book?'

'Yes, Sir.'

There was complete silence in the class.

'And who might this unfortunate other person be, McCauley?'

'My da, Sir.'

The class exploded. Even the Stupids were laughing and thumping their fists on the desk. Philson's veins were about to burst from his head.

'Ye see, Sir,' I shouted over the noise, 'my da curses a lot and spits on people he doesn't like and pushes them about, Sir, but only when he's drunk. And when he sobers up he doesn't remember anything so he told me always to write everything down for him that I see and hear so he can tell it all to the priest later. It's really his list, Sir. I wrote the list for him, Sir.'

Philson brought the cane down hard on the desk in front of the Smarts. I'd never seen him so angry. The stick broke into a million pieces and one of them shot up and stuck into Frankie Smart's face, just below his eye. It began to bleed and Frankie was squealing. Everybody shushed. Philson panicked and shouted at everybody to be quiet, even though nobody was making a sound. He took out his hankie and put it on Frankie's face to try and stop the bleeding. But it didn't. Part of the cane was still sticking out of Frankie and the desk was a mess of blood. Philson had gone white, even whiter than Frankie. He shouted at me to sit down, but before going back to my desk, I picked up the exercise book and the sin list, which Philson had dropped on the floor. He didn't notice. Philson was in big trouble and he knew it. I felt sorry for Frankie, but I was out of trouble – at least for the time being.

As Philson rushed out of the classroom with Frankie Smart, he shouted back to us to stay quiet. Five minutes later, Mr Johnston came in to take the class. He was younger than Philson and was training to be a teacher and was always smiling. He told us some jokes first and then made us get our books out for reading. Everybody read a paragraph except the Stupids. He gave them drawing paper and crayons. In the afternoon, we did sums and spelling. Before home time, he gave us homework to do.

Everybody liked Mr Johnston. If I didn't become a priest when I grew up, I would be a teacher like Mr Johnston.

CHAPTER 10

Clues Found, Mystery Solved

After school, me and Danny and Kevin and our Liam progged Daly's orchard. The apples tasted rotten. Small, hard and sour they were. It wasn't really the season yet for them. Mr Daly was old and you hardly ever saw him. His garden was a wreck. It wasn't really an orchard, either; it only had five trees. It had a high-wire fence around it with holes that you could climb through, but we always climbed over it because it was stupid just going through the holes, that would have been too easy. If Mr Daly repaired the fence, it would be a great place for prisoners when Hitler came. That's what I said to Danny and Kevin when we were climbing out again.

'What prisoners? Who's Hitler?' asked Danny.

'Policemen and soldiers and B-men and Philson would all be prisoners,' I told him. 'And Hitler is the leader of the Germans and they're bombing England now. They'll be here in a few weeks and then we'll get all our land back from the snobby Protestants.' At least that's what my da had told me.

'Don't be stupid,' said Danny. He was arguing with me again, but I didn't spit on him or knock him down. He was too much out of breath after the high fence.

Instead I shouted, 'Naw, *you're* stupid! Why do you think they're building all the air-raid shelters in the streets?' I answered for him. 'They're for the people to hide in for safety when the bombs are dropping.'

Danny kept silent at that; he just looked at me.

'Ye see?' I said. 'You know nothing.' But Danny wasn't finished yet.

'Billy and Cecil are Protestants. Are they going to be prisoners, too?' Danny thought he was being smart, but he wasn't.

'Naw,' I told him, 'Billy and Cecil are our friends, so they'll be safe, but their das are policemen, so they'll be prisoners. We'll rescue Billy and Cecil and tell Hitler that they're with us.'

'Cecil's da isn't a policeman, stupid, he's a B-man.'

'Same thing,' I said.

'It's not.'

'I'm going home,' I said. 'Our tea'll be ready. C'mon, Liam.'

I owed Danny two slaps. He'd get them when I felt like it. He knew that, too. Danny and Kevin ran off ahead of us. I think they were scared because of the invasion of Hitler and the Germans. I wasn't afraid. Not much anyhow.

'Did you hear that noise in our house last night, in the middle of the night?' I asked Liam when we were nearly home.

'What noise?' He was lying.

'When we were sleeping. It was like a dream to me. My ma and da and the twins and Uncle Jimmy, all shouting and arguing.'

'I heard nothing.' He was definitely lying, I could see it in his eyes.

'Did you see the bathroom all wrecked? Did my ma ask you if you'd taken anything out of it?'

'Naw.'

'She must've said something. You must've seen the bathroom.' Liam rushed on without saying anything. I ran after him, but he got to the house before me. It was too late to ask him anything else. Our Liam was acting strange, as if there was something he wasn't telling me. I didn't like that – people keeping secrets from me. It made me worry.

My ma was in the kitchen making pieces for us. She looked pale and tired. Me and Liam went into the living room. He just sat there with his head down.

'Do you want the wireless on, Liam?'

'Naw.'

'I'll put some music on for you.'

'I don't want it.'

'Why?'

'Just.'

'What does that mean, just?'

'It means naw, I don't want music.'

'So do you want me to go up and get you a comic?'

'Naw.'

He was still looking down at the floor. This was our Liam acting strange; he definitely had something to hide. I'd find out later.

My ma came in with two cups of tea and a piece each. 'Here ye are, boys, tuck in,' she said quietly, without smiling. She said nothing else; she just sat there, staring into the fire. After a while, when we'd finished our tea, she spoke. 'Liam, love, will you go to the hall to play? I have to speak to Dickie about something.'

Liam took his cup and the empty plate with him and closed the door behind him. She called me over to her at the armchair and told me to sit down beside her. It was the same as this morning. She put her arm around me and pulled me to her. It felt great. I was getting hugged by my ma twice in the same day. But if she was going to mention the gun, I still wouldn't tell her I'd seen it, because then she would know I had been lying to her. I might tell the priest about it in Confession. He wouldn't be allowed to tell anybody because of the vow of secrecy, but he could badger me about it afterwards if he recognised me. He might say I should report it, but I wouldn't because that would get everybody into big trouble.

'Do you remember this morning, Dickie, about your school-bag being down here?'

'Yes, Ma. That's right, Ma.'

'Let me explain, Dickie, because you should know what happened. You know that your da was drunk. He's just foolish like that sometimes, but last night he had a whole row with everybody after you went to sleep. He was searching mad for something. He started off in the bathroom, looking under the loose floorboard, and then he started in the other rooms: the girls' and Uncle Jimmy's and then yours. He grabbed your schoolbag and when he couldn't find what he was looking for in it, he threw the bag out the window and into the street. I forgot all about it for a good while, but when he went to sleep again, I went outside and brought it in.'

'That's all right, Ma, the bag was all right.'

So that was how Philson got the exercise book with the sin list in it. The book must've fallen out of the bag and my ma didn't see it when she went out to the street in the dark. Somebody must've picked it up in the morning, in daylight, and brought it to Philson because his name was on the front of it, below mine. Clues found, mystery solved. I was just thankful that my ma hadn't picked up the exercise book. I wondered should I ask her the big question now. I'd think about it for a minute.

'You're a good boy, Dickie. Why don't you take Liam out to play for a wee while?'

Before I closed the living-room door behind me, I asked her, 'What was it, Ma, that my da was looking for?'

'Ye needn't concern yourself with that, Dickie. Everything's all right now.'

I closed the door behind me. She didn't know that I knew, or if she did, she wasn't saying. My da hadn't blabbed. I was off the hook.

I took Liam outside and up the street. Kevin was standing at the lamppost. He looked as if he was praying. I spoke to him.

'Why do you not say "God bless the mark" when you see Danny's ma?'

'What mark?' asked Kevin.

'The big fat mark,' I said, 'and the moustache mark, and the big fat legs mark and the giant arse mark.' I wouldn't have said it if Danny had been there. At least not now, just at this minute, but if he ever called me Big Ears again, or stupid, I would, and he could just lump it.

'Those aren't marks that God would have to bless,' said Kevin. 'That's just the way she is.'

'Can you be born without legs?' I asked him. Liam laughed. I was glad.

'No,' said Kevin. 'Everybody starts off with legs, but they could get them cut off in an accident or something like that, like in a big machine or with a steam roller.'

'If you got your legs cut off in an accident,' asked Liam, 'would you get them back when you go to Heaven?'

Kevin and me stared at him. Our Liam had never asked an important question before, never mind a hard one like that. I liked that. I felt proud of him.

'Yes, you would,' replied Kevin, 'because you get back whatever you were born with.'

Then Liam went on, 'And if you were born with no legs at all, would you get new legs in Heaven?'

'I don't know,' said Kevin. 'You might, but I think you would have to have legs from the start. You can only get back what you had before.'

I was really pleased with Liam's questions. It showed he was smart: far smarter than Danny Doherty. Danny Doherty never got more than three sums right out of six and he always got less than half his spellings right. And now that Liam was in better form, he might tell me later about what happened in the house in the middle of the night. I wouldn't push him yet, I'd bide my time. You get better results that way.

CHAPTER 11

Sucking Varnish Wasn't Good

I didn't want to go back to the house yet. The mood my ma was in, and the way she was hugging me and all, I might accidentally tell her that I knew about the gun. That would spoil everything.

Billy and Cecil were playing football up the street. Tippity kick. Stupid stuff. Billy's da must be on duty somewhere or he would have killed him. He hated us playing football in the street.

'We'll go up and play shooty-in,' I said to Liam.

Kevin said he was going home. He hated football. His glasses always steamed up when he was sweating and he couldn't see the ball.

Liam followed me. I lifted a stone and scraped out goalposts on the barracks wall.

'Who's for shooty-in?' I shouted.

We played for about half an hour. They beat us twenty-four goals to eight but I didn't care, I was just passing the time.

'I want to go home now,' said Liam.

'Right,' I said, but before we left, Billy and Cecil said they would come down to the chapel with us on Friday evening. We would all go somewhere else after Confessions. We always did that.

As soon as we got home, Liam started to swing on the glass door. Danny's ma was in our kitchen and Danny was with her. She was cooking the dinner. Fresh herrings. I could smell them. I loved fresh herrings but I didn't like Big Fat Face in our kitchen. Or Fat Danny, either. I looked into the living room. My ma wasn't there; something was wrong.

'Your ma's a bit sick, Dickie,' said Mrs Fatso, when she saw me. 'She had to go up to bed. I'm making the dinner for youse all the night.'

I ran up the stairs and into my ma's bedroom. She was lying in bed, her face very red and sweaty, not pale like it was before. The belly disease must be worse. Her eyes were open and she smiled at me, but it wasn't a happy smile. It was a sick one. She put her hand out to me on the quilt. It was very hot when I touched her. 'We're going to get a new baby soon,' she said. 'The nurse is coming in a wee while and then we'll see if it's a boy or a girl.'

I didn't say anything. Nobody had told me about us getting a new baby. My ma had her handbag beside her. She took out a threepenny bit and told me to go down to the chapel and light a candle for her and the new baby, and she told me to take Liam with me and to be nice to Mrs Doherty because she would be helping us all for a few days.

'Okay, Ma,' I said. She gave me another smile before I left, but I could see the pain in her face.

We didn't go straight to the chapel because I told Liam that I was taking him to the shop to get a gobstopper first. If I had just told him that we were going to the chapel, he wouldn't have come. Liam got sick in the chapel sometimes. He said it was the incense at Mass that did it, but I think it was because he sucked the wood on the back of the seat in front of him. It was the varnish that made him sick. Sucking varnish wasn't good, but I didn't tell him that, because when he got sick, I always took him outside so I didn't have to stay the whole time.

The Mass was always in Latin and I didn't understand a word of it, but the sermons were in English, so that was okay. I always liked the sermon about the prodigal son. It was about a boy getting a whole lot of money from his da and spending it all when he went away. When he had no money left to buy food, he had to eat pig-swill. And when he came home again, his da was so glad to see him that he threw his arms around him. If my da had money and he gave me a whole lot of it, I wouldn't go away anywhere. I'd just buy things for Liam and the twins and my ma, and I'd keep a whole lot in my pocket as well, to rattle it, the same as Danny Doherty does.

I put the threepenny bit on the shop counter and asked for two gobstoppers, one for me and one for Liam. The penny change would be enough for the candle in the chapel. I didn't tell Liam about the new baby. I told him we were lighting a candle for my ma. He didn't say anything, just sucked the gobstopper. He held my hand on the way down. I liked that.

I slipped the penny into the box and took a candle from another box. If I hadn't bought the gobstoppers, I could have got three candles. I lit it from another old candle that was nearly burnt out and stabbed it into the wet grease of the old candle. I felt a bit sad because whoever had bought the dead candle, it could have been for a sick ma or a sick da, and they mightn't get better now. I lifted another new candle out of the box and lit it for all the sick people. I promised to put a penny in the box later. I told Liam to kneel down beside me and say a prayer for my ma. 'Why?' he asked softly.

'Because she's sick,' I whispered. If you talked loudly in the chapel, it was a venial sin. If you laughed loudly, it was a mortal sin. I wondered if Protestants lit candles in their churches.

'What's wrong with her?' asked Liam.

'She's got the big-belly disease.'

Liam didn't say anything at that. He just joined his hands and closed his eyes and started praying. The wet gobstopper was in his pocket. I'd told him it was a sin to suck a gobstopper in the chapel, but it wouldn't really have been a sin for Liam because he hadn't reached the age of reason yet. You had to be seven for that.

'Will we light candles for all the other mas who have the big-belly disease?' whispered Liam.

'Naw, it would cost too much,' I told him.

'Okay,' said Liam and we got up to go.

Father Mooney was standing behind us. We didn't know he was there until he spoke. 'Good boys,' he said. 'Aren't you the good boys?' He said it in a sort of low voice. Not a whisper. He had a big smile on his face. It mustn't be a sin to talk low in chapel because priests can't commit sins. They just hear other people's sins.

'You're Richard,' he said. I hated being called Richard, but it was all right for a priest to say it.

'Yes, Father, I'm Richard.' I felt a wee bit like vomiting.

'And you made your First Communion a couple of years ago. I remember you.'

'Yes, Father.'

'Good boy, good boy. And you'll be down to Confession as usual on Friday evening?'

'Yes, Father, I go to Confession every week.' I thought of the sin list. It was a long one this week and I still had more stuff to write into it. He mightn't be so pleased looking when he heard it all.

'And this is . . .?'

'Liam, Father – he's my wee brother. He's making his First Confession and First Communion next year.'

'Good, good. And how are your mammy and daddy?'

I just told him about my ma because I didn't want to say anything about my da in case it was a lie. You don't lie to priests. You could go to Hell if you lied to priests. So I just told him about my ma having the big-belly disease. I didn't tell him that the nurse was coming with a new baby.

'We were lighting a candle for her, Father, and saying a wee prayer.'

'Good boys, good boys.'

'The big-belly disease is going around, Father,' I said to him. 'Our Liam was down at the doctor's with my ma, and there was a whole crowd there. They all had it.'

I couldn't understand why the priest smiled, because you're supposed to look sad when you hear about people being sick.

'Ah yes, ah yes, yes, yes, yes,' said Father Mooney. And I even thought that his smile was going to change to a laugh, but it didn't, because that could be a sin, even for a priest.

'Is she in hospital, Richard?'

'Naw, she's up in the house, in bed.'

'That's good, that's good. Your mother will be better soon, boys. Don't worry. God is good.'

'Thanks, Father,' I said. It made me feel great, the priest saying that my ma would be better soon.

'And what are you going to be when you grow up?' asked Father Mooney.

'I'm going to be a priest, Father, but Liam doesn't know yet what he wants to be. He's too young to know.'

I could feel Liam tugging my hand. He wanted to leave. We turned to go. Father Mooney put his hand into his pocket and took out some change. I noticed that his hands were very smooth and his nails were very clean, not like my da's. He gave me and Liam a shilling each.

'There you go, boys. Get yourselves something nice.'

Liam and me genuflected properly before we left the chapel, in case the priest was watching. But he wasn't. He was going home to his big house in the chapel grounds.

Outside the gates, Liam took the gobstopper out of his pocket. It was covered in dirt but he kept licking it. He didn't say anything about the priest giving him money. He didn't seem too excited about it.

'Did you see the way the priest smiled when I told him my ma had the big-belly disease? You would have thought he would have been sad.'

Liam just grunted. The gobstopper was back in his mouth.

'He must have known something, Liam. Priests know things that we don't know. He said my ma would be all right soon. So that means that God was telling him that my ma was going to get better. That's what it is, Liam. Priests speak to God all the time.'

Liam still didn't say anything. Just kept sucking. At the corner of our street, Liam took the last of the gobstopper out of his mouth and threw it away.

'I know who has the gun,' he said.

Liam ran towards the house. I just stood there, shocked. How could he know about the gun? And how could he know who had it? I ran after him. He was swinging on the glass door.

'Who?' I whispered.

'I can't tell you.'

'Why not?'

'Because I can't.'

I sat on the bottom stair watching him. I could hear voices in the living room. I could smell the herring and the spuds. I was hungry. I asked him again about the gun.

'I can't tell you,' he said. 'It's a secret.'

'I'll give you a shilling if you tell me.'

'I have my own shilling.'

Mrs Fatso came down the stairs behind me. 'Ssssh,' she said. 'Your ma's sleeping. Youse'll waken her.'

'Fuck off,' I said under my breath. She didn't hear me. I moved over on the stair to let her past. She tried but she couldn't. She was too fat. Anybody else could have got past, but not big arse.

'Get up,' she hissed. She hit me on the side of the head. That made me shift. It was like being attacked by a whale. 'Clear the stairs, ye brat. The nurse'll be coming soon.' She went past me and into the living room.

'Why would the nurse be coming?' asked Liam.

'I'll tell you if you tell me the other thing.'

'The priest said my ma would get better so why is the nurse coming?' he asked again.

'I know why,' I said to him. 'I know why she's coming.'

'Why?'

I bent down to his ear and told him about the new baby and then told him he would have to tell me who had the gun.

'Fuck off,' he said.

'Don't say bad words,' I said and clipped him across the ear. He began to cry. I'd blown it. Now he'd never tell me. The living-room door opened. It was my da.

'Are youse two boys coming in for your dinner? Mrs Doherty has it all ready for youse.'

There were two plates of herring and spuds sitting on the table. 'Say thanks to Mrs Doherty,' said my da.

Thanks, Mrs Big Fatso.

'Thanks, Mrs Doherty.'

Me and Liam looked at the dinners. They looked cold. Liam whispered, 'Yuck.' I knew he wouldn't eat it. He hated herring. My ma wouldn't have given it to him. The twins were sitting on the couch, their empty plates beside them. Danny Doherty was sitting on his ma's knee. Big Fatso and Wee Fatso. They were on my ma's chair. I hated that. I ate the dinner. Liam just stared down at his and said nothing.

'Where were youse, boys?' asked my da.

'We were down in the chapel, lighting a candle for my ma.'

'Good, good, Son, good, good,' said my da.

There was silence then except for the wireless. Something was on about the war, something about bombs being dropped in England by the Germans. The man was saying that tons of bombs were dropped on some place in London and thousands of people were killed.

'Hell rub it up them,' said my da.

'God forgive you,' said Mrs Doherty. 'Those poor souls.'

'What about *our* poor souls?' shouted my da. 'What about what the British did in Ireland? Killing our people and burning us out and taking all our jobs and us having to emigrate to America and all.'

'Aye, and to England, too, for the work,' interrupted Mrs Doherty. 'It's a pity you didn't go as well like a whole lot of others had to.'

I looked at the twins. They were giggling. I didn't think it was funny, but I liked my da arguing with Danny's ma.

'So you were down at the chapel, boys?' said my da.

'Isn't that great?' said Mrs Fatso. 'Two wee boys going down to light a candle for their mother. Do you hear that, Danny? Would you ever do that for me?' Danny just grunted.

'We saw Father Mooney, Da,' I told him. 'He was asking about you.'

'Was he, now?' said my da.

'He said my ma would be okay soon. I think God told him that.'

'Did He now?' replied my da. 'Great, great.'

'Isn't that lovely?' said Mrs Doherty. 'Father Mooney talking to both of youse. You should have been there, Danny.'

'And what did you say to Father Mooney about my ma?' asked Kate.

'I told him she had the big-belly disease. A whole lot of mas have it. Liam told me, didn't you, Liam?' Liam didn't speak.

'Aye, she has the big-belly disease all right,' said Laura, glaring at my da. 'And Father Mooney's right, Dickie, it will get better soon, but if someone's not careful, it could come back again. Isn't that right, Da?'

My da gave Laura a bad look. 'We'll have none of that talk in this house!' he shouted. 'It's an act of God and a gift from Heaven. That's what it is.'

'Some act of God,' sniggered Kate.

'Aye, and some gift,' laughed Laura.

'Shush, shush now, will youse?' said Mrs Doherty. 'Sure isn't that some sort of talk in front of the three wee wans. Youse should be ashamed of yourselves, with poor Mrs McCauley lying upstairs waiting. We should all be thankful to God for what we have and what He sends us.'

They all kept quiet after that. The man on the wireless was still talking about people being killed by the German bombs.

'Are ye coming out, Liam?' I whispered as I pulled him by the hand. He didn't hold back and we went into the hall where Liam started to swing on the glass door. I slipped into the kitchen and made him a piece and a cup of milk. He stopped swinging when he saw the food and sat on the stair with me and gulped it all down. He was starving. When he finished, I gave him a gobstopper. I had another four or five tucked away in the bedroom, just for emergencies.

There was a light knock on the glass door. A big, dark figure. I opened it. It was the nurse. She had a long, dark-blue coat on her and a hat the same colour.

'Hello, boys,' she said as she came into the hall. 'And who have we here? Two nice boys who are good to their mammy?'

We just looked at her and said nothing. She had a big black bag with her. Liam and me looked at it at the same time then Liam pointed at it. 'Is the new baby in there?' he asked the nurse.

'You could say that, Son, aye, you could say that.'

Mrs Doherty came out from the living room. She must have heard us talking. 'Hello, Nurse,' was all she said. They went upstairs together. Me and Liam went back into the living room. The wireless was turned off. The twins were sitting there, saying nothing.

'You and Liam and Danny should go out to play for a while,' said my da. 'I'll call you in later before bedtime.'

We went to the street. Billy and Cecil were away. It was just me and Liam and Danny. It was getting dark. We saw Big Joey and Peter, Kate and Laura's boyfriends. They were climbing over a fence into Thompson's Field and waved when they saw us. Me and Liam waved back.

Joey and Peter had been coming to our house for nearly a year to see the twins. Well, to the porch anyway, they never got past the glass door. I liked them. They gave me money sometimes. I heard Uncle Jimmy telling my ma one time that the twins shouldn't be going out with them. He said they weren't the right type. When the girls heard that, they nearly went mad and told Uncle Jimmy to mind his own business.

'Those boys are up to no good,' said Danny.

'What are you talking about?' I asked him.

'My ma said they were dodgy boys and to steer clear of them. My ma says they're in the Movement.'

'What Movement?' I asked him. 'What Movement are ye talking about?'

'Just the Movement,' said Danny. 'That's what my ma calls it – the Movement.'

'You don't know anything. You just say things and you don't know what you're talking about. And your ma knows nothing as well, and she makes rotten dinners. And if you tell her I said that, I'll double the number of spits I owe you.' Danny said nothing more.

'You're stupid, Danny,' said Liam. Danny didn't say anything back to Liam, either, but he gave him a dirty look. I didn't say anything, because Liam would have to learn to look out for himself. A dirty look couldn't really harm you.

We could still just about see Big Joey and Peter in the distance. They had sat down on the grass and lit cigarettes. We turned away.

'It's getting cold,' I said. 'Let's go home.' Danny came with us because his ma was still in our house.

'I want to see the new baby,' laughed Liam. We ran the rest of the way down the street. Danny was puffing behind us.

As soon as we opened the glass door, we saw Kevin Doherty and his ma kneeling down saying the Rosary. Kevin's ma stopped praying and caught me by the hand.

'I'm sorry about your wee baby brother,' she said. 'God wanted him more than your mother. He'll be happy in Limbo now until God brings him to Heaven on the last day.'

I didn't know what she was talking about. Liam started to cry when he saw the crowd of neighbours in the living room. Some of them were shaking hands with my da and the twins. Uncle Jimmy wasn't there. The twins were crying and my da's eyes were red.

'Where's the baby?' I shouted.

They all stopped talking and looked at me. I ran out of the room and up the stairs.

'Where's the baby?' I shouted again when I went into my ma's bedroom.

'Ssssh,' whispered Mrs Fatso Doherty. 'Don't be upsetting your poor mother.'

'Where is it?' I cried. 'I want to see him.'

'He's gone,' said Mrs Doherty.

'Gone where?' I asked.

'The nurse took him away.'

'Why? Sure he's ours! Why did she take him away?'

I heard my ma crying out loud as Mrs Doherty pushed me out of the room. 'Because, Son,' she whispered when we were in the landing, 'the baby was dead, Son.'

'But the nurse brought it in the bag a wee while ago. Me and Liam were here when she brought it.'

'Yes, Son, you got the new baby all right, but it was dead when it came.'

Liam had come up the stairs after me and heard everything. Mrs Doherty went back in to my ma. We sat down on the landing floor.

'She must have smothered it,' said Liam. 'The bag was closed and it got no air.' Liam was right. The bag *was* closed when the nurse came. I was stupid and wee Liam was smart. Liam started to cry and I hugged him for a good while. I didn't cry out loud, but I sobbed sore in to myself.

My da came up the stairs then and told us to go to bed. We went into our bedroom but we couldn't sleep for a long time and I didn't read any comics; I didn't feel like it. All I could think of was the baby smothering in the nurse's black bag. That nurse was stupid and she killed our wee brother. Fifth, thou shalt not kill. She was a murderer, and she'd have to tell the priest in Confession about what she'd done.

That was the same night that the B-man's hut in Thompson's Field got burned to the ground. I could see the flames through the bedroom window and I didn't care. I heard the bells of the fire engine. Liam was already asleep, so I just went to sleep as well.

CHAPTER 12

The Baby With No Name

My da got us up and ready for school the next few days because my ma was still in bed. He said she was having a good rest because she was tired.

On Friday morning Kate and Laura were sitting on the couch. They were quiet and their eyes were red. They were still crying about the baby. My da was out in the kitchen. I looked at Kate and Laura. Liam was holding my hand.

'It was the nurse's fault,' I told them. 'Her bag was shut tight and the baby smothered in it.'

'Aye, and youse two should tell the police about her because she killed the baby,' cried Liam.

I told them that me and Liam would be witnesses because we were the first to see the bag. We'd tell the police everything.

'God Almighty,' said Kate, as she looked at us. 'What are we going to do with youse? Youse know nothing and youse are far too young to know anything. Come over here.'

Me and Liam walked over to them. They put out their arms, Kate's to me and Laura's to Liam. They hugged us. Nobody had ever hugged me before except my ma. Then they let us go, but held our hands. Laura spoke.

'Look, boys, all youse have to know for now is that the nurse didn't bring the baby in the bag. The baby was born upstairs.

So the nurse didn't bring it. It was nobody's fault. And that's the way it is sometimes. Sometimes babies are dead before they're born. And that's the way it was for your ma. That's all I'm telling youse now, so just go on to school. Me and Kate will be here all day to look after things. So youse aren't to worry now about anything. Your ma's going to be all right. So off youse go, now.'

There was still smoke rising from the burnt-out B-man's hut. Two policemen were standing looking at it. Bap Kelly was there as well, across the street with a group of men. He had his school-bag on his back. Nobody was saying anything, they were just watching the smoke.

'Hello, Dickie! Hello, Liam!' shouted Bap as we passed. 'Wait and I'll come down with youse.' I didn't know why Bap was there. He lived away down in the Bogside. He ran towards us.

'That was a great night's work, the B-hut and all,' he laughed, 'and if they build it again, it'll go the same way.'

'What are ye talking about?'

'The B-hut, the bastards' B-hut, and that's only the beginning,' said Bap.

I didn't know what he meant, so I didn't say anything.

'I heard about your wee baby brother,' said Bap. 'That happened in our house, too.' I still didn't say anything. I liked Bap all right, but he wasn't my friend. He had a gang in the Bogside, and everybody knew you didn't attack them because they were tough. He was called Bap because he had red hair. His ma came up to our house sometimes. She'd worked in the factory with my ma years ago.

'Why don't you come down to our house some day, Dickie? Bring the boys with you.'

'We might come down some day,' I told him.

We went into the classroom and sat down at our desks. Phil-son was writing something on the blackboard.

'Sir?'

'Just a minute.'

'Sir?'

'I said wait.'

It was Kevin's voice. 'Sir, Dickie McCauley's wee baby brother died last night. He was born dead, Sir.' Philson turned and looked at me.

'Is this true, McCauley?'

I put my head down. I didn't feel like saying anything. And I swore I'd kill Kevin Doherty before the day was over.

'Yes, Sir.'

Philson was standing beside me. 'I'm very sorry to hear that, Richard. And how's your mother?' *Big-arsed hypocrite.*

'She's all right, Sir.'

'Sir, should we say a Rosary for the dead baby?' said Kevin.

'I don't think that will be necessary, Doherty, but if we all bow our heads we'll say a Hail Mary for Richard's mother and father.' *Snot-nosed hypocrite.* And stupid Kevin Doherty. He knew how I felt about attention from Philson.

Philson didn't ask for my homework for the first time ever. At lunchtime I thumped Kevin. 'God forgive you,' he whimpered, 'I was only trying to get a Rosary said for the baby.'

Before going home, Philson reminded us about Confession time. We were to line up as usual in Helen Street for five o'clock. As we were leaving the room, he called me over to his desk.

'Richard, I'm very sorry about the baby.' I didn't say anything. 'And, Richard?'

'Yes, Sir?'

He put his hand into his pocket. I could hear coins rattling. He handed me a shilling. 'You don't have to do any homework this weekend.' When I was crossing Thompson's Field on the way home, I threw the shilling away, as far as I could. Nobody would ever find it.

The B-man's hut was still smoking when I reached Rosemount. There was nobody standing about, either, and it was starting to rain. I ran the rest of the way home.

My da was sitting on the bottom stair and Liam was swinging on the glass door when I went in. They were talking. I sat beside my da and he put his arm around my shoulder. It felt good.

'Where did the baby go, Da?' asked Liam.

'The nurse took him away because he was dead.'

'Why did he die, Da?'

'Because his wee heart gave up.'

'And will he be buried, Da, with a coffin and all, and a funeral?'

'He'll be buried, but there'll be no funeral.'

'Why not, Da? I thought everybody that died had a funeral?'

I just sat there, listening. I hadn't thought of the things Liam was asking. Liam was becoming very smart. He didn't say anything else, but I felt I should ask something.

'Did he have a name, Da?'

'Naw, no name, Dickie.'

'Can we not give him a name?'

'I suppose we could.'

'What'll we call him?'

'I don't know, Son. We'll have to ask your ma about that. Come on now, boys, and the twins will get youse your tea.' Liam stopped swinging and followed my da into the living room.

'I'll be down in a wee minute, Da. I have to go up to the toilet.' I was lying. I ran quietly up the stairs.

'Don't be long, now.'

I didn't go to the toilet. Instead, I slipped into my ma's room. I could hear her loud breathing. She was sleeping. I closed the door quietly and went into our bedroom. I took out the sin list and started to copy a new one. I had more to add to it:

✓ Fuck off – sixteen times
✓ Fuck – twelve times
✓ Big fart-arse – eighteen times
✓ Nose-picker – seven times
✓ Arse-scratcher – ten times

✓ Bastard – nine times
✓ Lies – thirty-four times
✓ Spat on people – twenty-three times
✓ Enjoyed hearing the Smarts cursing – three times

I memorised the list six times before I tore it up along with the old one. I had a good memory. If you left a sin out deliberately, it wouldn't be a good Confession and you'd have to go back again. That would then be an extra sin you'd have to tell. If you forgot one, that was okay and you could go to Communion if you promised you would tell it at your next Confession.

Liam came into the bedroom.

'Who taught you to say fuck?' I asked.

Fuck – thirteen times.

'Nobody,' he replied.

'Somebody must have.'

'I don't know,' he said. 'I'm not telling you.'

'That means you know. Who did you say had the gun?' I asked quickly.

Liam grinned at me before he spoke. 'Big Joey and Peter – they have it. The twins were hiding it for them under the bath.'

I couldn't believe what I was hearing. 'How do you know?'

Liam didn't answer and left the bedroom, smiling, leaving me with my big mouth wide open. I ran after him down the stairs. He wouldn't tell me any more. *Fuck,* I thought to myself. But it was still only thirteen times, I hadn't said it out loud.

Billy and Cecil were standing outside the shop in Helen Street when we were lining up across the road for Confession. Philson was counting heads, touching each one. He probably got rid of a few snots that way.

'Right, everybody,' he shouted, 'march in a straight line and no talking. Think about the sins you have to confess.'

We turned into Creggan Road. St Eugene's Cathedral was only down the hill a bit. I looked back. Billy and Cecil were following behind. Everything was organised for afterwards. We would capture a couple of the Marlborough boys and electrocute them at Cnoc na Ros. It wouldn't be a sin. It was only a small shock. We'd discovered bare electric wires months ago that workmen had forgotten about. They were hanging loose down the outside wall of the billiard hall. We told nobody about them because we knew they'd come in useful for torture purposes on our enemies.

We turned in at the gate of the cathedral. Billy and Cecil would wait there until we were all inside. They would then stand outside the porch door. They knew they couldn't come inside because a bolt of lightning would strike them. I'd heard that somewhere, about Protestants going into a Catholic chapel. If they did come in and there was a crowd there, the lightning would only strike *them*. It would pick them out from the rest of us. God would know who was who. Who the Catholics were and who the Protestants were. God knew everything.

There were five Confession boxes – three on the left aisle, and two on the right. Me and Danny and Kevin were picked for Father Mooney's box. It was the middle box on the left aisle. Father Kelly's was behind us and Father Martin's in front of us. I liked that. Father Mooney was nice. We were put in the front seats next to the Confession box. I would be the first to go in. Kevin sat next to me. Danny was opposite. Kevin's beads were rattling and he was praying out loud; I shushed him. Danny was picking his nose. I thought that must be a venial sin, picking your nose in the chapel. Everybody was quiet.

When Mr Philson got us all settled, he told us to kneel down and examine our consciences. Then he moved away to the aisle on the far side. After a while, Father Mooney arrived but he didn't look at us. He went straight into the box and shut the door behind him. I started to rhyme off my sins in my mind.

Father Mooney pulled back the blue curtain and nodded to Danny and me: Danny to his box and me to mine. Just as we opened the doors, there was a noise and a scuffle down the aisle behind us. I looked round. It was Father Martin coming up the aisle. He had one hand on Billy's ear and the other on Cecil's, dragging them along. I waited for the lightning bolt. None came.

Before I went into the box, I saw Father Martin pushing Billy and Cecil past us right up to the front of the queue for Confession, to his box. I felt weak and my stomach was turning sick. I could feel dizziness coming over me. I was in the biggest trouble of my whole life. Protestants going to Confession. They wouldn't know what to do. They wouldn't know what to say. I could hear giggling behind me as I went into the box. Everybody except the Stupids knew that Billy and Cecil were Protestants.

I was in the box, kneeling down in front of the closed grill. I couldn't think right. My Confession was about to begin and all I could think about was Billy and Cecil sitting outside Father Martin's box, the first two to go in. I could see no way out of this one. My life would be ruined. Me versus Philson was easy compared to this. Me versus priests was impossible. Or was it? The grill opened.

'Yes, my son, your sins . . .'

'Bless me, Father, for I have sinned. It's been a week since my last Confession.'

'Right, Son, off ye go.'

I couldn't remember anything. 'Bless me, Father, for I have sinned. It's been a week since my last Confession.'

'Yes, yes, boy. You said that. Now let's get on with it. We have a big crowd this evening.'

My mind was working in two different directions. It did this sometimes. My brain was trying to think of two different things at the same time. I found I could do that. Think in different directions.

'Fuck off.'

'I beg your pardon! What was that you said?'

'Fuck off – sixteen times.' I could hear them giggling outside. My voice was too loud. 'Fuck – thirteen times.'

'Who *is* this?' said Father Mooney, his voice angry. And he put the light on and looked through the grill. I put my head down so that he wouldn't recognise me.

'I'm sick, Father. My stomach's sick. I have to go out, Father. I'll come back again. I feel like vomiting.'

'Get out of my Confession box, boy, and don't come back until you have made a full examination of your conscience and you are properly prepared to receive the Sacrament of Confession.'

I got up from my knees and pushed the door open. I could hear the grill slamming behind me. Danny would be confessing now. I didn't look at anybody when I left the box, but a whole lot of them were still giggling. I was too perplexed to take a mental note of names.

I didn't care. I had a plan. I did a false stagger up the aisle toward Father Martin's Confession box. Billy and Cecil were still there. They looked pale, just sitting there, frightened. They should have run, but they must have been afraid of being struck by lightning. I put my two hands on my stomach as I moved towards them, staggering. The vomit was gurgling. The special vomit that was needed when things got desperate.

Father Martin's head appeared out of the box. 'Right, boys, I'm ready for you now.'

So was I. I staggered to my left, vomiting first on Billy, then turning round to vomit on Cecil. I made a loud noise to make it look better.

Father Martin shouted, 'Good God in Heaven, what's happening here?'

'I'm sick, Father. Sorry, I've just vomited on these two boys.'

'Take them outside, somebody, and get them cleaned up.'

'I'll do it, Father. I'm feeling better now.'

Billy and Cecil's trousers were covered in vomit, the best vomit of my whole life. Billy and Cecil were smiling and they looked very relieved. They didn't seem to care about the mess on their trousers, they were out of trouble.

I took them outside and told them to get on home quick. I told them I'd see them tomorrow, that I still had to go to Confession. They left, not saying anything. I went back into the chapel. I had business to attend to with a whole lot of extra sins on my soul. I went to a different priest – I thought it would be safer – and had to join the end of the queue. Philson was still there when I was leaving. He looked puzzled when he saw me. I looked innocent. I knew he hadn't seen the Billy and Cecil thing because he had been over in the far aisle.

CHAPTER 13

The Last Shall Be First

I got home around seven o'clock. 'You're late,' Kate said. 'You should have come straight home from the chapel.'

'I did,' I told her. 'I only got out a wee while ago. I was the last in. I had to wait to the end.'

'Why?' laughed Laura. 'You're usually the first in and the first out.'

'Not today,' I blurted out. 'I had to go twice.' It slipped out.

'The first shall be last and the last shall be first,' sniggered Kate. I didn't know what she was talking about but I'd heard it before.

'It's not funny!' I shouted again.

'Why twice?' asked Laura. 'I know you can be bad, Dickie, but I didn't think you were *that* bad.'

I didn't answer her.

'I saw Billy and Cecil coming up the hill over an hour ago,' chirped Liam. 'They had vomit all over their trousers.'

'What's all this about vomit?' asked my da when he came into the room.

I glared at Liam with a 'shut-up' look.

'I'm hungry,' I said. 'Is there any dinner left?'

He said nothing more. My da sat down and turned on the wireless. He didn't ask anything else; he just pointed out to the kitchen.

'Your dinner's in the oven, Dickie.'

It was fish and chips, all dried up and burnt looking. Two bad dinners in two days. But I still ate everything, I was starving. Then I went upstairs to see my ma. She was sitting up and looked better. I sat on the bed beside her. She put her arm around me, tight. I liked that.

'Did you get your dinner, Son?'

'Aye, Ma, it was lovely.'

'You're a good boy, Dickie, going to school every day and doing your homework and helping wee Liam. And you were at Confession today and all.'

'Aye, Ma, I was last in – that's why I was back late.' I didn't tell her I was first in as well. 'The wee baby's dead, Ma?'

'Aye, Son, it's God's will.'

'Will ye get another one in its place?'

I heard her take a big, deep breath. She didn't answer me. She hugged me tighter.

'The baby wasn't brought by the nurse, Ma; it was born up here in this room.' She looked at me. I didn't fully understand what born meant but I didn't say that. I'd have to look it up in the dictionary some time, or ask questions about it. 'Kate and Laura told me and Liam that, Ma.'

'Kate and Laura are good to youse, Dickie. Now youse make sure to do everything they ask youse to do until I get better.'

'Aye, Ma.'

'And you look out for wee Liam, won't ye, Dickie?'

She knew I would.

'My da said the baby was a gift from God. If it was a gift, why did He take it away again?'

'Aw, Dickie, there's a whole lot of things we don't understand and you shouldn't be worrying your head about it.'

'And why is the baby not in Heaven, Ma? Mrs Doherty told me it was in Limbo. Why didn't God take him back to Heaven with Him? How long will he have to stay in Limbo, Ma?'

'Dickie, Son, sure I don't have the answers for ye. Maybe ye should ask the priest sometime about it all. *He* might know. Now I'm going to have another wee rest, Son. I'll see ye later on.'

As I was closing the bedroom door quietly after me, I was thinking that my ma was really smart. About asking the priest about Limbo and all. Father Mooney's bound to know. I went into our bedroom. Liam was sitting on the bed looking at comics.

'Hello, Liam.'

'Hello, Dickie.'

'Are ye enjoying the comics?'

'Aye, they're great.'

'You can have them all to keep when I'm finished with them.'

'Thanks, Dickie, that's brilliant.'

'Remember you were telling me about the gun, about who owned it?'

'Aye, it belongs to Big Joey and Peter. I told you that before.'

'But how do you know?'

'I heard the twins telling my ma and Uncle Jimmy and my da, the night he was mad drunk.'

'And was there a whole row, Liam?'

'Aye, it wakened me, but you were having a nightmare. You didn't wake up. I heard everything.'

'What did ye hear, Liam?'

'I heard my da first, wrecking the bathroom and roaring out that somebody had stolen his gun. My ma and the twins and Uncle Jimmy came up the stairs. My ma was screaming at him. My da said it was *his* gun because he found it there last year, but the twins told him that it was Joey and Peter's gun, that they were hiding it for them.'

'And what did Uncle Jimmy say?'

'He shouted and roared at the girls and told them that they were stupid and they shouldn't have done it and they shouldn't

103

be going out with the likes of Joey and Peter because they weren't the right type for them.'

'And what happened then, Liam?'

'My ma was still screaming at my da and the girls were screaming at Uncle Jimmy. They told him to mind his own business, so he said he would and he left. And then my da came into our room, searching everywhere for the gun. He even looked in your schoolbag, and when he couldn't find the gun, he threw the bag out of the window.'

'And where was the gun, then, Liam?'

'The girls took it a couple of days before that and gave it to Joey and Peter. That's what I heard.'

'And did nobody tell my da that the gun wasn't his?'

'Aye, but he was drunk. He was just shouting all the time. The twins tried to tell him, but he wasn't listening.'

'And did you talk to anybody else about all this, Liam?'

'Naw, Dickie, it's a secret. I wouldn't blab. And nobody knows that I know. Except you.'

Liam went back to looking at the comics and I slipped downstairs. There were people standing in the porch. I could see two shapes through the glass and I knew who they were. I opened the door before they knocked.

'Hello, Dickie, how's it going?' said Joey.

I didn't say anything except that I would tell the twins they were there. I was thinking of the gun and the fire in the B-man's hut. And the big row the other night in our house.

'Thanks, Dickie,' said Peter.

I ran into the living room and told the girls that Joey and Peter were at the door.

'Right, Da,' said Laura, 'we're off to the pictures with Joey and Peter. Thanks, Dickie. You be good now.'

My da just read the newspaper. I heard him say 'fucking eejits' after the girls left. I followed them out to the porch and watched them walking up the street. Peter had his arm round

Laura, and Joey was holding Kate's hand. Yucky. Yucky. Yuki-ty-yukity-yuck.

***

On Saturday morning, Billy and Cecil were standing outside with their mas. I walked up to them. They were laughing and talking. I liked their mas.

'Hello, Richard,' Cecil's ma said. 'And how's your mother to-day?'

'Aye, sorry about the wee baby, Richard. I hope your mother will be all right soon,' smiled Mrs Burnside.

'Thanks,' I said. 'She's feeling better.' I looked at each of them as I spoke.

'Why don't youse go over and play in Thompson's Field for a wee while, boys?' said Mrs Colhoun. 'And, Richard, on your way back, call in, for I've got a wee cake for your mother.'

'Thanks, Mrs Colhoun,' I said, 'I will.'

Danny and Kevin were there. They weren't playing or anything, just looking at the burnt-out hut. We walked over to them.

'The IRA did that,' said Billy, 'because it was a Protestant hall.' I looked at Danny. He didn't say anything; he just kept looking at the rubble. Kevin, too.

'Is that right? How do you know?' I asked him.

'I heard my da telling my ma.'

Billy Burnside was blabbing. I would never blab on my da. And I wouldn't blab on Joey and Peter, either, even if I knew definitely that they did the fire.

'What did your mas say about the vomit on your trousers?' I asked them.

'Nothing,' said Cecil. 'When we were coming up from the chapel, we decided to tell them that we had sore stomachs from eating fish and chips and that we just vomited. We didn't tell them we were in the chapel.'

'Aye, and Cecil's ma didn't know about the vomit on me and my ma didn't know about the vomit on him,' Billy laughed.

'Great,' I said. 'That was good thinking.' And that's why I had them in the gang. They were smart.

'It wasn't your fault,' said Cecil. 'We should have run off when we saw the priest coming, but he was too quick for us.'

'Aye, and he had us up the aisle before we knew it,' said Billy.

We all had a good laugh about the priests and the vomit.

'They're starting the air-raid shelter in our street on Monday,' Cecil said. 'My da told me.'

'It'll take them just a week to build it,' Billy chirped in. 'I heard my da telling my ma.'

That was the first I heard about an air-raid shelter in our street. Protestants knew everything that was going on. My da told me that. But they didn't really know everything. I mean, nobody could know everything. Even I knew that.

When we were walking back home, down our street, Billy told me to wait a minute while he went into the house for something. When he came out he slipped me a bunch of comics from under his coat. I hid them up my jumper. Nobody saw us. Billy's brilliant and he's definitely my best friend.

I then called in to Mrs Colhoun and got the cake she promised. My ma would be pleased, but my da wouldn't. As usual, he would say that he didn't like stuff that came from a B-man's house, that it would choke him, so when I got home I told him I got it off Kevin's ma. He ate a big slice of it and it didn't choke him. My ma and Liam loved the cake, too. We left some for the twins who were over in the park with Joey and Peter. We didn't leave any for Uncle Jimmy. My da said he was away on some business and he didn't know when he would be back.

***

Liam and me went to ten o'clock Mass the next morning. I hadn't cursed or hit anyone since Friday night, so I was able to go to

Holy Communion. My soul was as white as the driven snow. I looked over at Father Kelly's Confession box. That's where I had gone after I'd brought Billy and Cecil outside on Friday evening. Father Kelly had coughed a lot when I was telling him my sins. When I'd finished, he was quiet for a good while. He then asked me about my family. I told him that our wee baby had died and my ma had the big-belly disease and that Father Mooney had told me that she would get better soon because Liam and me had lit a candle for her.

Father Kelly told me that I was a good boy, but that I would have to watch my bad language and bad habits. I told him I would. He made me say a whole Rosary for my penance. That took nearly half an hour extra. And that's why as well I was so late getting home from the chapel on Friday evening.

I hated Sundays, except for going to Mass. You didn't see Billy and Cecil much, and Danny and Kevin just stood about doing nothing. I played Ludo and Snakes and Ladders and Tiddly-winks with Liam. It was boring. The Marlborough boys wouldn't be about much, either, but that was all right because you needed the full gang to capture even one or two of them. We'd see to that during the week.

I went upstairs to do my homework. Philson had said I didn't need to do it, but I did it anyway. It was easy. And I hadn't cursed all day or hit anybody or pushed anybody. And my ma was getting better so I was feeling good. Things were looking up.

CHAPTER 14

Was Jesus A Catholic Or A Protestant?

On Monday morning, Mrs Big Lardo Doherty came to our house before eight o'clock. Wee Danny Lardo was with her. He had his schoolbag with him. My da was just leaving for work. The twins were already away so that meant Mrs Lardo was staying with my ma, and Danny was going to school with us. Fair's fair, she gave us bread and tea, Danny as well. Danny said that this was his second breakfast. Mrs Lardo was stuffing herself, too, with *our* bread as we were leaving. Her mouth was full when she was trying to say bye-bye to Danny. She had a bigger belly than my ma but she wasn't sick with it.

Liam went into his own class. He was laughing. Danny had just farted in the corridor, a loud one. I was laughing as well. Philson didn't hear us. You could see him through the open door, writing stuff on the board. We were early.

Philson was in a good mood. He must have had a good breakfast. Probably bacon and egg and sausages. He was smiling at everybody when they came into the room. 'Okay, boys,' he shouted, 'settle down now. We're having a special visitor this morning. Father Mooney will be here shortly to give us all a talk about God.'

I liked that. I liked learning about religious stuff, about God and all. And about the miracles of Jesus. Jesus was brilliant. He

108

cured sick people just by putting His hands on them. He cured a blind man one time after putting muck and spittles into his eyes. And He brought people back to life, but then the baddies captured Him and killed Him. They nailed Him to a big cross, and even when He was dead, they put a spear into His side, just to make sure. But He beat them all, because He came back to life and they couldn't kill Him again. Jesus died for our sins and that's why when we sin, it's like putting another nail into His hands or feet. But when we confess our sins, He forgives us and the nails come out again. I always forget about that when I say bad words and things.

Father Mooney's a very old man. He's in charge of all the other priests in the cathedral. But not in total charge. The bishop is, and the bishop lives in the same house as them. When Father Mooney came into the classroom, we all stood up and said, 'Good morning, Father.' Then we sat down quietly. Father Mooney was smiling. He always smiled at us. Everybody liked him, even the Stupids.

'Good morning, boys,' he said. Philson looked happy as he stood beside the priest. 'I want to talk to you this morning about when Jesus was a little boy, when He was about your age. You all know that He lived with his mother, the Blessed Virgin, and with His father, Saint Joseph. And He grew up with them, and He was subject to them. Does anybody know what "subject to them" means?'

The three Smarts put their hands up. I knew the answer but I didn't bother to put my hand up. Nobody else did, either. Father Mooney pointed to Frankie Smart.

'It means that Jesus knew that Mary and Joseph were in charge of Him.'

Father Mooney then pointed to Timothy Smart.

'It means, Father, that He always did as He was told because Mary and Joseph were His parents.'

'Well done, boys,' said Father Mooney. Philson had the big

hypocrite smile on his face. It was the smile he always used for the priest.

'So, now,' continued Father Mooney, 'we assume also that if Jesus was subject to His parents, and always did as He was told, that meant that He would have helped around the house. He would have studied hard and most importantly of all, He would have said His prayers every morning and every evening.'

John Smart's hand was still up. He hadn't taken it down since the first question.

'Yes, boy?' said the priest.

'Would Jesus have gone to school like us, Father?'

Philson was still smiling and nodding his head down at John Smart.

'We are not told that, but we have to assume that He learned to read and write and talk well, so in a sense, He had schooling.'

'And did Jesus have any friends when He was a boy?' asked Frankie Smart again.

'Of course He would have had friends. All little boys have friends.'

Philson's smile was beginning to sicken me. And I was fed up with the Smarts. I put my hand up.

'Yes, boy?'

'Was He in a gang, Father?'

Philson stopped smiling and went to move forward in front of the priest as if he was going to shush me. But Father Mooney stopped him.

'As I said before,' continued Father Mooney, 'He would have had friends and He would have played with them, but I don't suppose you would have called it a gang. Not the way you mean it anyhow.'

Philson glared at me. He wasn't smiling now. Kevin Doherty put his hand up. Philson's smile came back on because he knew Kevin was always praying.

'Yes, boy?' said Father Mooney.

'Did Jesus go to Confession every week like us, Father, and to Mass every Sunday? And did they say the Rosary every night?'

Philson looked at the priest, not sure what to make of that question. I was a bit shocked myself because that was the first time Kevin had ever asked a real question in the class. The priest smiled down at him. Philson smiled, too. Hypocrite.

'No, of course not, Son. Jesus did not commit any sins and there was no Mass as we know it in those days, but He would have prayed a lot, even though Rosaries weren't said at that time. And the Last Supper would have been the first Mass that was ever said.'

'Was Jesus a Catholic or a Protestant, Father?'

Father Mooney stared at Kevin. His brow wrinkled a bit. Philson stepped forward again.

'Now, I think you've had enough questions, Kevin,' he said.

But Father Mooney interrupted. 'It's all right, Mr Philson. There were no Protestants and Catholics in those days, my son. There were many sects and religions, of course, and different faiths, but it was Jesus himself, when He was older, who set up the Christian faith.'

Kevin wasn't finished yet. He had his beads out now, his fingers moving back and forward across them. His jam jars were steaming up.

'Are Protestants Christians, Father?'

'Yes, they are, boy. They believe in Jesus Christ, so if you are a follower of Christ, you would be a Christian. Now, just one more question.'

I put my hand up. Philson couldn't stop me. He looked worried, but Father Mooney was still smiling. I really wanted to ask a question.

'If Jesus had died before He was baptised by John the Baptist, would He have gone to Limbo?'

'Of course not. Jesus was God made man. He would have gone straight back to Heaven.'

'Dickie McCauley's wee baby brother died before he was baptised, Father,' said Kevin, 'and he went to Limbo. My ma told me that. And she said he could be there for millions of years. That's not fair, Father.'

Father Mooney didn't say anything this time, and I was annoyed with Kevin for talking about my wee brother. It was none of his business. Father Mooney's face went very red and Philson looked angry and annoyed. Some of the class were giggling.

'That will do now,' said Philson quickly. 'Father Mooney has been very good to come along this morning and talk to us. Now, boys, I would like you all to thank him.'

'Thank you, Father Mooney,' everybody said at the same time. Well, nearly everybody. As usual, the Stupids shouted it out at different times. Father Mooney smiled at us before he left the room and Philson went with him. We all kept quiet. Philson was back in two minutes and his eyes were blazing. He went mad. He began to roar and shout at us about our bad manners and our stupid questions and about the giggling and lack of respect for the priest.

'You're not fit to be Catholics, the lot of you. You're a shocking bunch. I never met the likes of you before in my life.' He banged his cane down on an empty desk, far away from the Smarts.

'Come up here, McCauley.'

I left my seat and walked towards him.

'It was you, McCauley, that started the rot.'

'What rot, Sir?'

'Don't be impertinent, boy! You know the rot I mean – the silly questions about a gang and then Limbo, and encouraging Kevin Doherty's foolishness.' I looked down at Kevin. His face was white. He'd never been in trouble with Philson before. 'And only for the sensible responses of Francis and Timothy and John here, the whole morning would have been a total catastrophe.' The Smarts' faces didn't look pleased, just ordinary.

You could smell Kevin from the front. People were holding their noses. Everybody knew his smell. Philson, too. 'Get out, Doherty,' he shouted at Kevin, 'and don't come back for ten minutes.'

'It was me, Sir. It was me that farted,' said Danny with his hand up. I couldn't help it, Sir.' Danny had taken the blame. I liked that.

'Get out the two of you. You're both a disgrace.'

Philson couldn't prove anything. Danny and Kevin shuffled out of the room. Kevin was still white, his Rosary beads rattling in his hands. Now Philson turned to me but before he could say anything else, Denis Harley from Marlborough Road had his hand up.

'Yes, Harley?' Philson snapped.

Harley was in the wee stupid Marlborough gang. They just dug holes in the Wee Green and played kick-the-tin and ran after girls. I hated him.

'Sir, Dickie McCauley brought two Protestants into the chapel on Friday evening. To Confession, Sir.'

The whole class went silent. So did Philson. For a minute. His face went dark grey. I didn't like it. His fist was white around the cane. 'What?' he shouted.

'I did not, Sir.'

'Shut up, McCauley. Say that again, Harley.'

'Sir, Dickie McCauley brought two Protestants to Confession on Friday evening.' Harley was grinning. I'd kill him later.

Philson took a deep breath as he turned to me. I looked up at him.

'Is this true, McCauley?'

'No, Sir. Protestants don't go to Confession. Harley's a liar, Sir.'

'How dare you say such a word about anybody in my class! And the priest here a few minutes ago, too.'

'But it's true, Sir. I didn't bring anybody to Confession.'

He raised his stick as if he was going to hit me. But he didn't. He was swinging it up and down. Harley had his hand up again. I looked down at him and he was still grinning. I was thinking about how he would be killed. Death by electrocution at Cnoc na Ros. Then I'd spit on him a hundred times and get Danny to fart in his face fifty times or maybe a hundred times as well.

'Sir, the two Protestants, they're friends of Dickie McCauley's and Danny Doherty's and Kevin Doherty's. They all live in Rosemount, Sir.'

Philson turned to me again. His other hand was tight on my shoulder.

'Is this correct, McCauley?'

Yes, you big arse-scratching, nose-picking hypocrite.

'Yes, Mr Philson.'

'And were those two boys in the cathedral on Friday evening?'

'Yes, Sir.'

'And did they go to Confession?'

'No, Sir.'

'They were sitting outside Father Martin's Confession box, Sir, right up beside the front, and McCauley came up and vomited on them.'

Harley's death would be slow and painful. I would see to that personally. Electrocution at Cnoc na Ros might be too quick.

'Is this true, McCauley? Did you vomit in the cathedral?'

'Yes, Sir. I was sick, Sir. It was an accident, Sir.'

I looked up at Philson as I spoke. His eyes were bulging as if they were going to shoot out of his sockets. He couldn't believe what he was hearing. Neither could I.

'Let's get this straight, McCauley: you brought your two friends who are Protestants to Confession on Friday?'

No, snot-nose.

'No, Sir.'

'And these friends of yours, were they in the cathedral?'

'Yes, Sir.'

'I've heard enough, McCauley,' Philson shouted as he lashed his cane at me. I ducked. He missed. 'Sit down, McCauley. The Church authorities will have to hear about this. And your parents, too. This is a most serious business altogether. Much worse than you've ever done before. Your time has really come, McCauley.'

After school, when me and Danny and Kevin were walking home, we met Bap Kelly. He was holding Denis Harley like a prisoner.

'He's all yours, Dickie,' laughed Bap. He pushed the crying Marlborough snob over to us. When Bap left, we dragged Harley up the lane to Cnoc na Ros and electrocuted him. I then ordered Danny to fart in his face. Harley swore he'd never blab again.

CHAPTER 15

A Fine Day's Work

Uncle Jimmy was back by the time we got home. He'd brought a big bag of meat with him and a sack of flour and a full bag of spuds. Even my da looked pleased to see him. Uncle Jimmy said he was sad to hear about the baby dying, but that it was probably for the best. My da didn't argue with him, but the twins were annoyed when he said it. Laura shouted at him.

'Aye, *you* would know what's for the best, Uncle Jimmy. You always know what's best for everybody.'

'I'm only saying, with the war on and all, and your da out of work most of the time, and with the small money you girls get in the factory, there's hardly enough to go around as things stand.'

'A wee baby wouldn't take up much,' shouted Kate, 'and don't you dare say to my ma that it's all for the best. Because it's not, and we would have managed, even without you. And my ma's in a bad enough way without you making things worse. Come on, Laura, let's get the dinner on.' They went out to the kitchen.

Uncle Jimmy didn't say anything else and my da said nothing, either. They knew it was useless arguing with the twins. Me and Liam just sat there listening to everything. My da turned on the wireless and Uncle Jimmy started reading a newspaper. There was nothing else to hear except stupid war news.

'I got youse a wee present,' said Uncle Jimmy after a minute or two. 'It's in the hall.' We rushed out. It was a fifty-piece jigsaw puzzle.

'Wow,' said Liam. 'Brilliant.'

'It's rubbish,' I told him, when I looked at the tattered box. 'There's probably about twenty pieces missing.'

'Will we try it?' asked Liam.

To please him, I opened the box and emptied everything out on the floor.

'Get the four corners first and then all the straight edges,' I said. 'That's the best way to start.'

My da had showed me that trick last Christmas when I got a jigsaw puzzle from Santa. But that was a new one. I still had it under my bed. I'd give it to Liam later when he was a bit older.

There was a knock on the door. I knew before I looked who it was. Snot-nose Philson and Father Martin. Showdown time. I opened the door.

'Hello, Richard,' said Father Martin. Philson didn't speak. 'Can we have a word with your father?'

'Da!' I shouted. 'Father Martin and Mr Philson want to see you.' I wasn't nervous or afraid. My conscience was clear.

'What's that, Son?' said my da as he came out to the hall. 'Oh! Hello, Father. Hello, Mr Philson.'

'Could we have a wee word with you, Mr McCauley?'

'Aye, surely. Come on in here.'

He led them into the sitting room. He closed the door behind him, but it opened slightly again because the lock was broken. It had always been broken. I sat on the bottom stair to listen. Liam played with the jigsaw.

'We've come at a bad time,' said Father Martin, 'what with your wife being sick and all.'

'That's all right,' said my da, 'she's coming round now, thank God.'

'That's good, that's good,' replied Father Martin. 'We hope and pray that she'll have a full recovery soon.' It went quiet for a wee while then he said, 'But we're really here about another matter, Mr McCauley. It's about your son Richard.'

'Ah, Dickie? What's the wee rascal been up to now, Father?'

'Well, it's like this, Mr McCauley. For a start, his language and behaviour in school leave a lot to be desired.'

'What sort of language and behaviour is that now, Father?'

'Well, today, for example, he shouted very loudly in Mr Philson's class and called another boy a liar.'

'Is that so? Well I'll be damned. Imagine our Dickie doing that. And this other boy you're talking about – *was* he a liar, Mr Philson?'

'Well, that's not the point, Mr McCauley,' said Philson, 'whether he was or he wasn't. And with all due respect, Richard shouldn't have said it and he shouldn't have shouted.'

Father Martin coughed before he spoke again.

'I agree with Mr Philson, Mr McCauley. A young boy of Richard's age coming out with language like that is most disrespectful and uncharitable, and the manner in which he did it, too—'

'This other boy,' interrupted my da, 'did he accuse Dickie of something?'

'Well, yes, he did,' replied Philson. 'He claimed that Richard brought two young Protestant boys down to Confession on Friday evening.'

'Well, well, well,' said my da quickly. 'And what could be wrong with that now? Sure some of them Protestants have a lot to confess, when you think what they've done to Ireland. A lot of confessing, I'd say.'

'With all due respect again, Mr McCauley,' said Philson, 'that's not the issue here. The fact is that these two Protestant boys, who are friends of your son's, were sitting outside Father Martin's Confession box, and would have been first to go in, I might add, if there hadn't been an unforeseen, unfortunate occurrence.'

'An unforeseen and unfortunate occurrence?' queried my da.

'Yes, Mr McCauley. It so happens that before they had the opportunity of entering the Confessional, Richard walked over to them and vomited all over them.'

My da didn't say anything just then, but it was in my mind that he might now be remembering about hearing Liam mention on Friday night something about seeing Billy and Cecil coming up the hill with vomit on them. I felt like running into the sitting room and telling my da what really happened, but I didn't. I just sat there and listened some more.

'Mr McCauley,' said Father Martin, 'these actions of your son amount almost to blasphemy and sacrilege.'

I didn't know what blasphemy and sacrilege were but they didn't sound good. And I was thinking, too, that my da was no match for Father Martin and the arse-scratcher. I might have to do something about that.

'And besides that, Mr McCauley,' Father Martin continued, 'besides the incidents in the cathedral, which, of course, are of a most serious nature, there is the matter of which I spoke earlier – the hurtful language in the school and the shouting. So what it all amounts to, Mr McCauley, is that your son needs a lot more discipline and he would need to mend his ways immediately. You'll see to that now, Mr McCauley, won't you?'

My da was too quiet. He was stumped or else he was thinking hard. Father Martin and Philson had beaten him. It was time for me to jump to the rescue. Either that or run away to the Free State and stay in Aunt Minnie's for the rest of my life. And I didn't feel like doing that.

I began to sneeze and cough. Liam looked over at me and laughed. He knew it was a put-on job. But my da heard me. He must have known it was a put-on job, too. My da wasn't stupid.

119

'Come in here, Dickie,' he shouted. 'I've been hearing some terrible things about ye and I think maybe it's only fair that ye should have the right to reply.'

I came in and stood beside my da. Father Martin and Philson were sitting on the couch.

'Is it true, Son, that ye brought two Protestants into the chapel on Friday evening?'

'No, Da, I didn't.' I could see him relaxing. He knew I was telling the truth.

'What happened, Da, was that Billy and Cecil came down as far as the chapel. They were to wait outside until Confessions were over. We were all going to go somewhere afterwards. They waited outside the door. It was Father Martin who brought them in. He took them up the aisle and put them in the seats beside his Confession box. I saw him, Da.'

My da turned from me to the priest. Father Martin had gone white and Philson had gone grey. And I knew by my da that he wasn't stumped any more.

'And what about that, Father?' asked my da.

'He could be right, now, he could be right. The boy could be right,' stammered Father Martin. 'I'm just remembering now that I *did* bring two boys in from the cathedral porch that night. I thought they were skiving.'

I heard my da taking a big deep breath before he spoke again.

'So, there we have it, then – it wasn't Dickie at all that did it. And as well as that, sure he wouldn't be the first person to get sick in the chapel. Sure doesn't it happen all the time?' Father Martin and Mr Philson got up from the couch. 'So, there we have it,' repeated my da. 'There was no sacrilege and no blasphemy, and there was no lying, either, and the shouting in the class was probably to clear his name. The boy's innocent, Father. Wouldn't ye agree, Mr Philson?'

'It looks like it,' said Father Martin. 'I think maybe we've got the wrong end of the stick. What do you think, Mr Philson?'

Philson didn't say anything. He gave a low grunt and kept his head down. Guilty like.

'And we're very sorry to have troubled you, Mr McCauley,' continued Father Martin, 'especially at this time, with your wife being sick and all. We'll just be off now, Mr McCauley.'

'And would you be sorry at all for troubling Dickie here?'

'Of course, of course, of course,' stammered Father Martin. Philson headed for the door. They all stepped over Liam in the hall before they opened the glass door and left. He was still doing the jigsaw puzzle on the floor.

My da saw them to the street and I heard him calling after them. 'And another thing! Now that the two of youse are out and about, will youse be calling at that wee liar's house? The boy that started the whole thing?'

He slammed the big front door after them. On the way back in, my da caught me lightly by the back of the neck with his hand and rubbed my hair with his other hand.

'A fine day's work, Son, a fine day's work altogether. And wasn't that the crafty move on the two wee Protestants – the Dickie McCauley vomit trick? A nice one, Dickie. Aye, a nice one, Son, but you be watching yourself after this. That Philson boy's a right bastard.'

My da went back into the living room. Liam started to laugh. 'That's two curses my da has taught me now: fuck and bastard,' he said.

I rubbed his hair, the same way as my da had done on me. I noticed, too, that he had Uncle Jimmy's jigsaw puzzle nearly finished. I was thinking when first looking at it that there would be about twenty pieces missing. I'd been nearly right. It was Uncle Jimmy that was stupid and my da was the smart one.

I went upstairs to do my homework. I wanted to look up some words in the dictionary as well. Words like blasphemy and sacrilege; I needed to know these things. The smell of the dinner coming from the kitchen was making me very hungry. I could hear my ma singing in the bedroom. I didn't disturb her. She was getting better and I had plans to make. The invitation from Bap Kelly couldn't be ignored. Bap Kelly was a big-time gang leader. Famous in Derry and feared by everybody. And he had done me a favour as well, capturing Denis Harley for electrocution. I owed him a visit.

CHAPTER 16

The Tale Of A Missing Eye

After dinner, me and Liam went up to see my ma. She was sitting up, reading *The People's Friend*. My da bought it for her every week. Her empty dinner plate was on the bedside table.

'Hello, boys,' she smiled. 'Wasn't the dinner lovely? The twins brought it up for me. It's the first I've eaten in nearly a week. I'm nearly better now.'

'Aye, Ma, it was lovely,' said Liam. 'Far better than Mrs Doherty's dinners, but not as good as yours, Ma.'

'Ah, now, sure we can't say a bad word about Mrs Doherty. Wasn't it great that she came in to help when I was sick? Maybe I'll be all right to get up tomorrow.'

Me and Liam climbed onto the bed beside her. She put her arms around us.

'Ma, I forgot to tell you that Frankie McElduff invited me to his birthday party in December.'

'And me, too,' said Liam.

'Aye, and the rest of our friends, too, Ma,' I added.

'Well, well, isn't that the best news I've heard all week? Our Dickie and our Liam going to a party in a doctor's house. Now, aren't we coming up in the world? Wait till your da and the twins and Uncle Jimmy hear about this. And isn't it grand, too, that Uncle Jimmy's back again?'

'Aye, Ma,' I said. 'Will he be staying now?'

'For a while, I suppose. But he'll still have to go away on business sometimes.'

When me and Liam were talking to my ma like that, and feeling cosy and all, I was thinking that it was very strange that my ma didn't know that *we* knew all about the gun belonging to Peter and Joey. And that *she* knew all about the gun. And Uncle Jimmy as well. And about the twins being the first to know about it because it was them that hid it under the bath in the first place. And it was very, very strange that there had been no talk about it since the night of the big row. At least no talk that I had heard. And I heard a lot of what was said in the house. Except when I was sleeping. Maybe they all talked about it then, or when I was out of the house. That must be it. But there was no fuss about it anymore and the gun was gone now anyway, so maybe that's why it was never mentioned. And I was glad it was away because my da might start about it all over again if he got drunk.

'Now, boys,' my ma said, 'why don't youse go out to play for a wee while? Your friends are probably still in the street.'

We got up to go. 'Ma,' I said to her before we left, 'will it be all right if I call down to the Bogside to Bap Kelly's house some day? He said we could come.'

'Surely, Son, but don't stay too long because Mrs Kelly has enough to do without having to entertain you boys as well. And if you do see her, tell her I was asking about her.'

'Okay, Ma.'

I was going to Bap Kelly's anyhow, but I thought it would be better to mention it to my ma because she would hear some time that I had been there, so it was definitely better that she knew before I went. This was me working things out in advance. Planning things before you did them was better. That way, there wasn't as much chance that you could get into bother. Especially with my ma. It didn't matter about telling my da. He wouldn't care anyway.

My ma was right. They were all in the street. They were looking at the part of the air-raid shelter that the workmen had built. The place was a mess. There was sand everywhere, in loads, like mountains, and loose all over the street, too. Younger ones had been playing with it after the workmen left, throwing it at one another and sliding down it. Liam ran to the top of a sand pile.

'What are youse all looking at?' I said to them.

'The air-raid shelter,' they said.

'Don't be stupid,' I told them. 'It's not an air-raid shelter yet; it's only a wee wall. And listen,' I whispered so that only they could hear me, 'we're going down to the Bogside tomorrow to Bap Kelly's house.'

'I'm not going down there,' Kevin said quickly. 'There were ghosts in that house. It used to be haunted.'

'Great,' said Liam. 'I'm going.'

'What are ye talking about?'

'I'm telling you, Dickie, a ghost used to live in Bap Kelly's house – a devil ghost.' Kevin's eyes started to rise.

Before I could say anything, Danny spoke. 'I heard that, too. My ma told me one time about it – that Kelly's house was haunted. It was Bap who told her and your ma the whole story one night when they were down in Kelly's house before Bap's ma came home with the shopping.'

Billy and Cecil started to laugh, but I wanted to hear more, even though I felt like laughing, too. I had heard a lot about Bap, but nothing about ghosts.

'And the devil took Bap's eye,' wailed Kevin. As he was speaking, he suddenly took the Rosary beads from his pocket and held them up in front of us all, praying out loud. 'And may God protect youse if youse go, and may His Holy Mother intercede for youse if the devil comes back when youse're there.'

'I would like to see a ghost,' laughed Billy.

'So would I,' said Liam.

'Same here,' said Cecil. 'What time are we going, Dickie?'

'Shut up,' I said. 'What else did ye hear, Kevin?'

'My ma said that all the Kellys were going to leave the house one time because of the ghost, but they had nowhere else to go, so Bap's ma and da and all the wains went up to the Parochial House to see the priest. It was Father Mooney they saw, and they told him what was happening. Father Mooney went straight down with them. My ma said he had black hair on the way down, but after what happened, it turned pure white.'

'And what happened?' asked Danny in a scared voice. I felt a wee bit scared myself, but I didn't say anything. Liam was excited. He was too young to be afraid.

'Father Mooney took his prayer book with him, and a big bottle of holy water. The Kellys all followed behind him. It was raining that night and Father Mooney had his umbrella up. All the Kellys got soaked.'

'Get on with it,' I said.

'Well, when they reached the house, Mr Kelly opened the door. The priest went in first and everybody followed him. As soon as they went in, there were loud screeches and all the furniture started to move round the house.'

'That's stupid,' I said. 'Furniture doesn't move by itself.'

'It didn't move by itself – it was the ghost. It was the devil that was doing it.'

Kevin's face was sweating. Danny was staring at him and he was looking scared. Even Billy and Cecil had gone quiet. Liam was all ears.

'My ma said that Father Mooney started to splash holy water about and he held up the crucifix and started to pray out loud.'

'And did that make the devil disappear?' asked Billy.

'Naw, it didn't. Not then. The screeching got worse and stuff was flying all over the place, clothes and all. And the furniture was smashing into walls in the living room. That's when Father Mooney told everybody to kneel down and pray. And when they were praying, the furniture went back into place and the only screech they heard was from a black cat that was sitting on the landing. Everybody looked up at it. It had red eyes and its fangs were twice the size of an ordinary cat's. And its claws were long and sharp.'

'That's stupid!' shouted Danny. 'I'm not listening to any more of this rubbish.'

'Fuck off, Danny,' I hissed at him. 'Go home if you want to.'

'Fuck off,' laughed Liam. 'Big cowardy custard.'

But Danny didn't, he just walked up the street and then came back again. He wanted to hear more. Kevin's jam jars were steamed up and you could see the big whites. He was holding his Rosary beads very tight.

'What age was Bap then?' I asked Kevin.

'He was six, the same age as Liam there.'

'And how did the devil take his eye?' Danny wanted to know.

'I'm coming to that now,' whispered Kevin. His voice was hoarse.

I said nothing, just waited, the same as Billy and Cecil and Liam and Danny. You could see the sweat dripping off Kevin's face.

'Father Mooney told all the Kellys to move to the street. He held up the crucifix and walked towards the stairs, praying out loud and shouting to the cat to leave the house and never come back.'

'And when did the priest's hair go white?' asked Cecil.

'Shut up,' I told him. 'Go on, Kevin.'

'I have to sit down a minute,' whispered Kevin. 'I'm exhausted.'

We took him over to the wee wall of the air-raid shelter. He was breathing very hard and his face was pale. Billy reached into his pocket and pulled out a gobstopper. He gave it to Kevin to suck. Billy was kinder than I was, because I just gave away gobstoppers to keep people from blabbing.

'Thanks, Billy,' Kevin said and he sat on the wall for another minute or two. He took the gobstopper out of his mouth and handed it to Liam. 'You can have that,' he said. Kevin was kinder than I was as well.

'Wow, thanks, Kevin,' said Liam before he put it in his mouth.

Kevin was praying quietly on his beads. He was still pale.

'And did the priest get the cat out?' Danny asked.

'The devil was inside the cat,' whispered Kevin. 'He had taken over the cat's body.'

'Aye, but did he get rid of it?' For a boy that didn't want to know, Danny was asking a lot of questions now.

'The cat was roaring down at the priest, shouting at him that he couldn't leave until the priest went first. So the priest backed out, still praying and holding up the crucifix.'

'And how did the devil get Bap's eye?' Danny asked.

'I'm coming to that now if ye give me a chance,' said Kevin. 'Ye see, what happened was that when the priest reached the street, the devil-cat came down the stairs, slow like, but he started screeching again when he got as far as the hall stand. He screeched out that he couldn't go any further because the priest's umbrella was still in the hall. Anything that belongs to a priest, ye see, is holy.'

'And what about Bap?'

'Shut up, Danny!' I shouted to him. 'What happened then, Kevin?'

'Father Mooney whispered to Bap to run in and get the umbrella and run out again as fast as he could. Father Mooney knew that Bap was very brave. He sprinkled him with holy water first. Bap rushed in and grabbed the umbrella and was out again in seconds. But that's when Bap made the mistake. When he reached the street, he gave the umbrella to his da and then he rushed back to look in the doorway to see what the devil was doing. And just at that second, the cat came flying out, its eyes blazing and its claws swinging everywhere. As it flew past Bap, it reached for his eye and pulled it out of his socket, laughing and screeching at the same time. When it got to the street, it disappeared in a puff of black smoke, Bap's eye and all.'

Everybody was quiet when Kevin finished. His eyes were back up in his skull. 'Is he going to faint?' asked Liam.

'Fuck off,' said Danny to him. 'Are ye all right, Kevin?'

'And what about the priest's hair?' Cecil was at it again.

'Give him a chance,' I said.

'It's all right, Dickie. The priest didn't know his hair had turned pure white until he got home and looked in the mirror.' Kevin's eyes were back to normal but he was praying into himself.

'Right, boys,' I said. 'See youse all at half-four tomorrow. We'll be in the Bogside at five.'

Nobody seemed too excited about it, except for our Liam. Billy and Cecil said they couldn't go the next day for some reason to do with a church visit or something but they could go on Wednesday so we all agreed to go then.

I was feeling hard done by because my ma hadn't told me the story about Bap's eye before Kevin did. I should have been the first in the gang to know about these things. That's the way it should be. But I was glad anyhow that before we went to the Bogside, we all now knew what happened to Bap's eye.

CHAPTER 17

Cecil The Blabber Spills The Beans

In the playground at lunchtime on Wednesday, I told Bap we'd all be calling down to see him after school. He looked pleased. 'See you then,' he said. I couldn't help glancing at his glass eye and thinking about the devil stealing his real one. Bap was tough. He probably had bodyguards in case of attacks from gangs. I'd check that out later.

My ma was up when we got home from school. The twins were with her, but my da and Uncle Jimmy were out working. She was sitting in her armchair reading *The People's Friend*. She smiled when she saw me and Liam. Father Mooney was right – the big-belly disease was starting to go away.

'There they are, girls, the two best boys in Derry.'

'Aye, right,' laughed Kate. 'If they are, I wouldn't like to see the rest of them.'

Me and Liam laughed as well. Liam was learning fast not to upset the applecart. But he was beginning to curse more. If my ma heard him, she would blame me and I'd be the worst in the world again, never mind the worst in Derry.

'How about a piece and a cup of tea, boys?' asked Laura. 'The kettle's on the boil.'

'Thanks, Laura.'

I prodded Liam. 'Thanks, Laura,' he said.

After the tea, Liam blurted out, 'Dickie's taking me down to Bap Kelly's house today.'

'That's nice,' said my ma.

'Watch out for the big black cat,' laughed Kate.

'Aye, and if youse see an eyeball lying on the road,' said Laura, 'give it to Bap for a spare to see if it fits him.'

I didn't think that was funny, talking about Bap's eye like that. You don't laugh at things that have to do with the devil or with religion. God could strike you dead. That was mocking.

'That'll do now,' said my ma when she saw my face. 'That wee lad went through a bad time and you shouldn't be making light of it.'

I was glad my ma said that. It saved me from shouting back at Kate and Laura. But I was still annoyed with them that they hadn't told me about Bap before Kevin did. They should have known better.

Me and Liam went upstairs. I did my homework and Liam looked at comics. There were five policemen in the yard of the barracks. I could see them through the window. I was really glad now that the gun was away because my da might have shot at them some day when he was drunk. They could hang you for doing that, even if you missed.

***

Me and Liam were the first in the street. Then Billy and Cecil. I said that maybe Danny and Kevin wouldn't come because they might be afraid. It was nearly half-past four.

'Don't worry,' said Liam, 'they'll be here okay.' He was right. Danny and Kevin came down the street together from Kevin's house. Danny had a grey balaclava on his head. Kevin was wearing a brown leather pilot's hat. The two of them looked stupid, but I didn't tell them that.

'Those hats look stupid on youse,' laughed Liam.

'Shut up,' I said to him. He was beginning to annoy me.

'What have ye got there?' I asked Kevin. He had a glass bottle in each hand.

'This is Lourdes water and this is holy water,' he replied, 'just in case.'

'Time to go,' I said.

At the top of the Bogside, Kevin told us all to stop. We were outside the gate of the slaughterhouse. You could see a bunch of cows in the yard, making a racket. They knew their time was up. That's what Danny told us: that cows could smell death, and that's when they kicked out.

'We should all say a prayer now for Danny's da,' Kevin said. 'That's where he was killed by the cow.'

'I'm saying no prayer,' said Cecil. 'His da's dead and that's that. Ye don't pray for the dead. It's only the living ye pray for.'

'Shut up,' I said to him. 'Ye don't know what you're talking about. Right, Kevin, start your prayer.'

As Kevin began to pray, Cecil walked away. Halfway through the prayer, he came back. 'And another thing,' he said to me, 'you would be far better praying for those two boys that are going out with your twins, and for your uncle as well.'

'What are ye talking about?' I asked him as I pushed him away.

'And may his soul and the souls of all the faithful departed rest in peace. Amen,' finished Kevin.

'What are ye saying about Peter and Joey?' I asked Cecil again.

'I'm only saying that you'd be far better off praying for them boys because they could be in big trouble.'

'What are ye talking about?'

Everybody was listening now. Cecil had an audience. 'I heard my da talking to Billy's da about them.'

'What did he say?'

'He said they might have burned the B-man's hut.'

'They did not!'

'Billy's da thought the same. I heard them talking about it. And he said they would be keeping an eye on your uncle as well.'

'Is this true, Billy?' I asked as I turned away from Cecil.

'I dunno. I never heard them talking.'

'See? You're talking rubbish, Cecil.'

'I'm only telling you what I heard. Billy wasn't there.'

Cecil was a blabber, but I'm glad he was. We headed down towards Bap's house. I had never been in the Bogside without my ma before. It was a very long street. There were shops and a bakery and a big coal yard. It was a better street then ours. All the houses were painted different colours. It was great. I was watching for lookouts. Bap might have them about the different corners in case of an attack. I didn't see anybody. They were probably well hidden. I felt a bit excited, but I didn't say anything to the rest.

Bap's house was number fifty-eight A. That meant there must have been a house numbered fifty-eight somewhere. Everybody went quiet except Kevin when I knocked at the door. He was praying and sprinkling Lourdes water and holy water on the front step. I told him to stop and put the bottles away.

The door opened a wee bit. A wee boy about Liam's age peeped his head round it. He had red hair, the same colour as Bap's.

'What do you want?' he asked.

'Is Bap in?'

He looked at us all before he opened the door fully and turned back into the house. There was a long hallway with stairs going up to a landing. That must have been where the cat sat. There was no hall stand. They must have got rid of it. We stood there waiting.

Mrs Kelly came to the door, smiling. She had red hair, too. So had the five others who were with her, three boys and two girls. She shushed them all back into the house.

'Hello, Dickie,' she said. 'Hello, boys. Come on in. Charlie's expecting youse. And how's your ma, Dickie? I'm sorry to hear about the wee baby. It's God's will.'

'She's getting better, Mrs Kelly. She's up out of bed today. She was asking for you.'

'That's good, I'm glad to hear it. Charlie's out the back. He's making a cart to carry the coke from the Gasyard. And next week, if we can get corrugated iron, he's going to build a shed.'

We all followed her into the house. Kevin was sprinkling holy water and Lourdes water everywhere. She didn't see him. I gave him a dirty look and he put the bottles back in his pocket. We went out through the back door and into the yard.

Bap was nailing a piece of wood onto a frame. He stopped when he saw us. 'Hello, Dickie, how are ye doing? Hello there,' he said to the rest of them.

'Your ma said you were making a coke cart,' I said.

'Aye, the other wan's broke,' he said. 'It's old.'

I couldn't have done it. I was useless at making things. My da never showed me anything like that. 'This is Billy and Cecil,' I told him. 'They're not at our school.'

'Hello there, I know youse. I've seen youse about. Protestants, aren't youse?'

Billy and Cecil said nothing but they were staring at him. I was hoping that they wouldn't mention his eye.

'Sorry to hear about your eye,' said Billy.

'That's all right, it happened a long time ago.'

I was raging at Billy. I'd thump him later.

'Can I help you to make the cart, Bap?' I asked him. I was trying to get them onto something else.

'And were you afraid after the devil took it?' Billy again. I cringed.

Bap laughed. Billy was soon to get a slap in the face as well as the thump I'd promised.

'Naw,' Bap said, still laughing. 'It didn't worry me. Wan eye's as good as two.'

Liam and Danny and Kevin stood there saying nothing, but Kevin's lips were moving quietly. He must have been praying.

I thought Bap was brilliant. He handed me a piece of wood. Liam was holding his nose. Kevin had done a silent job. Nobody else cared.

'Would ye saw that for me, Dickie, across the line I've marked?'

I'd never done anything like this before but I was willing to try anything. To show off. The rest were watching. Perfect. I put the wood on an old box and put my foot on it. I started to saw. Careful like. I was a natural. It took less than a minute. Bap took it off me and nailed it to the frame.

'Do another, Dickie. Just four more needed. We'll be finished soon.'

The rest lost interest. Liam climbed a ladder against the yard wall. 'Pigs!' he shouted.

Bap laughed. He said the old boy next door kept pigs. The rest got their turn up the ladder to see them. I didn't bother, I had work to do.

Mrs Kelly brought tea and biscuits on a tray and we all sat in the yard and had a picnic. It was great. Bap was brilliant. We watched him nailing the rest of the wood and fitting it all onto a set of pram wheels. When the coke cart was finished, he wheeled Liam up and down the yard in it. Even Kevin was smiling now, he'd forgotten about the devil thing.

Before we left, Mrs Kelly told us to come back some other day. I said we would. Maybe Bap's gang would be there the next time, but I didn't ask him about it. On the way up the Bogside Road, I couldn't see any lookouts. They were good. I wished I had a gang like Bap's but I didn't say that to the others.

CHAPTER 18

Everybody Salute Uncle Jimmy!

Liam ran into the house, excited about the pigs down in the Bogside and about Bap's coke cart. My ma and da were in the living room. The kitchen table had been brought in and set up for dinner. They did that sometimes if there was a crowd in, because you could get extra chairs round the table. They laughed at Liam when he asked if we could keep pigs.

'Can we make a coke cart, Da?' I asked. 'Then me and Liam could go to the Gasyard for a bag.'

'Naw, we only use coal,' my da said. 'Coal's the best.'

Coal was five shillings for a bag. We got two every week. That was ten shillings just for coal. They owed the coal man a whole lot of money. Some weeks they couldn't pay for it, but he left it anyway. I knew they'd never get it paid off. Maybe Uncle Jimmy would pay it. He got the use of the fire as well.

You could buy coke for a shilling a bag. That's because it used to be coal before they took the gas out of it. And they put the gas through to all the houses for cookers and things. The gas was tuppence a go in the meter. It came through the pipes to under people's stairs. Me and Liam used to hide under the stairs in our house sometimes. You could smell the gas there. It was rotten. Maybe I'd get Bap to get stuff for another coke cart. We could make it in our back yard some time. Coke would be cheaper, even *I* could buy a bag when I gathered up the money.

You could smell the stew cooking in the kitchen. Stews were great. Even if the twins were cooking. But the dinner wasn't ready yet so I played Ludo in the hall with Liam. You could see into the sitting room. The door was open a wee bit. The twins were laughing and giggling.

'Peter and Joey are in there with them,' whispered Liam. He was sniggering. I thought it strange. They'd never been in the house before, only in the porch. I looked in. The girls were sitting on the boys' knees with their arms round their necks. It was yuckity-yuck time again. Liam was peeking as well, sniggering even louder. I whispered to him to be quiet or they'd hear him. They did.

Kate came to the room door and tried to bang it shut, but it just opened even wider. 'Bloody lock,' I heard her saying.

'Anyway,' shouted Laura at her, 'it's dinnertime.' The room door was opened and they all trooped out. Me and Liam were still on our knees on the floor.

'Hello, Dickie. Hello, Liam. Are youse at the Ludo again?' Peter and Joey had big grins on their faces as they looked down at us. I felt stupid. We stood up so that they could get past us. We thought they were heading out the front door, but they weren't. They followed the girls into the living room and sat down at the table. Laura then brought the pot in from the kitchen and Kate dished out the stews onto plates.

Liam looked at me, puzzled. 'They're having their dinner in our house,' he whispered.

'Shush,' I warned him as we followed them.

'Right, Ma, Da,' said Kate, 'the food's ready. And, Dickie, Liam, your dinners are out!' she shouted.

Me and Liam waited a minute to see what my ma and da would say. My da said nothing, but I noticed that he hadn't looked surprised when they'd gone into the room. He must have known they were coming. My ma smiled at Peter and Joey. Liam looked at me again, still puzzled.

'It's nice to see you, boys,' my ma said. 'It's not often we have company for dinner.'

'It's only stew, Ma,' laughed Laura. 'You'd hardly call that a dinner.'

'It's as good a dinner as you'll get anywhere,' said my da.

'It is, Mr McCauley,' Peter said.

'Grace first,' said my ma as me and Liam sat down at the table. 'Bless us, O Lord . . .'

'Now we can all tuck in,' said my da after Grace was finished. You could smell the Guinness off him, but he wasn't drunk. I was glad. He wouldn't fight with anybody. And he wouldn't be singing *Kevin Barry*.

Halfway through the dinner, the front door opened. It was Uncle Jimmy. He walked to the living-room door. He didn't say anything at first, just looked at Peter and Joey. When they saw him, they jumped up and pushed their chairs back from the table and saluted him. They stood to attention, like the soldiers do over in Brooke Park when the British Captain comes.

Me and Liam began to laugh. We jumped up as well and saluted him the same way. Then my da jumped up and saluted him.

'Ma, salute Uncle Jimmy!' shouted Liam. 'Everybody salute Uncle Jimmy!' repeated Liam.

But the twins or my ma didn't rise from the table. My ma looked a wee bit scared. She wasn't laughing. The twins looked annoyed. Me and Liam sat down. Something was wrong.

'What the fuck are you two boys doing in this house? Get out! Get out now, and don't ever come back! That's an order.'

Kate and Laura jumped up now, shouting at Uncle Jimmy to mind his own business, that it wasn't his house and he had no right to order anybody about. But Peter and Joey were already at the glass door. Uncle Jimmy followed them, shouting after them, 'I'll see you boys in half an hour! Be there. You know where.'

Laura and Kate ran past him to the street. They were raging.

'Well, well, well,' said my da when Uncle Jimmy came back in. 'So what have we here? The big-time captain of a big-time army ordering two wee lads about. Bossy Boots Jimmy. Bossy Boots from Donegal coming up here to Derry to throw his weight around.'

'You know nothing, Barney,' said Uncle Jimmy. 'Just sit down and eat your dinner and let me take care of the likes of them.'

'And who the fuck do you think you're talking to, Jimmy, telling *me* to sit down?' shouted my da. His eyes were blazing. 'You come into *my* house, ordering everybody about, shouting your mouth off and thinking you're the king of the castle. You're nothing but a bloody second-hand clothes seller and you'll never be anything else, you jumped-up bastard.'

My ma rose from the table. 'Jimmy, Barney, will youse stop all this shouting! And in front of the wains, too. Youse are a disgrace, the two of youse, and the language of youse. Nothing but disgraceful.'

My ma was great. She was standing between the two of them. She looked small, but she was tough. She looked a bit scared as well. Liam was grinning. I thumped him, but not hard. I just wanted to know what was going to happen next. I was worried. Really, really worried.

Uncle Jimmy wasn't finished yet and neither was my da. They were at it for nearly five minutes. It made me sick. My ma couldn't stop them. But I could, because I knew things. And so did our Liam. They all shouted at each other for another while. Then my ma sat down. She was exhausted. And very pale. She put her head into her hands. The half-eaten stews were all on the table, going cold.

'Shut up!' I screamed out. 'Shut up, Da! Shut up, Uncle Jimmy! Youse know nothing, and the cops know everything!'

'That's right!' shouted Liam. 'The cops know everything. Cecil Colhoun told us. He heard his da talking to Big Burnside.'

'What are you talking about?' my da asked and Uncle Jimmy went quiet.

'We're talking about you, Uncle Jimmy. They're watching out for ye, and they know that Peter and Joey burned the B-man's hut. Cecil told us.'

'Dear God in Heaven!' cried my ma. 'Dear Jesus Christ and His Holy Mother protect us.'

'When did youse hear this?'

'A wee while ago, Uncle Jimmy, when we were going down to Bap's house. About two hours ago. Cecil didn't mean to tell us, but he did. He told everybody. He blabbed.'

'Jimmy!' my ma shouted as she rose again from the table. 'Get out there this minute and tell them two young fellas to head across the border right away. And, Barney, you go and get the twins and bring them back here right now. And after that, Jimmy, you get across the border yourself. And if youse don't go this minute, I'll kill youse myself.'

My ma was as white as a sheet. My da and Uncle Jimmy left without saying anything. They banged the glass door behind them. It nearly broke. I felt that there was no way that Uncle Jimmy would be taking orders from my ma and crossing the border – he must be just going outside to let her calm down. And I felt that there was no way, either, that Peter and Joey would be heading for the Free State immediately. Not without seeing our Kate and Laura again. Uncle Jimmy and Big Burnside were no match for the twins. And threats didn't go down well with our Kate and Laura. Even I knew that.

'Come here, boys,' my ma said quietly when they had all left.

We went over to her. She was still pale and shaking a wee bit. She put her arms around our shoulders. She didn't say anything else; she just kept hugging us. But we knew she was scared. I

140

looked up at her for a good while; I just kept staring at her. I was scared, too. Very scared.

'I'm going out, Ma,' I said suddenly as I jumped up. 'And here, Ma, I forgot to give you this. Kevin gave it to me.' I slapped the pouch with the Fatima Rosary beads down on the table. I ran to the street. My ma was calling after me.

'Dickie, Dickie, where are ye going? Come back here, Dickie! Come back this minute!'

But I didn't. I just kept running. I had never done that before. I didn't know why I was doing it. My brain wasn't working right. Right now I couldn't control what was happening in the house. I was scared of it all. But maybe I could control what was happening outside, or what was going to happen. Then I wouldn't be scared. I was never scared when I was in control. As I ran faster, a plan was forming in my mind.

I could still hear my mother shouting when I reached the top of the street. Billy and Cecil were there. They looked round when they saw me. 'Your ma wants you,' said Billy.

'Shove off.'

'She's calling ye, Dickie,' said Cecil.

'You shove off, too.'

'We're only telling you.'

'Mind your own business!' I shouted.

'Why, what's up?'

'Nothing's up.' I knew a lot was up, but I wasn't for blabbing, especially not to Billy and Cecil. I was getting smarter about things every day, but what I was seeing and hearing was making life harder. Harder for everybody. Well, I could make life hard for people as well. But I didn't know exactly what was going to happen next. Not until I shouted, 'Get Danny! Get Kevin!'

'Why, where are you going?'

'I'll tell youse in a minute.' I didn't fully know myself yet, but I would when Danny and Kevin arrived.

'What's happening, Dickie?' asked Kevin when he came out of the house. Kevin was first there. Danny was after that, wheezing as usual.

'We're going to attack the Marlborough gang,' I ordered. 'Is everybody with me?'

'Aye,' they all said.

'When?' asked Billy.

'Now.'

'We need a plan,' said Cecil.

'I have a plan. Just follow me, and keep quiet the whole way.'

I knew I had to do something different right now to get things out of my head and think things through. Things that were happening; things that I had no control over; things that spelt danger, big danger. Like what was going on back there at the house a while ago. And even before that. With my ma and the twins and Uncle Jimmy, and my da, and Peter and Joey and about what the cops were saying; about what me and Liam had heard from Billy outside the slaughterhouse when Kevin was praying for Danny's da. I had no control over any of this and I needed to be in control if I was to do anything about anything. Just for the moment, I would put it all out of my mind. Now I was in control.

I ran across Creggan Hill and into Thompson's Field. They all followed, even Billy and Cecil. I was glad they were with us. It wasn't dark yet, so we'd have to be careful. Nobody was about. It was clear as far as the school wall. The Marlborough crowd didn't have lookouts. Not like Bap Kelly. They were stupid.

'Now, over the wall,' I whispered. Billy and Cecil helped Danny, he couldn't climb it by himself.

We were in the school grounds. The caretaker would be away home. He stopped at six o'clock. It was now after seven. We'd go across to the far wall and into the back lane behind Marlborough Road. It was a low wall, easy to get over. Then we had to be really careful. We would be in enemy territory. I knew it would be stupid just to walk down the back lane and into Marlborough Road. They'd spot us straightaway. I wasn't stupid.

My idea was simple. We'd go through the back garden of the house that faced onto the Wee Green in Marlborough. The Wee Green was a square patch of waste ground between the houses on the other side of Marlborough Road. Go down the side of this house and then we'd be in the front garden. Hide behind the front garden wall, opposite the Green, with a clear view of the Marlborough crowd. It was a good scheme. It should work, but I'd look stupid if it didn't.

'Right, boys,' I whispered, 'this is what we're going to do.' I told them my plan.

'Brilliant,' said Kevin, but he still had the beads out.

'Stupid,' hissed Danny. 'What if there's a dog there?'

'There's no dog,' I lied. 'I checked it out.'

'When?'

'Yesterday,' I lied again.

'But it might have been away yesterday.'

'They don't have a dog, Danny.' I gave him a dirty look. It shut him up.

We didn't have to climb the back wall of the house. The gate was open. We slipped in – me first, the others followed. Quiet, the way I told them. Down the side. Nobody was in; I could sense it. And there was no dog. I was lucky. The plan was working.

The Green was a good bit across the road and the Marlborough crowd were busy digging stupid holes. They were using shovels and picks. We watched them for a while. You could see the plots behind them.

'My da's over there,' whispered Cecil, pointing.

'Over where?' asked Kevin.

'In the plots, stupid; he's weeding turnips.'

'That's all he's good for, weeding turnips,' laughed Danny. 'Weeding turnips isn't a job, and if you're a B-man, that's not a job, either.'

'Shut up, the two of youse,' I whispered, 'or the attack is off.' They kept quiet.

'They're building trenches,' said Danny.

We all kept quiet and watched. They had a long hole dug down the side of the Wee Green. It was over two feet deep. It must have taken them weeks to do it. Two of them were putting sheets of corrugated iron over the trench and two others were putting clay and sods on top of the iron. The rest were digging another tunnel to connect with it. They had a whole pile of iron sheets sitting at the side of the Green, ready for more tunnels. It looked brilliant. But another plan was needed. There were too many of them to attack. I had to think fast.

'I'm going to the Bogside,' I whispered to them, 'to get Bap and his gang to help.'

'Great,' said Cecil. 'We'll wipe the lot of them out then.'

'Just keep quiet till we come back, and keep your heads down.'

I ran the whole way. It was beginning to get dark when I reached the slaughterhouse and turned down into the Bogside. I couldn't see any lookouts. Bap had them well trained. I knocked at his door. It was Bap's ma. 'Come on in, Dickie,' she said. 'Charlie's out the back; he's hammering away there as usual.'

Bap was nailing a big frame together. 'Hello, Dickie,' he said. 'What do you think? My da got me a load of wood the day. I've started a shed for the greyhounds. Do ye want to give me a hand?'

'I've no time, Bap, but if ye want a load of corrugated iron, I can get it for ye now.'

'Great,' he said. 'Where is it?'

I told him. I said he would need to bring the gang with him because of the big Marlborough crowd. And bring the coke cart as well to carry the iron. He looked at me. I could see his glass eye glinting. I knew he was thinking. He must have a plan coming.

'The problem is, Dickie, the gang's away on a raid. They won't be back until late. You and me'll go. It'll be nearly dark anyway by the time we get there and the Marlborough gang will probably be away.'

Something didn't sound right. Away on a raid; without their leader. And no lookouts and no bodyguards? It didn't add up.

Bap ran in to tell his ma and da what was happening, about him getting sheets of iron. He was excited about it. I pushed the coke cart through the hall and into the street. Before we left, Mrs Kelly called me back into the house. Bap was already pushing the cart through the Bogside towards Creggan Street. He couldn't get to Marlborough quick enough.

'Here's a wee scone I baked the day, Son. Will ye give it to your ma and tell her I'll be up to see her soon?'

'Thanks, Mrs Kelly.'

'And, Dickie, will ye watch out for Charlie on that old corrugated iron? We don't want him losing another eye. As ye know, he lost that one about four years ago when a crowd of slags were throwing stones over the yard wall. You look out for him now, won't ye?'

I didn't say anything. Just nodded and ran off in shock after Bap. I was learning a lot of things this day and I didn't like what I was learning, not one little bit.

When we reached the slaughterhouse, I let Bap see me throwing the scone over the wall. Maybe some poor cow would get it before she was slaughtered. Bap made no comment.

I said nothing to Bap the whole way up the hill, about his eye or about him not having a gang. I was too clever for that. Everything was lies and I knew it now. The worst thing was that he must think I was stupid, and I was far from stupid. I now had another plan, but in the meantime, I needed Bap to help. Liars could be useful. And lying could be useful sometimes as well. And I was the best liar I knew.

'Right, boys,' I told them when me and Bap got up to Marlborough again, 'let's get ready.'

'Where's Bap's gang?' whispered Danny.

'They're coming round by the lower plots' end,' I lied, 'and when they're in place, we'll make the charge. I'll give the signal.'

Bap looked at me, puzzled. I didn't give him my special look. I didn't need to. And he knew in that second that I didn't need to. He knew now that I was no fool. Bap kept his mouth shut. His game was finished. Over with.

'There's no need for them,' snapped Danny. 'There's no need for Bap's gang. The Marlborough crowd have left. They went before youse got here. They left when it got too dark. We may as well go home ourselves. It was a useless plan, McCauley,' he went on. Danny's words didn't annoy me. I would have felt the same, but I still told him to shut up. Plan B then went into operation.

'What do we do now, Dickie?' asked Cecil.

'We load up the sheets of corrugated iron onto the coke cart, that's what we do, and then we take them to Rosemount – to our back yard.' I looked at Bap, challenging him to speak. He said nothing.

'Are they for trenches, Dickie? Are we going to build some trenches?' asked Billy.

'I'll tell you later.'

We slipped across the road to the Wee Green, careful not to fall into any holes. One by one, the sheets were loaded onto the cart. Even Bap helped. I kept watch. They worked quietly. It was dark, but sometimes the moon came out between the clouds.

Just as the last sheet was being loaded, we heard loud banging noises from the plots. Everybody's head went down. Except mine. And Bap's. I looked over to my right where the noises came from. There were two more bangs and flashes. Within seconds, I saw two figures running across the lane at the side of the plots. I saw their silhouettes. I looked at Bap. He saw the silhouettes as well.

'Let's go,' I hissed. 'Now!' They were scared. They didn't have to be told twice.

It was even darker when we reached Rosemount. It was slow work. The iron was a heavy load. It took a long time to push it up the hill. Afterwards, Bap took his empty cart back home. He could sweat for a while for the corrugated iron. It was safely stored in McCauley's back yard. I was sweating for another reason.

I went into the house. They were talking in the living room. The table was back in the kitchen and there was music from the wireless. I stood listening. It was ordinary – they didn't know anything. I opened the door.

'And where were you to this time of night?' Kate asked. Liam was sitting on my da's knee, sleeping. My da was snoring. I looked at the clock. It was nearly half-past eight.

'Down at Bap Kelly's.'

'In the dark, in the blackout?'

'I know my way.'

'Hitler could have got ye.'

'That'll do, Kate. Leave Dickie alone.' It was my ma and she sounded okay. There'd be no kneeling in front of the Sacred Heart picture tonight. That's the way she sounded. And there was no scold in her voice. I wouldn't have cared anyhow. But she was glad to see me, I knew that by the way she spoke. And I noticed that things in the house looked normal when there was no way they should have been, especially after the big row earlier.

'And look at the state of ye,' laughed Laura. I looked at my clothes and shoes. Full of muck. 'Ye should have been in by eight.'

'Quiet, Laura,' said my ma softly. 'Are ye all right, Dickie?'

'Aye, Ma, I'm okay. We were out playing.'

'That's all right, Dickie. Get a wee wash and I'll get ye a glass of milk and a piece. Ye didn't finish your dinner before ye left.' There was nothing said about me running out.

'Naw, nobody did,' snorted Kate. 'Nobody had any stomach for eating. Have ye any more information for us, Dickie? You're the one that seems to know everything about the place.'

'Leave him be,' said my ma. She took me out to the kitchen and made a piece and poured me some milk. I washed my hands.

'Take your boots off, Dickie, and I'll clean them.' I did as she asked.

'Is Uncle Jimmy away, Ma?'

'Aye, Son.'

'And Peter and Joey?'

'Aye, they're away, too.'

'Are they coming back, Ma?'

'Aye, they'll be back sometime, I suppose.'

'When, Ma?'

'I don't know, Son, I don't know. Uncle Jimmy left this for ye.' She reached into her apron pocket. It was a half-crown. 'He gave one to Liam, too. Aren't youse the lucky boys?'

If Liam agreed, I was thinking, we could buy five bags of coke between us in the Gasyard, and borrow Bap's cart to take them home.

I took the half-crown and put it in my pocket. I wasn't really listening to the rest of what she was saying. It was something about me and Liam being good boys. My mind was back on the Wee Green and the plots. And on Bap. And on what we heard – and saw.

'We should have brought a rope,' Bap had said. 'We'll have to hold the iron when we're pushing the cart.'

'Aye,' I'd replied, whispering to him so that the others wouldn't hear me, 'and you watch your good eye when you're pushing it. We don't want ye going blind altogether, do we, Bap? Your ma told me, Bap. All about your false eye. About what *really* happened to you.'

He didn't say anything. He didn't have to. His lying games were over – at least with me they were. And he knew it.

That was just before the bangs and the flashes had started in the plots. And Bap had definitely seen the two silhouettes.

I knew he had, the way he looked at me afterwards. Bap Kelly knew who the silhouettes were. And I knew as well.

After I got the milk and the piece, I went to bed. Somebody else could see to Liam.

Who did they all think they were, trying to act normal down in the living room after all the shouting and arguing just a while ago? It wasn't normal when I got thran and ran out of the house, and it wasn't normal when I came back that nobody mentioned anything about anything. And it wasn't normal that the two silhouettes me and Bap saw in the plots were Peter and Joey when they were supposed to be across the border in the Free State. And it wasn't normal that the banging in the plots was from a gun, or guns. I wasn't stupid, but everybody must have thought I was.

Now, that couldn't be normal. Most definitely not.

CHAPTER 19

Prayers For The Dead

Philson was reading a big thick book in class the next day. You could hardly see his face behind it. He did that sometimes. Sitting at his desk, he would read it to himself the whole day. Just give you work to do and tell you to get on with it. He hardly noticed what ye were at. This morning, he told us to get our reading books out. It was *Kidnapped* by Robert Louis Stevenson. I hated it. I'd read it six times after Uncle Jimmy bought it to me about two years ago. It was great at first when you didn't know what was going to happen next. But I knew every page now. I was sick of it.

'Right, Francis, you begin – the first three pages. Then Timothy, three pages, and John, and so on . . .'

It was always the same. We knew what to do. Keep Philson happy and give him peace. Even the Smarts played the game. So did the Stupids. Quiet life for everybody. For a whole day.

It came to my turn. Philson's nose was still in the book. 'Page ten,' I started. 'Page ten is the best page in the book because it means that Mr Philson isn't listening to a word we say. It means that Mr Philson is deaf.'

The sniggers got louder. This was the sniggering I liked. Sniggering at Philson. If the sniggers got too loud, he would look down at us. I was always ready. The sniggers did get too loud.

He looked down. He banged his stick on the desk. The giggling stopped.

'Manners!' he shouted. 'Have the manners to listen when, when . . .' he looked down to see who was reading, 'when McCauley is reading. Not that *his* manners are anything to write home about, but everybody deserves to be heard. Now, McCauley, continue . . .' He went back to his book.

I began to speak another few lines, real ones, before I felt it was safe to say anything else about Philson. 'Philson is also a very smelly man because he only takes a bath once a month . . .' Some more giggles. Philson hit his cane on the desk again but didn't look up. He still wasn't listening. I mumbled on for another couple of minutes until Kevin took over, then Danny, and then the rest of them, except the Stupids.

In the playground at lunchtime, I made sure that Danny and Kevin were with me when I called Bap over. 'About the corrugated iron,' I said to them, 'Bap here is building a shed for his gang. Isn't that right, Bap?' He looked at me, puzzled, and nodded, but not saying anything.

'Wow,' said Kevin, 'a gang shed! Why can't *we* have a gang shed, Dickie?'

'Because we don't need one. And Bap has a massive gang, isn't that right, Bap?' Bap just looked down and shuffled his feet a bit.

'And Bap's coming to Rosemount this evening with his gang to bring the corrugated iron to the Bogside. Isn't that right, Bap?' Bap nodded.

'Right,' I said to him, 'we'll see youse at six o'clock. You and your gang. Youse can load it all on the coke cart and take it with youse. Six o'clock, Bap. We'll be waiting.'

Bap shuffled away. He knew it would take him at least three trips to Rosemount and back down to the Bogside, four sheets at a time on his cart. Without any gang to help him, he was going to have a busy evening. And I would order Billy and Cecil and

Danny and Kevin to watch. Maybe Liam, too. Nobody gets off with trying to make a fool out of me.

It was nose-in-the-book time again for Philson after the lunch break. This time he gave us a composition to write. 'Heads down,' he said, 'and no noise from anybody.'

He gave the Stupids paper and coloured pencils. I wrote a page. It took me twenty minutes. It would do. He wouldn't read it anyway. The rest of the time, I just sat thinking about the big row between my da and Uncle Jimmy before me and Liam told them about what the police had said. It was the worst row in the house for a long time. I'd never forget it.

'And them two young fellas, Peter and Joey,' my da had shouted at Uncle Jimmy, 'ye have the shit scared out of them, ordering them about the way ye do! That'll get the British out of Ireland all right. It will, my arse. And from what I know of ye, ye don't know wan end of a gun from the other. Call yourselves IRA men. The whole lot of youse would run away at the first sight of a B-man.'

Uncle Jimmy's eyes were blazing. He had pointed his finger at my da and warned him not to speak bad about the IRA. 'The day's coming soon when you'll need them—'

'Barney McCauley,' my da interrupted, 'needs *nobody* to fight his battles, and especially not the likes of you.'

Only for me and our Liam, they still would have been arguing. And only for the row, I wouldn't have known a whole lot of things that I know now.

Philson slammed his book shut. People jumped. 'Right, everybody, write out your homework for tomorrow. The information is all on the board.' Then he hesitated before he spoke again. He smiled and looked down at the three Smarts. 'Francis, Timothy, John, I'd like you to stay behind after school today. I've some information for you.'

Nobody knew what it was about. Most people didn't care.

'Kelly, Harley, Dickson, McCauley – you lot wait quietly in

the corridor until I'm finished with these three boys. Then come back in and see me.'

Now everybody went quiet. There must be something big brewing. The bell went. Everybody left the room except the three Smarts. Me and Bap and the other two waited outside. None of them looked worried. I hadn't done anything wrong, so I wasn't worried, either. But it was still a puzzle why Philson wanted to see me.

After a couple of minutes, the three Smarts came out of the room. They were smiling and had large white envelopes in their hands. They didn't say what was happening, just told us to go on in.

Inside, Philson wasn't smiling or anything, but he didn't look annoyed. 'McCauley,' he said, 'I want you to sit down in the back seat while I deal with Kelly, Dickson and Harley.'

I went to the back and sat down. Philson was talking to the others. It was more a quiet mumble. I couldn't hear what he was saying. After a minute, he gave them an envelope each. The same kind as the Smarts. Then they left the room.

Philson got up from his desk, took a duster out of his drawer and wiped the board clean. He then tidied his desk and put his book into his briefcase. I thought for a minute he had forgotten all about me. I remembered what my da had told me about Philson. 'Watch that boy,' he'd said, 'because he's a crafty bastard.'

Then Philson looked down at me. 'Ah, McCauley,' he laughed, 'the last but not the least. The last shall be first and the first shall be last.' I remembered our Kate had said something like that to me once. 'Come up here, McCauley. I wanted to speak to you by yourself. I think, under the circumstances, it's only fair.'

When was the big nose-picker ever fair? He was after something. Information? He wouldn't get it from me.

'Now, McCauley, I know that you come from a difficult background and that you have many troubles and hardships. I also

153

know – yes, I'm convinced of it, McCauley – that children such as you, in those circumstances, often rebel against authority.'

I didn't know what the arse-scratcher was talking about. It must be something about my da. That was it. My da had sorted him out and now he's going to get back at me in some way. *Crafty bastard,* I thought.

'The thing is, McCauley, even with all the problems that you are experiencing, and even with your constant bad behaviour and your bad manners and your poor background, you do have a modicum of intelligence which could set you apart from many others who might find themselves in the same circumstances as yourself.'

I still didn't know what he was talking about. And I'd remember to look up 'modicum' sometime in the dictionary. *Watch the bastard,* I thought.

'Taking everything into consideration, especially your high academic record at this school, I have recommended that you should be allowed to sit for the entrance examination to the College this coming May. That's for a scholarship, McCauley. To the College. What do you think, McCauley?' I said nothing, just grunted what sounded like a 'thank you' but wasn't.

Philson handed me a big white envelope, the same as the others got. 'This is a letter, McCauley, to inform your parents of our decision, when the examination will be and so on. I suggest you give it to your mother to read.'

I noticed right away that he didn't suggest that my da should read it as well. I didn't like that.

'Oh, Sir,' I lied, innocently, 'my ma can't read. It's my da who does all the reading in our house, Sir. My da has hundreds of books, Sir, and he reads all the time: French books and German books and Irish books. My da can speak three languages as well as English. It's just that my ma never learned to read, Sir.'

Philson took a coughing fit. He couldn't speak for a minute. I could see wet snot on the end of his nose. He could wipe that one, there'd be no need to pick it.

'Of course, of course, McCauley, whatever. Just give the letter to your parents. Now, go on home.'

I left the room. Bap Kelly was in the corridor waiting on me.

'What are you doing here?' I asked him.

'What did Philson want?' said Bap.

'None of your business, Kelly.'

'Was it about the entrance exam?' Bap Kelly was a puzzle. He didn't have to ask me. He saw the envelope in my hand. I put it into my pocket.

When we were outside the grounds, Bap took out his own envelope and tore it in two. 'That's what I think of Philson,' he said. 'He can shove his scholarship.' He put the two pieces back in his pocket.

I didn't say anything. But before he turned the corner to go home, I shouted to him, 'Don't forget, Kelly, you be up for the corrugated iron at six o'clock. If you're not there at six, I'll give it to somebody else.'

'Right, Dickie,' he said. 'Thanks, Dickie.'

I thought it was strange that he didn't talk about the bangs and the flashes in the plots last night. Bap Kelly really was a puzzle. Maybe I was a puzzle to him, too. I reached our street. The men were working at the air-raid shelter which was half up.

'You're late, Dickie,' said my ma when I opened the glass door, 'Liam's had his piece.'

'It's all right, Ma, I'll make my own.'

'Good boy, Dickie.'

My da was there. No work today.

'I see ye got a load of corrugated iron, Dickie,' said my da. 'What's it for?'

'It's for Bap Kelly, Da. He's calling up for it this evening. He's making a greyhound shed.'

'Where did ye get it, Dickie?'

'Over in Marlborough, Da.'

'And what did it cost ye, Dickie?'

'Nothing, Da. We got it off the Marlborough crowd. They were going to use it for tunnels, Da, but they're not now.'

I went out to the kitchen before he could ask any more questions, but I heard him laughing, 'That Dickie's some pup, Kitty.' I didn't hear what she replied, I didn't want to know.

I was making my piece when I heard a loud knock on the glass door. I looked out and saw the silhouettes of Mrs Doherty and Kevin. They could wait. The knocking got louder, then the door was pushed open and Mrs Doherty and Kevin rushed in. Kevin had the Rosary beads in his hand. His eyes were in his skull. He was saying the Rosary out loud. They looked scared.

'Hail Mary, full of grace . . .'

'Ma!' I shouted. 'There's Mrs Doherty.' She opened the living-room door.

'Hello, Mrs Doherty. Hello, Kevin. Come on in.'

'Did ye hear, Kitty? We've just heard it ourselves. Poor Mr Colhoun . . .'

'May his soul and the souls of all the faithful departed rest in peace,' Kevin said out loud. 'Hail Mary, full of grace . . .'

'He's dead, Kitty, poor Mr Colhoun's dead.'

'My God, what happened?'

'They found him in the plots, Kitty, God rest his soul.'

'Our Father, who art in Heaven . . .'

'He was shot, Kitty. The poor man was murdered, but they didn't find him until today. He must have been there all night, lying dead, God rest his soul.'

My heart was thumping. I could hear what they were saying, but I wasn't taking it all in. I walked into the living room. I felt dizzy. The piece was still in my hand.

'May God forgive them, Kitty, murdering a nice man like that, and him just minding his own business in the plot . . . and that poor wee Cecil . . . oh, my God!'

The last I heard was Kevin praying, louder now, 'Glory be to the Father . . .'

156

My head was spinning. Voices were all mixed up. Nothing was making any sense. I felt weak and dizzy and I was falling to the ground. I couldn't help myself. Then blackness.

CHAPTER 20

The Facts Of Life

I opened my eyes. I felt sick, weak, I couldn't move. I was lying on the floor and my da was kneeling beside me. He was throwing water on my face. I could hear my ma crying.

'Is he all right, Barney? Is our Dickie all right? Dear God in Heaven, make our Dickie all right.'

My eyes blinked but I couldn't move. Something was wrong. It must be TB or diphtheria or polio. That's what it was: polio. And my da throwing water over me would make it worse. They'd take me away in an ambulance, wrapped up in a red wool blanket. I saw them doing that with other people, carrying them out of houses and putting them into the backs of ambulances. It happened all the time. Some of them never came back.

'He's all right, Kitty, he's coming round. His eyes are open.'

'God Almighty, what happened him, Barney?'

'He just fainted, Kitty, but he's all right now.'

'Dickie, Dickie.'

I could see my da staring down at me, calling my name. I couldn't say anything. I was paralysed. I couldn't talk. My lips wouldn't move.

'Angel of God, my guardian dear, to whom God's love commits me here . . .'

I could hear Kevin praying but I couldn't see him.

'Is the wee lad all right, Barney?' It was Mrs Doherty. That made me feel worse. Kevin and his ma in our house when I was dying. I could feel something crunched up in my hand. That meant I wasn't paralysed all over. I lifted my hand up to look. It was a squashed piece. There was jam on my fingers. Like blood.

'Look at the poor wee soul,' wailed Mrs Doherty, 'with the wee piece in his hand.'

'. . . ever this day be at my side, to light and guard, to rule and guide. Amen.'

I turned my head to Kevin. I could see the two big whites behind the jam jars and his frightened look. My da was lifting me off the floor. Putting me on the couch. A coat over me. My ma putting a wet towel on my head. 'He's all right now, Kitty. He'll be back to normal in ten minutes.'

My da and ma were great. They were bringing me back to life. I asked for a drink. I could speak. I wasn't paralysed and I hadn't got polio, I'd just fainted. People fainted all the time in school and in the chapel. I closed my eyes. I could feel my ma sitting beside me. She was holding my hand. Liam was holding my other hand. 'Are ye all right, Dickie?' he asked. I opened my eyes and smiled at him.

'There you are now, the wee lad's coming round okay. It must have been the shock about wee Cecil's father.' It was Mrs Doherty speaking again. I hated her. I closed my eyes. I closed my mind from her. I didn't want to hear her any more.

'That'll do now, Mrs Doherty; we'll not talk about it now.'

'Aye, you're right, Kitty, but wasn't it terrible? Them bastards in the IRA have a lot to answer for. May God forgive them for what they done to poor Mr Colhoun. And him only doing a wee job at the plots.'

I felt sick again. But I didn't feel dizzy, just stomach sick. Not vomiting sick. My mind could hear the bangs in the plots and see the flashes in the dark and the silhouettes of Peter and Joey running across the lane. And the dead B-man lying on the turnips with a spade in his hand. And blood all over him. And Mrs Colhoun screaming when she heard about it. And Cecil crying and holding on to his ma. And Uncle Jimmy driving his van across the border to the Free State. And the gun that used to be under the floorboards in the bathroom. Maybe the same gun killing Mr Colhoun, with either Joey or Peter pulling the trigger. The same gun that my da had allowed me to touch in the bathroom. And Bap looking at me watching the silhouettes. And me looking at Bap watching the silhouettes. And my da shouting at Uncle Jimmy that he would run at the first sight of a B-man.

Although my mind was still whirling, I sat up. I was feeling better, stronger. Liam was still holding my hand and my da had a cup of water for me. 'Here, Son, drink this,' he said. 'And how are ye feeling now, Dickie?'

'Better, Da. I think I fainted, Da. I never did that before.'

'There's a first time for everything, Dickie.'

I drank the water. 'Can I have tea and a piece now, Ma? I'm hungry.'

'There ye are. Ye see, Kitty? Dickie's back to normal.'

'I'll get it for ye now, pet; it must have been the hunger that did it. And I'll get the dinner on, too.'

My ma was wrong. It wasn't the hunger that made me faint. Kevin's ma was right. It was hearing about Cecil's da being killed in the plots. It was about Cecil without a da. And about me knowing who did it. Me and Bap. I'd have to see him before he came for the corrugated iron. I looked at the clock. It was half-past four. He was coming at six.

After the tea and piece, I really did feel normal. I had things to see about. I told my ma and da I was going outside for a while. I headed for the Bogside. On the way, I called into the chapel. I hadn't meant to. I was inside the gate before I knew it. I went up the middle aisle and sat down on the front seat. The red light was on above the altar. That meant Jesus was present. I learned that from Father Mooney. If the red light was out, Jesus was away somewhere. I knelt down and said a prayer that my ma taught me. It was a short one.

'Oh, Most Sacred Heart of Jesus, I place all my trust in Thee.'

I looked up at the altar and thought about what was happening. God knew everything, so you didn't have to tell Him. You just thought about different things. I was thinking of Cecil, and about what Peter and Joey had done to his da, and I knew it was bad, because it was a mortal sin to kill anybody, and if they didn't confess it before they died, they would go to Hell. I was thinking of Uncle Jimmy, about the time he told me that it wasn't a mortal sin if you killed somebody in a war. And I was thinking that Uncle Jimmy knew that Peter and Joey were going to kill Mr Colhoun. Maybe he even told them to do it. But Mr Colhoun wasn't our enemy, and there was no war, not like the Germans and the British. Mr Colhoun was only weeding turnips in his plot. Mr Colhoun was Cecil's da. He wasn't the enemy. And I was thinking as well that if I knew who did a murder and didn't tell anybody, that could be a mortal sin, too, and I could go to Hell if I didn't tell the priest about it in Confession.

'Hello, Richard.'

I looked up. It was Father Mooney. He was smiling down at me. I didn't see him coming.

'Hello, Father.'

'Are you paying a wee visit, Son?'

'Yes, Father, I'm just saying a prayer.'

'Good boy, good boy.' He sat down beside me.

'Is there anything bothering you, Son?'

'I was just thinking about things.' I didn't want to tell him about Mr Colhoun because it wasn't a Confession and he might badger me to go to the police. If I told him about it in Confession, he couldn't do that.

'And how's your mother, Richard?'

'She's getting better, Father. The big-belly disease is going away.'

'That's good, that's good.'

'I have to go now, Father.'

'Before you go, Richard, there're a couple of things I wanted to talk to you about.'

'Yes, Father?'

'The first thing is . . . and what age are you, Richard?'

'I'm nine, Father, nearly ten.'

'Good, good. Now, Son, have you ever heard of a thing called "the facts of life"?'

'Naw, Father, I haven't.'

'Well, you know, Richard, that babies are born?'

'Yes, Father. Kate told me. She said that our wee baby was born up in the bedroom. Me and Liam thought it was brought by the nurse in the black bag.'

'And you know what love is, Richard?'

'Yes, Father. Love is a good feeling between people.'

'Very good, Son, very good.'

'Well, you see, Son, when mammies and daddies feel love, and get very close together in their love, if they're very lucky, God will send them a new baby.'

'Who brings it, Father?'

'Well, that's what I'm explaining to you, Richard. This love that I'm talking about, between a mammy and a daddy, is what starts the baby off. And it grows from a very tiny speck inside the mammy. And it takes nine months for it to become a baby. And then it's born, from the mammy. Do you understand now, Richard?'

'I'm not sure, Father.'

'It's not a disease as you thought it was, Son. It's the baby getting bigger and bigger as the months go by, inside the mammy, if you know what I mean.'

I stared at the priest. My mouth was open. I was shocked. I'd been stupid, a fool. I knew nothing. But I did now. I was learning stuff. Fast.

'Yes, Father, I know what you mean now.'

'Good boy, good boy.'

'And the other thing, Richard, is this. Up at the school the other day, your young friend with the glasses was getting very annoyed about the question of Limbo.'

'Yes, Father. Kevin should mind his own business.'

'Well, it was a very good question and I think he deserved an answer, because a lot of big people are asking the same question as well. About Limbo, I mean. Well, let me tell you, Richard, what I think. I think that your wee baby brother is with God now, at this very minute, in Heaven, Son, with all the angels and saints.'

'He has no name, Father.'

'Why don't you give him one and then ask your mammy and daddy about it?'

'Could I call him Johnny, Father? I like the name Johnny.' I could see Father Mooney smiling at me when I said that. It was a very friendly smile.

'I think you couldn't have picked a better name, Richard. Johnny, after John the Baptist, eh?'

Before I left the chapel, I took Uncle Jimmy's half-crown out of my pocket and put it into the candle box. I lit twenty-nine candles for Cecil's da and one for our baby Johnny, even though he was in Heaven. I said another short prayer and headed on to Bap's house.

Bap's ma came to the door when I knocked. 'Come on in, Dickie.'

'Naw, it's all right, Mrs Kelly. I'll wait for him here.'

'Isn't it great, Dickie,' she said, 'about you and Charlie?'

'What about us, Mrs Kelly?' I didn't know what she was talking about.

'About you and him doing the scholarship exam for the College. Isn't that the great thing, now?'

I didn't say anything. Bap Kelly really was a puzzle. A real big, giant puzzle. That's all I could think of. So much for shoving it up Philson. The scholarship, I mean.

'Charlie!' she shouted over her shoulder. 'Dickie's here for ye.'

She then turned back to me. 'And, Dickie . . .'

'Yes, Mrs Kelly?'

'Aren't you the great boy for getting Charlie the corrugated iron?'

'It's up in our back yard, Mrs Kelly. It's all mucky, so every sheet has to be washed before he can bring it down.'

'Well, isn't that good of ye, Dickie?' She laughed before she went in. 'Do you hear that, Charlie? All the iron's going to be washed before ye bring it down. That's the best ever I heard.'

It was the best I ever heard, too, because I had just thought of it. And it would be Bap Kelly who would be washing every sheet with a bucket of water and a brush before he put them on the coke cart. And into the bargain, he'd be doing three journeys with them to the Bogside – all on his own!

'I just wanted to ask you one question, Bap,' I said to him when he came to the door, 'before ye came up to Rosemount.'

'What's that?' He looked worried.

'Did you see who ran across the lane after we heard the bangs in the plots last night?'

'I did, aye. It was big Joey and Peter, the two boys that are going with your twins. And I'll tell you something else.'

'What?'

'Colhoun's not the first bastard they shot.'

I didn't want to hear any more of what he had to say. I was shocked. I turned and walked away. I might know a whole lot of things but I knew I still had a lot more to learn. But nothing more to learn about Bap Kelly, or so I thought. The fake Charlie Kelly, Charlie the liar, Charlie Bap Kelly, the one-eyed fake. For him, it would soon be payback time.

In my heart, I knew that Bap Kelly knew a lot more about life than I did. But I was determined to catch up. Nobody outwits me that way. And Bap Kelly was soon to find that out.

CHAPTER 21

A Whole Mess

When I got back to the street, there was nobody about. Blinds were pulled down in a whole lot of houses. People did that if somebody died. Cecil's and Billy's big front doors were closed. I walked on into the house. My ma and da and Liam were in the living room.

'Had ye a nice walk, Dickie?'

'I had, Ma. I feel better now.'

'That's great, Son. Your da has the dinner on. It'll be ready soon.'

'Thanks, Ma.' It was strange, them not mentioning anything to me about Mr Colhoun. Mr Colhoun was Cecil's da. And Cecil Colhoun was my friend. I went through the kitchen to the yard. Liam followed me.

'What are ye doing, Dickie?'

'I'm getting a bucket of water and brush for Bap. He's going to wash the corrugated iron before he puts it in the cart.'

'It's not dirty, Dickie.'

'It's dirty enough.' I laughed, 'And, Liam . . .'

'What?'

'Would you go up the street and tell Danny and Billy and Kevin to be down here at five to six? And to come down the back way. Remember, Liam, five to six exactly. That's important.'

'Right, Dickie. And what about Cecil? Will I tell him, too?'

'I don't think so, Liam, since his da was killed.'

'Who killed him, Dickie?'

'I don't know,' I lied.

As soon as Liam left, I went upstairs to do my homework. Another composition, sums, spellings and algebra. They were all easy. When I'd finished, I started my sin list for Friday. This time in code, in case it got into the wrong hands:

✓ 10 FOs
✓ 8 Fs
✓ 6 Bs
✓ 8 Ls
✓ 2 Ss

When I finished the list, I put it under the lino. Before I went downstairs again, I looked through the window. The air-raid shelter was nearly finished. It just needed a roof. It would probably be ready next week. I looked into the barracks yard. I counted ten policemen there, all lined up. I never saw that before. They must be drilling or something. Big Burnside was one of them. Liam came upstairs to tell me Danny and Kevin would be down in five minutes. He said Billy wasn't allowed to come.

'His ma told me that, Dickie. She said he wasn't allowed to play with us anymore.'

'Did she say why?'

'Naw, she just said it and then closed the big door on me, Dickie.'

'Liam, would you like to go down to the hall and play Ludo before we get our dinner?'

'Great, Dickie. And will you be down in a minute?' I nodded. Liam reached under his bed for the box and rushed downstairs.

I stood looking out the window again at the barracks. The policemen marched quickly into the police station. The drill must be over. I went downstairs. Liam had the game set out on the hall floor. 'You start,' I said. He threw the dice.

Halfway through the game, there was a knock on the glass door. I saw the silhouette. It was Bap Kelly. I looked at the clock on the front-room mantelpiece. It was six o'clock, he was exactly on time. I got up and opened the door but didn't say hello. He made to come in the front door with the cart. I put my hand up. 'Take the cart round to the lane,' I told him. 'The back gate's open for ye as well. Wash each sheet of tin before you put it in the cart.'

Bap didn't look pleased. He went back down the street, pushing the cart ahead of him. I closed the glass door. 'Right, Liam,' I hissed, 'out the back, quick.' Danny and Kevin were there as ordered. Liam had done well. He was learning fast.

'What's up?' Danny asked.

'Aye, what's happening?' asked Kevin.

'Aye, what's up, Dickie?' Liam was excited.

It was great, everybody wanting to know my next move. I had already told them that we were giving Bap the sheets of iron. That was enough for them to know at this stage. I ordered Kevin and Danny to just stand and watch him for a while, and not to help him in any way, and say nothing at all to him when he was washing and loading the first four sheets. I told them as well that it would take him the rest of the evening to do the whole job.

'Don't forget, now,' I said again. 'Just stand there, all quiet, and when he's finished the first lot, and when he leaves with it, I'm going to tell youse the biggest secrets about Bap Kelly youse ever heard in your life.'

'Wow,' whispered Kevin.

'Sounds good to me,' said Danny.

They looked excited. They knew something was brewing. Something serious between me and Bap Kelly. They knew it was me getting my own back about something. And Bap Kelly was going to be the one to suffer. They sensed it. And they'd soon learn why. We heard the cart coming up the back lane.

'Right,' I said to them, 'you know what to do.'

They nodded, animated. I quickly took Liam back into the house to finish the game of Ludo, but his mind wasn't on it. He wanted to know what I was up to with Bap. He was so excited when I told him he would be the first to find out.

And that was the very moment that things began to happen which, I swear, will stay with me for the rest of my life. It all began in a strange kind of slow motion, and then it was like lightning immediately after that.

The first thing was that Kate and Laura opened the glass door coming in from their work. They were very quiet. I knew they weren't saying anything because of the shooting last night. They didn't even say hello. They just stepped over me and Liam and the Ludo board and went into the living room. They had shut the door behind them, but within two seconds it all began. And it was shocking.

The first noise I heard was the door bursting open onto Liam's back and then these five cops rushing through our porch with batons in their hands, roaring and shouting. There was a crash as the glass on the door smashed into pieces, a whole lot of it landing on Liam and some on me. Liam screamed with the shock of it all and he put his hands to his face. He was cut. There was a lot of blood running out of his right cheek and his neck.

I jumped up but before I could reach Liam, two of the cops lifted me and Liam and threw us into the sitting room, but not before I saw more cops coming in from the back yard, through the kitchen, roaring and shouting and pushing Danny and Kevin and Bap in front of them. Danny and Kevin were squealing with fright. Bap didn't look frightened, just annoyed. I heard Big Burnside's voice. I hadn't noticed him before.

'Put them there in the sitting room with the other two!' Burnside shouted. 'And you stay with them, Johnstone. The rest of youse, look for guns.' So that was it. A raid. My heart sank. If the gun was back under the bathroom floorboards we'd all hang. Like Kevin Barry. It was worse than a nightmare.

I tried to get back out to the hall to see what was happening. I only got as far as the door. Liam was holding on to me, crying loudly.

A cop I had never seen before then pushed the five of us roughly into the sitting room. When Danny and Kevin saw the blood pouring out of Liam, they screamed even louder. Bap just stared, staying cool, as if he were just watching it all happening to somebody else. I'd remember that. Liam was in hysterics by this time, so I went straight over to try to help him. His face and neck looked terrible. A whole mess. I could see wee bits of glass sticking out of him. Now it was my turn to scream – at the policeman.

'Liam needs my ma!' I shouted to him as I moved towards him. 'He's bleeding bad.'

The cop pulled me away and forced me to sit on the floor with Danny and Kevin and Bap. Liam was on the floor in the corner of the room, screaming even worse now because he knew nobody was helping him. I made another rush towards Liam. It seemed the right thing to do. But the cop was too quick. He caught me by the arm and forced me back again.

'Sit down there, ye wee bastard, or ye'll get worse than him.'

'He needs my ma!' I screamed. 'If ye don't get my ma, he could bleed to death.'

The cop just laughed.

It was only then that I heard all the other roars and shouts from outside, in the hall. The door was a wee bit open because of the faulty lock. The only roar from inside the room was from Danny. He was shouting for his ma and roaring at the policeman at the same time that he was nothing but a black bastard and that the IRA would get him and cut his throat. I gave him a dunt in the ribs. We were in enough trouble without stupid threats like that from Danny. Kevin was praying out loud. His beads were rattling. The cop was just glaring at us. His eyes were bulging and his face was red and sweaty.

The sitting-room door suddenly burst wide open. Somebody's foot had hit it. I could hardly believe what I saw, but I had to because I couldn't miss it. There was my da and Kate and Laura rolling about the hall floor, wrestling with what looked to be about six policemen. Everybody was all over the place, with the cops swinging their batons and my da and the twins roaring and screaming as they fought with them. I could hear my mother crying loudly, but I couldn't see her. She must still have been in the living room or the kitchen.

Upstairs, the other cops were wrecking the place, throwing furniture about and hammering loudly from one room to the next. And when all this was still happening, I noticed that Liam wasn't screaming any more. He seemed to be sobbing and moaning in to himself, and his hands were still up at his face, and you could see all the blood on his fingers. I felt sick. I felt useless. I was a prisoner in my own home and I couldn't even help my ma or my wee brother.

The roaring and screaming in the hall went on and on as the cops got the better of my da and the twins. They were now dragging them along the hallway. I heard Burnside shouting again: 'Get them three into that back room and keep them there! I want to speak to these articles in the other room.'

I could hear them all scuffling and still screeching as they banged the living-room door shut behind them. Burnside was looking mad. Really angry. His face was red and blotchy and he shouted to the cop who was guarding us: 'Get you upstairs and help the others!' The cop left the room.

'Mr Burnside!' I shouted. 'Our Liam's bleeding bad. He needs my ma. He needs treatment.'

'I'll give youse treatment all right if youse don't tell me what I want to know.'

'We know nothing!' shouted Danny. 'And I'll tell my ma on you if you don't let us go. We don't know anything. You have no right to keep us here.'

'I have every right, and youse won't be leaving till youse answer my questions.' Burnside put his two hands up towards us. 'Now, let's all calm down,' he said. 'We have a serious situation here. Four possible witnesses to a terrible murder over in the plots. That's what youse are, witnesses.'

'Liam wasn't there!' I shouted. 'Let him go. Let him go in to my ma.'

'He stays,' said Burnside.

'Your Billy was there, too,' squeaked Danny, 'and Cecil Colhoun.'

I elbowed Danny's ribs again. I didn't want him blabbing. I hated blabbers. I don't know if Burnside heard him or not because Kevin was still rattling his Rosary beads and was now reciting the third decade out loud. If he did hear him, he didn't take him on. But Billy and Cecil must have blabbed about us being near the plots last night. You couldn't blame Cecil for blabbing, it was his father that was shot dead. Even *I* might have blabbed if I'd been in his shoes. And into the bargain, after all this, the Marlborough gang would know who stole their stupid sheets of corrugated iron. Word was bound to get out. But I didn't care. We could handle them.

But handling Burnside now was a different kettle of fish, what with all his questions, his wee black notebook and pencil out, and the screaming and all still going on in our living room. And worst of all, Liam was moaning all the time and we weren't allowed to see about him. Big Burnside must be the worst bastard in the whole world and this must be the worst day in my life.

That's what I was thinking anyway as we sat there listening to Burnside. We were prisoners in our own house. The whole McCauley family, as well as Danny and Kevin and Bap.

Chapter 22

God Bless The Mark

The arse was out of my trousers. They must have caught on a nail sticking out of a floorboard. Fuck the cops. I only had one pair of trousers. I shouted to Liam to get up, but he wouldn't move.

'Ma!' I roared down the stairs from the landing. 'My trousers are ripped! I'll be late for school.'

She shouted back, 'Throw them down, Dickie! I'll sew them.'

I pushed them over the banister rail. To pass the time, I looked into my ma's and da's room. It was wrecked, the same as ours; and the twins' room, and Uncle Jimmy's attic room – all wrecked as well, with floorboards pulled up and holes in walls and torn wallpaper lying everywhere. Everything was in a mess, even the bathroom. The cops had found nothing or we'd all be in jail by now. And we'd told Big Burnside nothing, either.

'Liam,' I shouted again, 'if you don't get up now, you'll not be in time for school!' He didn't answer. I shook him and pulled the blankets off him, but he still didn't rise. I had other things to worry about now.

I had already cleaned the blood off him last night, because nobody else was bothering about him, and I'd taken out a couple of wee bits of glass that were sticking to his face and neck. The cuts weren't as bad as you would think, what with all the blood, but it was very scary for him. That's why he was screaming a lot in the hall and in the sitting room. And he didn't even cry when I was fixing him up and cleaning his cuts with Dettol. He was very brave. I didn't bother telling my ma or da about what happened to Liam because they were fussed enough with what happened to them. I just put Liam straight to bed after the cops had left.

I went downstairs with my shirt in one hand and holding my vest between my legs with the other, like in the dream I get sometimes. I ate a slice of toast that was on a plate and drank a taste of cold tea from my ma's cup. It would do for now. It was five minutes to nine. I was going to be late for school. I hated that because it would give Philson a chance of saying something stupid to me.

My da was sitting in his armchair, not reading the paper or listening to the wireless or anything like that. Just sitting there. His eyes were staring at nothing. He didn't say hello to me. And the twins must have been away to work. Their dishes were still on the table.

'Here, Dickie, they're finished,' my ma said, handing me the trousers. 'Get off to school now or you'll be late. Where's Liam?'

'He wouldn't get up, Ma. I shouted to him, but he wouldn't move.'

'You go on. I'll see to him,' she said. But I ran back upstairs, fumbling at the same time to get my clothes on. As I grabbed my schoolbag, I shouted to Liam once again to get up, but he still wouldn't move. My ma would have to sort him out. He was going to be very late.

As I left the house, I thought it was strange that they didn't talk about the police raid last night or even ask me about what happened in the sitting room. It was as if it was a normal morning. But it wasn't. Nothing was normal any more. The whole street would know by now, or maybe even the whole of Derry, that our house was wrecked, and about all the cops fighting with my da and the twins, and keeping us prisoners in the sitting room, and about our Liam getting cut, and all the screaming and shouting. Naw, nothing was normal any more.

It was a couple of minutes past nine when I knocked at the classroom door and walked in. The Stupids never knocked. They just barged in and sat down when they were late and never a word from Philson. He just took a quick look at me and turned away again when I entered the room.

I'm late, you big nose-picker. It's because the cops raided our house last night and wrecked the place and tore my trousers and messed everything up. Jumped us, they did. That's why I'm late. Are you satisfied now?

'I'm late, Mr Philson.'

'Sit down, McCauley. We haven't started yet. Collect the home-works, Harley, and take out your reading books, everybody. It's eyes down and a quiet room for the rest of the morning.'

Just like that, as if I hadn't been late, as if nothing had happened, as if everything was okay, as if it was just another ordinary day. But I knew it wasn't, and nearly everybody else knew it wasn't. As I headed towards my seat, I glanced over at Danny and Kevin. They were pale and scared looking. I looked at Bap. He seemed the same as usual and gave me a thumbs-up with a nod and a bit of a smile. Aye, Bap Kelly was a puzzle all right. I hadn't him fully figured out yet. And his corrugated iron was still lying in our back yard.

'You okay, Dickie?' whispered Harley as he lifted my home-work book. I stared up at him without replying. Blank like. I made a mental note not to electrocute him anymore. He'd learnt his lesson. But he wasn't getting the corrugated iron back. I'd promised it to Bap Kelly, and to his ma, and to all the Kelly brothers and sisters. They needed it more than the Marlborough gang. But Bap Kelly would still have to earn it. I didn't check, but I bet he hadn't even one sheet of iron scrubbed when the cops grabbed him and Danny and Kevin from our back yard last night. I opened my reading book at the first page.

But I couldn't get wee Liam out of my mind. This was only the second time he hadn't gone to school with me. I'd even taken him to school on his first day. I remember it well. Halfway there, he'd peed his trousers and wanted to go home, but he was okay when I told him that I'd peed my trousers twice on my first day. And I was thinking now that he'd be at least half an hour late for school by the time my ma got him up and got his breakfast into him. He'd never been that late before.

'McCauley, when did you do this homework? Was it before the shenanigans or after the shenanigans in your house last night?'

A couple of boys sniggered, but I didn't even look. I knew who they were.

'I don't know what you mean, Sir.' *You big nose-picker.* 'What's shenanigans, Sir?' I knew what shenanigans were. I was being thran. I heard the same boys sniggering but I didn't care. I'd get them for something else later. Philson didn't answer me.

'What time did you do your homework, McCauley?'

'As soon as I got home from school, Sir.'

'So it was *before* the shenanigans, then?'

I didn't answer him. He was just trying to be smart. And I didn't feel like playing games with the arse-scratcher. Not just now, anyway. I had too many other things to think about. Philson was on to somebody else now, so I turned to the second page of my book as if I were reading. It gave me time to think again about last night. It had been like a bad nightmare, worse than the last one. But it wasn't a nightmare, it was real. And I knew it wasn't finished yet.

My mind suddenly went back to Burnside, the bastard. I could still see everything and hear everything as if it was still happening.

***

Burnside had eventually ordered us all onto the couch in the front room – Liam in the middle, still holding his face. Seeing the blood had made me feel sick. I had asked Burnside again to let Liam go in to my ma. He said he'd let him go when we answered his questions. Liam wasn't screaming or crying then, just sort of moaning in to himself. And you could still hear the noises in the rest of the house.

'Right, Richard,' said Burnside, 'I'll start with you.'

'I don't know anything!' I shouted.

'Listen, McCauley,' hissed Burnside through his teeth, 'your family's in big trouble this night, and that means your *whole* family – that means you as well, brat. Do you understand this, McCauley? And these other boys here that were with you at the plots the other night—'

'We saw nothing, Mr Burnside,' interrupted Kevin. 'Honest to God, we saw nothing. It was dark, Mr Burnside. Ask Billy – he'll tell you, and Cecil, too. All we saw were flashes, and then we heard some bangs. We didn't know what it was, Mr Burnside. That's when we ran, Mr Burnside.'

Kevin was on his feet, pleading with Burnside and rattling his Rosary beads, but Burnside pushed him back onto the couch. 'Sit down, brat!' he shouted. 'I'm talking to McCauley.' Kevin was smarter than I thought. He was giving me time to think things out.

Burnside turned back to me. 'Right, for the last time, Richard – and I'm trying to be civil here, before things get really serious for you – what time did you crowd get to the Wee Green last night?'

Burnside didn't have to tell me that this was serious. I knew it was serious. If they found the gun upstairs, it was serious, and if they could prove it was the same gun that killed Mr Colhoun, then it was even more serious. So no matter what I said to Burnside now, it wouldn't really make a blind bit of difference.

But there were four things that were rushing through my mind when Burnside was speaking. One, Burnside isn't as smart as Philson; two, I'm smarter than Philson; three, if they haven't found the gun upstairs, the McCauleys are in the clear, for now; and four, if Bap Kelly doesn't blab about what *he* knows then there's really nothing to worry about, because I know for certain that *I* won't blab. I was ready now for the bastard Burnside.

'And I'm warning you, Richard,' Burnside went on, 'if I find you're telling me lies, the whole McCauley family could be in very big trouble.' This was it: McCauley versus the bastard. 'For the last time, McCauley, what time did you crowd get to the Wee Green last night?'

'About eight o'clock.'

'How do you know it was eight?'

'That's easy, Mr Burnside. When the Guildhall clock started to strike, your Billy looked at his watch. He asked me to light a match so that he could see it. Just ask him if you don't believe me.' The bastard gave a rough cough as if he wasn't listening to that last part about Billy.

'Right, and was it dark when you were there? In the Wee Green, I mean?'

Stupid question, stupid cop. For two reasons. One, it was always dark at eight o'clock near the end of September, and two, hadn't I just told him that I had to light a match to see his son's watch?

'Yes, it was dark.'

'Right. And how long was it before you heard the shots?'

'We didn't hear any shots, just some bangs, and then there were some flashes. We didn't know what was happening. That's when we ran, Mr Burnside – honest, Mr Burnside – your Billy and Cecil Colhoun and the rest of us. All of us ran. You can ask Billy and Cecil if you don't believe—'

Before I had even finished what I was saying, Burnside had another question as his eyes blazed with anger.

'And how long after that did you see the men running down the lane?'

Burnside was a crafty cop. But still stupid.

'We didn't see anybody. It was pitch black – I told you that before.'

'Don't be cheeky with me, McCauley!'

'It's the blackout, Mr Burnside. You can't see anything in the blackout.'

'There was a moon out, McCauley. You must have seen something, heard somebody running?'

'I told you, Mr Burnside, we didn't see anybody. We didn't hear anybody. Honest. We ran away. The bangs and flashes scared us. Ask Billy and Cecil if you don't believe me. The moon was covered then. Honest, Mr Burnside. Ask Billy and Cecil.' I knew I was sickening the bastard talking about Billy and Cecil all the time.

Burnside knew he was getting nowhere with me, but as I sat there lying to him, I could still see the silhouettes of Joey and Peter running down the lane.

'That's all for now, McCauley. I'll be speaking to you again. You can be sure of that.' He turned to Kevin. 'Now, Kevin,' he said in a soft voice, 'you're a good religious boy. I know I'll get the truth from you.'

Kevin went pure white. He just stared straight at Burnside, his Rosary beads shaking in his joined hands. 'Honest to God and His Blessed Mother, Mr Burnside, I saw nothing, I just heard the bangs. Poor Mr Colhoun! May his soul and the souls of all the faithful departed, through the mercy of God, rest in peace.'

I thought for a second that Burnside was going to say 'amen', the way he was staring at Kevin, but then I remembered that Protestants don't pray for the dead, only the living. Burnside's eyeballs were bulging and his face was sweating.

'Shut up, Doherty,' he roared, 'with all that religious rubbish! You papishes are all the same, with your Rosary beads and your packed chapels and that priest-ridden country across the border. Youse would think by the way youse go on that youse are all saints. But I'll tell youse what youse are, youse are nothing but murderers and liars and thieves.'

'Oh, my God,' cried Kevin as he stood up, holding the crucifix in front of him. 'May God and His Blessed Mother forgive ye, Mr Burnside, and I'll pray for ye, Mr Burnside, so that God will look down upon ye and take pity on ye and forgive ye for what you're saying.'

'Just tell me what you saw, Doherty!' shouted Burnside, and he pushed Kevin back roughly into the couch. 'And stop all the mumbo jumbo!'

'I told you, Mr Burnside, I saw nothing. Sure it was pitch black.'

'And the two boys that were running?'

'I didn't see anybody. I told you, Mr Burnside. I saw nobody. And if you don't believe me, why don't you ask your Billy and Cecil Colhoun? They'll tell ye that nobody saw anything.'

Kevin was brilliant, even if he didn't mean to be.

Burnside's face was getting redder and his eyes were bulging worse than Kevin's, and there was spit at the two sides of his mouth. He took a big deep breath and turned to Bap.

'And you, boy, what's your name?'

Bap just stared at him and looked puzzled. He said nothing. But Kevin did. He shouted out, 'He's deaf and dumb, Mr Burnside!' Bap was more amazed than me. 'And he has only one good eye, Mr Burnside; the devil took the other one.' Bap stayed quiet.

'What's his name?' roared Burnside. 'And where does he live?'

'He collects brock, Mr Burnside,' spluttered Kevin. 'His next-door neighbours have pigs and he collects brock for them around Rosemount. The brock is to feed the pigs, Mr Burnside.'

Burnside stood up from his chair. His face was red and sweating and his eyes were even bigger than Kevin's whites behind the jam jars.

'I didn't ask you what he does!' screamed Burnside. 'I asked you his name and address!'

'We don't know, Mr Burnside. We think it could be Doherty from the Bogside, Eddie Doherty. He was out in Dickie's back yard with his cart when the police came. They took him in here. He's deaf and dumb, Mr Burnside. He was born like that, Mr Burnside. An act of God, Mr Burnside.'

I knew when this was all over, if it ever would be, that Kevin Doherty would never be spat on again, and I would never boss him about like the rest of them and I might even get a religious medal from the Holy Shop in William Street and pin it to his jumper when everybody else was watching. His ma would be as proud of me as I was of Kevin.

Burnside stood up. His spittles were still hanging from his mouth and the sweat was dripping off him. I thought his eye-balls were going to fall out. I would have smiled to myself if I hadn't heard our Liam moaning again. Danny Doherty had now hidden behind the couch. Burnside didn't notice. Stupid cop. He turned to me again.

'Just two more questions for ye, McCauley,' he hissed, 'and then that's everybody for now. Those two boys who are going out with your twins, do ye know where they are now?'

'Who?' I asked him.

He slapped me hard across the face and told me not to be smart.

'You know very well who I mean, ye wee Fenian bastard! And your uncle, where would he be now?'

'He's away on business, Mr Burnside. Uncle Jimmy's a businessman.'

'I'll bet he is!' roared Burnside as he lifted me up close to his big red face and his bulging eyes and his spittle mouth. I could smell Guinness and whiskey off him. It was rotten. Even more rotten than the smell from my da. 'Yeah, I'll bet he is, McCauley. I'll bet he's a big-time businessman.'

Burnside threw me back onto the couch and before he left the room, he shouted, 'Just stay there, the lot of youse, for now! And there'll be more questions another day. Youse got off light for now.'

We all stayed quiet, even Liam, until the cops had gone. We could hear their boots crunching on the broken glass on the hall floor on their way out.

***

Somebody was nudging me. 'I'm sorry to hear about what happened, Dickie, the cops wrecking the house and all, last night. I hope wee Liam will be okay.' It was Harley whispering to me as he handed me back my homework book.

'Thanks,' I whispered back. Maybe the Marlborough crowd weren't as bad as I thought. As the bell rang for lunchtime, Philson shouted to us to file out quietly. I put my reading book into my schoolbag. I hadn't read a single line all morning. I had too many more important things to be thinking about right now.

We sat eating our lunches on the steps at the back of the school. You could smell the burnt cake that Danny was devouring. His ma had made it. It was rotten but Danny loved it. We always told him that his ma's cakes were made of burnt lard. Now and again she brought one down to our house, but my da always threw it in the bin when she left. Except when it was half-decent.

Kevin was eating blackberry-jam sandwiches. You could smell them, too, but they were nice. Sometimes Kevin would give you a sandwich if he had too many. He hadn't too many today, but he gave me one anyhow because he knew I had forgotten to bring a lunch with me, and you weren't allowed to leave the school grounds at lunch break.

Bap Kelly was playing shooty-in at the school wall. He waved. I waved back. Maybe I shouldn't have but I did. Maybe it was the way he had acted dumb with Big Burnside in our sitting room that made me wave. Maybe Bap Kelly had more sides to him than I knew about. And maybe I was just playing it cool until I was more certain about him.

Frankie Smart walked over to us. 'About the birthday party, Dickie.'

'Yeah, what about it?'

'You know I wanted you to come? You and Kevin and Danny and Liam and Billy and Cecil and Bap?'

'Yeah?'

'Well, my father thinks it would be a good idea if you didn't come this year. Maybe next year. He told me to tell you.'

'Fuck off, Frankie,' said Kevin.

'Aye, fuck off,' repeated Danny.

I didn't say anything. I just gave him a look that said it all. And anyway, I had spotted Miss Lafferty taking her class out to the covered area. That's where all the wee ones sat down to eat their lunches. I stood up and walked over a bit. I wanted to see how Liam was. Maybe he had no lunch, either. If my ma forgot to give me my lunch, she probably forgot Liam's as well. Miss Lafferty saw me and came over. I liked her; she had been my teacher as well for my first two years here.

'Hello, Richard,' she said. 'Is Liam sick today?'

'He is, Miss,' I lied.

'That's too bad,' she said, 'because he's a very healthy little boy and I've never known him to be off school since he started. I hope he'll be all right soon.'

I felt rotten as I turned away. Rotten that I'd lied to her and rotten that I didn't know what was happening with Liam. Bap had heard us and he knew by my face how I felt. He had seen the state of Liam last night. 'Do you want to go home, Dickie?' he said. 'I'll go with you.'

'We can't,' I replied. 'Philson would kill us.'

'Not if he doesn't know.'

'What do you mean?'

'We can slip over the wall, go through Thompson's Field and out to your house in five minutes. We'll be back before the bell goes.'

I stared at Bap for a minute. It was a good plan and I hadn't thought of it. Aye, there were more sides to Bap, all right. More than I could count.

'Okay,' I whispered as I looked about to see if Philson or any of the other teachers were watching. We slipped over the wall and ran the whole way home. Nobody saw us – as far as I could make out.

Our front door was closed. It was never shut, except at night. I banged the knocker loud and kept on banging it, but my ma or da didn't come out. Something was wrong. My ma was always in the house, and my da, too, when he wasn't working or in the pub. We looked in the front sitting-room window, but nobody was there. I felt lonely. I wanted to cry, but I couldn't because Bap was there. I hated Liam for messing things up.

'Round the back,' Bap said. We ran fast. The back gate was shut, so we climbed over the wall. The back door was closed as well. We looked through the yard windows, but nobody was in the kitchen or the living room, either. Bap climbed up on the wall again and started running along it, his arms out like a tightrope walker. I followed, copying him. I had never done this before. You could see into every back yard. They were all differ-ent. Suddenly, a voice shouted, 'Get down from there!' It was Big Burnside. He wasn't dressed as a cop. He ran to his own back gate and out into the lane. He caught us before we could get down and away. His big face was up close to mine. His breath was still smelly. Rotten. Rotten smelly Burnside.

'Have youse no respect for the dead,' he shouted, 'youse wee blackguards? Naw, youse wouldn't have. Youse know no better.' He turned to Bap. 'And what have we got here? The deaf and dumb rascal from the Bogside? Deaf and dumb, my arse; do you think I'm a fool? What are youse doing here anyway? Shouldn't youse be in school?'

'We just came up to see if Liam's okay. He was sick this morning.' I did a false plead. 'We have to get back to school, Mr Burnside.' I felt sick pretending to plead with the likes of Burnside. But it worked. He released his grip, but we didn't run. We just stood there waiting for Burnside to go back in. He didn't. He hesitated a wee bit before he spoke.

'Your mother and father took him away in somebody's car this morning. Somebody said they were going to the hospital.'

My stomach felt sick when he said it. I began to cry in to myself. Bap didn't guess. He pulled at my sleeve and whispered, 'Let's go. We'll be late.'

'Get off to school with youse, now,' shouted Burnside, 'and don't let me catch youse up on that wall again! Youse are nothing but trouble, the whole clan of youse.'

Bap and me raced the whole way back. Halfway across Thompson's Field, the bell rang. We ran faster. Sweating. Stitch in my side. Stomach sick. Still crying in to myself about our Liam. Maybe he was dying with polio or tuberculosis or scarlet fever or some other disease? I didn't care if Liam had messed things up. I didn't hate him. I loved him. He was my wee brother. The only one I had.

Nobody was there. Nobody was in the playground. Everybody was back in the school. We ran up the steps and through the front entrance. The corridor was empty. We were late and probably in big trouble. Philson versus Dickie and Bap time.

'I'll say you were sick,' hissed Bap. He didn't need to. Philson wasn't in the class yet. Nobody noticed us coming in except Kevin and Danny and the three Smarts. I wiped my sweaty face. My clothes were sticking to me. The stitch was away, but my legs were still numb. Liam was dying and I was in school sweating. It wasn't right. You shouldn't be in school if somebody in your family is dying.

'Settle down!' Philson shouted as he came into the classroom. 'Get your reading books out, but before you do, write tonight's

185

homework down in your jotter. I've written it on the board.' Not again. More reading. Philson was having an easy day of it.

I didn't read anything. I just turned the pages. I looked over at Bap. His face was nearly as red as his hair. But he'd done me a favour and I wouldn't forget that.

I felt like telling Philson I was sick. I could vomit on the floor and run out of the class. I could pretend to faint and then moan in pain. I didn't do anything. I just sat there thinking that Liam could be dead for all I knew and nobody came to tell me. It was the longest afternoon of my life.

When the bell went, Philson asked me and Bap to stay behind. When the others left, we stood in front of his desk. He made us wait a long while before he looked up and spoke. He turned to me first.

'Richard, Kevin Doherty's mother called with me at lunchtime on a private matter. In the course of our conversation, she told me that your young brother Liam was ill and had to be taken to hospital. I'm very sorry to hear that and I hope he will be better soon. And regarding your trip home at lunch break, I am aware of it, and although I understand your anxiety about Liam,' he continued as he turned to face Bap, 'I must warn both of you that rules are rules, and they are there for your safety. And in future, I will not turn a blind eye to any further infringements of school law. Do you understand?'

'He said that deliberately,' shouted Bap when we got outside, 'about not turning a blind eye! He was looking straight at me when he said it. And the bastard had a smile on his face, too. Even with only one eye, I could see that. He's a nose-picking bastard, Dickie, probably worse than Big Burnside.'

Bap swore about Philson all the way down Helen Street, but I wasn't really listening because I was anxious to get home to find out about Liam. I just nodded to him as he turned down the hill and I ran the whole way up to the house. And I swore again that if God made our Liam better, I'd never say another curse.

CHAPTER 23

Can't The Doctor Make Him Better, Da?

When I turned the corner into the street, I saw a green van outside our door. It wasn't Uncle Jimmy's, his was blue. I heard banging coming from the house. It made my heart thump. I thought for a second it was another police raid. A man was coming down the stairs carrying a bucket filled with rubbish. I didn't know who he was. My ma was out in the kitchen, singing.

'Hello,' the man said to me, smiling, 'you must be Dickie.' I didn't say anything, but he ruffled my hair as he passed me in the hall. I didn't like that. He called out, 'We'll have that cup of tea now, Kitty, and Charlie takes no sugar.'

'Right!' shouted my ma from the kitchen. 'Just give me two minutes.'

Even though I was thinking of Liam when all this was going on, I was glad when I heard my ma singing because last night, after the cops left, she was in a terrible state. I never heard her cursing before. She'd shouted 'bastards' at least sixteen times when all the screaming was going on. I counted them in case she would ask me the number later when she was going to Confession. And this morning after she had fixed my trousers, I noticed that she was very pale and tired looking. Now she seemed to be okay.

And this morning, as well, before I left for school, I'd noticed that the whole living room was bashed up, drawers out of the cupboard and all, and things all over the place. The clock and the two delft dogs and the Child of Prague on the mantelpiece were completely smashed. The Sacred Heart picture was turned back to front. My ma must have done that because she didn't want Jesus to be looking down at the mess.

But now it was all cleaned up and I could see our Liam sitting at the table in the kitchen with a cup of tea and a jam piece in front of him. The wee fart. I hated him again. He had messed my day up and had made me sick worrying about him, and there he was, stuffing himself as if it were a normal day.

And there was my ma acting as if it were a normal day, too, and workmen in the house with my da as if life were normal; and there was my mind thinking about all this, and there was me, too, watching it all happening and at the same time thinking about the terrible day I'd had with Philson and with Burnside, and about me lying to Miss Lafferty about Liam, and about Bap helping me, and about the stitch in my side when I was trying to get back before the school bell.

A fit of unreal rage suddenly came over me, which my ma noticed immediately, because, before I could reach our Liam to strangle him, she had caught me by the shoulders and bundled me into the front sitting room. She threw me back onto the couch, rougher than Burnside had done last night, and I did something then that I never thought I would ever do. I went really mad. I spat on my ma's face and screeched at her with a load of curses, and I gathered more spit and curses for a second attack. But before they could leave my mouth, my ma had thrown herself on top of me, smothering me with her body. Her arms held me down, pinning me, and she began to ssssh me, and ssssh me and ssssh me.

'There, there, there,' she kept saying. 'There, Dickie, there, there, there. Ssssh, Dickie, everything's going to be all right, Son. Ssssh, ssssh, ssssh.'

'Is he all right, Kitty?' I heard my da's voice from the hall.

'He's going to be all right, Barney. It's just the shock of everything. Ssssh, ssssh, ssssh,' I heard her whisper.

I began to calm down a bit, but my ma still held me fast to the couch.

'It's them bastards, Barney. They don't care who they hurt – men, women or children. They're the scourge of Ireland.' It was the voice of the man who'd ruffled my hair in the hall and I felt embarrassed because I didn't want anybody else to know our business. The whole street knew it already, and now a total stranger, a workman in our house, was making remarks about us. I would have to calm down and sort out this situation.

'It's okay, Ma, I'm all right now. I was just raging about that wee shite Liam making mugs out of the whole lot of us. Let me up, Ma. Please.'

I heard my ma taking a big deep breath before she allowed me to rise from the couch. I lay there, looking up at her, and I could see her red eyes and the tears dripping from them.

'Christ, what have we done to deserve all this?' cried my ma suddenly. 'In under God, can we not live a normal life like everybody else?' She started to shout hysterically. 'Barney, will ye for Christ's sake help me? I can't take any more of it!' And she ran out of the room sobbing. She went out the front door, slamming it behind her. She was probably going up to Kevin's ma or Danny's ma. She always did that when she was badly upset.

Now it was my da's turn to take over, even though he wasn't very good at it. 'Right, Dickie,' he shouted from the hall, 'get a grip on yourself! We're having enough bother without you fucking us up as well.'

I was already standing up by the time my ma had left. My da was now standing just inside the door of the sitting room, glaring at me. I could see a workman behind him. I could see my da's big belly and his big nose and his big ears and I could nearly smell his big Guinness breath mixed with his big whiskey breath. And I hated him, more than I hated Liam, because I knew in my heart that it was my da that was always making my ma cry. More than me or Liam or the twins did.

It was my da that had showed me the gun under the bathroom floorboards, lying to me that it was his, and that he would free Ireland with it. It was my da that allowed Peter and Joey into our house. At least he could have stopped them coming in. And it was my da who had allowed Uncle Jimmy to stay in our house, even after Uncle Jimmy had ordered Peter and Joey to kill Mr Colhoun in the plots. And it was my da who had told me that Hitler was our friend and the friend of Ireland when Father Mooney had told me that Hitler was an evil man and that the devil was living inside him. Aye, I really hated my da then.

I put my head down and rushed towards my da's big belly. If I got him in the middle of it I knew I would hurt him and make him cry. And he would have nobody to run to like my ma did when she was hurt and when she was crying. I shouted 'bastard' as I ran, hoping that I wouldn't hurt my head when I landed on the big Guinness gut.

I never reached him. All I could feel were his two big arms around me, not hurting me, but hugging me. Not roughly, but gently, almost like my ma. He swayed back and forward with me as gently as my ma ever did, and I could hear his voice saying, 'Oh, Dickie, oh, Dickie, I'm sorry, I'm so sorry. Oh, Dickie, my son, I'm so sorry.'

And his arms tightened around me without hurting me and I knew what I always knew – that my da loved me and that I loved him, even when I hated him at times. But I was still sobbing a bit with the rage that I had felt about Liam and about my ma and my da and everything.

I saw the workman going upstairs as my da was half-carrying me into the kitchen where Liam was still sitting at the table. The cup of tea and piece of bread were still in front of him, untouched. My da put his fingers to his lips after he had placed me gently in a chair. He then bent close to me. 'I have to tell you something,' he whispered. 'It's about our wee Liam there. He's not well, Dickie. We had to bring him to the doctor.'

'He looks all right, Da. He doesn't look sick.' I was still sobbing and shuddering a bit.

'Naw, he doesn't, Son, but it's the kind of sickness that's brought on by shock.'

'Can't the doctor make him better, Da?'

'Aye, he gave him medicine, but he says it might take a good while for him to come round. It could take hours or it could take days or even weeks, Dickie, for him to come out of it. That's what the doctor told us, Dickie. He needs a whole lot of rest, too. We know you're good to him, Son, and with your help and our help, he'll soon get better. Okay, Son?'

'Right, Da,' I said as I slipped off the chair and walked quietly over to Liam. He was still staring down at the piece and the tea. My da stood watching.

'Will I feed ye, Liam?' I asked him, but he didn't reply. I broke off a bit of bread and pushed it into his mouth, but he wouldn't chew it. And when I put the cup to his lips, the tea dribbled down his chin. I felt rotten in the stomach – and sad, the saddest I'd ever been in my life. Liam's eyes were blank when I turned his face round to mine. It was as if he were sleeping with his eyes open. I whispered into his ear did he want to play Tiddlywinks, but he didn't say anything. That's when I began to cry out loud as I hugged him tight. I kept holding him until I couldn't cry any more. Then my da came over and hugged the two of us. My whole body was still shuddering.

'The bastards!' roared my da suddenly. 'It was them fucking bastards of cops that did it, and they'll pay for it!'

Now it was my da's turn to cry. I could see the tears coming out of his big red eyes. I had never seen my da crying before. I had seen him with red eyes, but that was when he was drunk. But he wasn't drunk now and there was no big smell of whiskey or Guinness off him. We stayed like that for a good while, saying nothing, just me and my da holding each other and Liam. After another wee while, I looked up at my da and whispered to him, 'When's Hitler coming to get the bastards?'

He didn't answer me. And when I saw more big tears coming out of his eyes, I began to cry again because I knew in my heart that Hitler wouldn't be coming – not to Derry, anyhow. And I felt stupid, too, talking about Hitler like that, as if he were our friend, when I knew in my heart that Hitler was evil, just like Father Mooney had told me.

'Right, Son,' my da whispered to me. 'Seeing your ma has gone out for a while, it's up to us to get these workmen a cup of tea.' As he filled the kettle, I looked at Liam. He was still sitting there at the table, staring down at his piece, but his eyes were dead.

Even before the water in the kettle was boiled, my ma was back. Her eyes were red as well, but she wasn't crying anymore and I felt rotten because I'd spat on her face and cursed at her just ten minutes ago. Father Mooney wouldn't be too pleased when he heard all about it in Confession. But my ma wasn't angry with me because she came straight into the kitchen and gave me a long hug without saying a word about what happened.

'Okay, boys,' said my ma after a while. 'Barney, you take Liam into the living room. And, Dickie, you and me will get this tea ready for the workmen.'

It made me feel a lot better, my ma asking me to help her, and when everything was ready I followed her upstairs. She had the tray with two cups of tea and I carried a plate of biscuits.

We went into my bedroom first. All the floorboards were nailed back. The lino was ripped and piled in a corner with bits of torn wallpaper. My sin list was somewhere inside it but I didn't care. And I didn't care if anybody had seen it, either: it was in code. There was a man plastering the wall. He smiled when we walked in. He had red hair. I could hear another workman hammering in the other room. Everywhere still looked a mess.

'Ah! Thanks for the tea, Kitty. Just what the doctor ordered.'

'Well, Charlie,' my ma said to him, 'it looks as if we'll soon be back to normal.'

'Aye, a couple of days and you'll be as good as new,' said the man.

'Isn't that great, Dickie? Do you hear that? You'll be all ship-shape soon, thanks to Charlie here, and thanks to young Charlie as well. Isn't he the great boy?'

I looked up at my ma. I didn't know what she was talking about, but I soon would. It was staring me in the face and I hadn't seen it. But a second later, I did.

'This is Charlie's da, Dickie – your wee friend Charlie. Sure aren't they the spitting image?' laughed my ma.

I stared at the workman. He had red curly hair, and my ma was right. He was the spitting image of Bap, except that he was bigger and he had two good eyes. He laughed when my ma said that.

'Hello, Mr Kelly,' I said, a wee bit shocked.

'Well, isn't that the good-mannered boy ye have there, Kitty? It's not often I'm called Mr Kelly.'

'And ye have a good wan of your own, Charlie. And isn't it great that he's our Dickie's friend? For if it hadn't been for him, sure you mightn't have heard about the house being wrecked last night. Aye, that wee Charlie of yours is the bee's knees, all right, arranging all this.'

Once again, my mind was trying to cope with a whole lot of things at the same time. And trying not to let them mix me up. There I was, standing in my own wrecked bedroom, thinking stupidly that somebody might have found my sin list for Confession, the same sin list that I now suddenly spotted lying with the rest of the rubbish in the corner. Aye, there I was, with my stupid mouth still wide open, looking up at Bap Kelly's da smiling down at me and me saying 'hello, Mr Kelly' and at the same time thinking about Bap Kelly arranging to get our house fixed. The same Bap Kelly who, last night before the raid, was going to be forced to wash twelve sheets of corrugated iron that didn't need to be washed, and be made to carry them by himself on a home-made cart to his house in the Bogside. The same Bap Kelly that I was going to tell Kevin and Danny and Liam about; about his eye, and about no ghost or no devil, and about him having no gang at all, so that they would laugh at him and make fun of him. That was my stupid plan that was backfiring like everything else around me at this very minute.

Aye, there I was, saying 'hello, Mr Kelly' when I was feeling rotten about his one-eyed son, and even more rotten about spitting on my ma's face. But the worst of all was our Liam downstairs going mental and being looked after by my da with the big red eyes, and me thinking, through everything, that our Liam would never get better at all, no matter what my da or ma said. And as I said thanks to Mr Kelly and walked as slow as I could down the stairs, clutching my sin list, different good plans were going through my mind about how I could sort a whole lot of things out by myself if people didn't keep interrupting me and if I was left alone to think everything through.

Before going into the sitting room to do my homework and get my full sin list together, I juked into the living room. My da was dipping bread into the cup of tea and pushing it into Liam's mouth. Before I did anything, I said a prayer that Hitler would drop a bomb on Big Burnside's head for what he did to Liam and that it wouldn't hurt anybody else. But I knew that was stupid, so I took it back and instead offered it up to make our Liam better. I knew Hitler was even more evil than Burnside, because bad and all as Burnside was, as far as I know, he hadn't killed anybody.

Of all the new sins I had to add to my list, I think the worst of the whole lot was spitting on my ma. And I'd have to ask Father Mooney as well if I'd sinned against Bap Kelly. I'd tell him everything if he asked me. That's the best thing you can do in Confession. Tell everything that you can remember.

When I memorised the lot, I did my homework. It was easy. Sums and spellings. When I was putting the books back in my schoolbag, my ma came in with a cup of tea and a piece.

'Take this, Dickie,' she said, 'because you got nothing to eat since you came home from school and you'll be heading off to Confession in five minutes.'

You would have thought that, with everything that had happened in our house since last night when the cops raided – and especially because of our Liam – that the last thing on my ma's mind would have been that I had to go to Confession.

I thanked my ma for the tea and told her that I would light a candle for Liam. She hugged me before I left and it made me feel good, especially when she didn't mention that I had spat on her. She must have known that I was sorry and that I would tell it in Confession. As I was leaving the house and pulling the glass door behind me, I noticed that there was new glass in the door. I hadn't seen it when I came in from school. Bap's da must have done that, too.

So I went back into the house, up the stairs and into my bedroom, where Bap's father was still plastering. My ma or da didn't hear me, but I made an arrangement there and then with Mr Kelly that should begin to put things right with Bap. Out of the six or seven things that had been crowding my mind less than an hour ago, I had now dealt with three or four of them. And when I got to the chapel, and after Confession when I lit the candle for Liam, I knew he would begin to get better. And that would be the most important thing I had to deal with: getting Liam better. I didn't want him to go mental full time. And Father Mooney had told us plenty of times that if you pray hard enough to God for something, you'll get it.

Before I closed the glass door behind me, my ma was in the hall. She'd heard me running down the stairs.

'I thought you were away, Dickie. You're going to be late if you don't hurry.'

'It's okay, Ma, I just forgot something.'

'That's all right, Son, the dinner'll be ready when you get back.'

'Isn't the new glass in the door great, Ma?'

'Aye, Dickie, it's great. Now run on or you'll be late.'

I began examining my conscience as we turned out of Helen Street to go down Creggan Hill. I didn't speak to anybody, not to Bap or Danny or Kevin. I had so many sins to remember and I didn't want to forget even one, because after Confession, when I lit the candle for Liam and said a special prayer, I wanted nothing standing in the way of him getting better. God wouldn't listen to you if you still had stains on your soul. It needed to be pure white so that you would have a look-in with Him.

When I had rhymed the sins all off to Father Mooney, he just gave me my penance and absolution without remarking about any of them. But before I left the Confession box, he spoke to me about what had happened last night in our house. Priests know everything. He even knew about our Liam going mental, but he didn't call him that. He said he would pray for Liam and he told me to tell my ma and da that he would call up to see them soon.

I stayed in the chapel for a good while after Confessions were over. I didn't want to be talking to anybody yet about the police raid. And I didn't want anyone seeing me lighting a candle, either, and then kneeling down again to pray some more. They might think I was going soft.

When I was walking down the aisle after finishing my prayers, I looked up at the big clock on the wall below the gallery. It was twenty minutes past six. I could hardly believe it. I'd been in the chapel for ages. My dinner would be in the oven now, drying up. They'd be mad with me when I got home, but I knew now that I had something else to do before I went back to the house.

It was getting dark when I left the chapel. There were no lights on in the street because of the blackout. Instead of heading up the hill to Rosemount, I turned left and ran towards the Bogside. I just wanted to check on something with Bap Kelly.

There was a green van outside his door, the same van that had been at our house. His da must be home. I knocked. Bap's wee brother opened the door and stared at me for a while until he was sure he knew me. His name was Toby. I thought that was a strange name for a person, because there's a boy in our class who has a dog called Toby.

'Charlie!' he shouted over his shoulder. 'It's your man from Rosemount. He's looking for ye.'

'Hello, Dickie,' said Bap as he walked through the hallway. 'Come on in.' And then, 'Get you back inside!' he shouted at his young brother and pushed him away roughly. The wee fellow reminded me of Liam and I felt sad for a minute.

'Fuck off!' Toby shouted at Bap. 'You're not my boss.' Bap just laughed.

At this very minute, I wished that our Liam would be able to say 'fuck off' when I got back to the house. I would be glad if he did because it would mean he was getting better. He could say it for the rest of his life for all I cared.

As I walked into Bap's hall, I didn't want to say thanks to him about the work that was going on in our house or about him going home with me at lunch break to find out about Liam. Saying thanks was something I wasn't used to. I didn't have to anyway. And Bap didn't have to say thanks, either, about getting the corrugated iron. He just told me that his da and the other workman were taking it in from the van and out to his back when he got home from Confession. I could see he was pleased as he spoke. From the scullery doorway you could see the sheets of corrugated iron piled neatly in Bap's yard beside the wooden frames of the greyhound hut.

'My da says it'll need another dozen sheets but he knows where to get them,' said Bap. 'You were good with Burnside last night,' he went on, 'not blabbing or anything, and not being afraid. I told my da about it all.'

'Did ye?'

'Aye, and my da said that it was lucky your uncle wasn't in the house or they'd have got him for sure.'

'Aye, he's away on some business,' I said. 'He was lucky he wasn't there.' I wasn't too sure why I said that, but it sounded good anyhow.

'They're getting youse new lino for all the ripped stuff,' Bap continued. 'They did the same for us after we were raided last year.'

I knew I was out of my depth here and I was glad when Bap's ma arrived with two glasses of lemonade. She handed one to Bap and one to me.

'Thanks, Mrs Kelly,' I muttered.

'Ah, sure you're the great lad, Dickie McCauley. Wasn't Charlie just telling us about how ye handled Burnside during the raid? Is your mother okay, Son?'

'Aye, she's grand, Mrs Kelly,' I lied. People knew enough about the McCauley family without me giving any more away.

'You'd have thought she'd had enough bother without that carry-on last night. Charlie, my husband, was telling me how upset youse all were and about how it affected your Liam. God knows, that bastard Burnside has a lot to answer for. Anyway, he'll not be bothering youse again, ye can be sure of that, Son. The Movement'll soon see to that.'

As I was handing her back the empty glass, I was trying to work out how Mrs Kelly could know that Burnside wouldn't be bothering us anymore and who it was that was arranging it. And the other thing I was still trying to work out was who or what the Movement was. I didn't want to sound stupid by asking Mrs Kelly, although Bap might have noticed the puzzled look on my face when his ma was talking to me.

As soon as I said I had to leave, Bap walked with me out to the front street and let me into the secret that Peter and Joey had stayed in his house last night. He'd heard his da saying to his ma that it was a good job they hadn't stayed in their own houses or with the McCauleys in Rosemount, because the cops would have got them.

'They didn't know I could hear what they were saying, Dickie. They didn't know I was listening. My da said that the boys would be heading across the border in a couple of days, that they'd be safe as soon as they reached Jimmy's house in Donegal. He said they'd be staying for another couple of nights in Derry first, in a different safe-house, until things cooled down. And before they go, they want to have a last wee visit to your house again to see the twins.'

I was going weak at the knees as Bap was speaking. I could hardly take in what he was telling me, but a whole lot of other things were now falling into place. About what the Movement was, who was in it and the things they did. About the killing of Mr Colhoun. That the twins probably knew what was going to happen to him in the plots. And even my ma – she might have known as well. And definitely Uncle Jimmy, he would have known. But not my da. *He* couldn't be in on it. Not after the fight he'd had with Uncle Jimmy.

As I walked on up the Bogside after leaving Bap, my head was spinning about everything, especially about murder being a mortal sin. And if you didn't tell it in Confession before you died, you'd definitely go to Hell. It was all something I'd have to speak to Father Mooney about, but only in Confession, because if I told him outside the Confession box, he might have to blab to the cops, and then everybody in our house, except my da and Liam and me, would be hanged.

But the thing was, I'd already been to Confession with the school just a few hours before. It was another dilemma for me, but I'd have to do something. I just had to speak to Father

Mooney again. That's when an idea struck me. The adult Confessions would be starting at seven o'clock. It must be nearly that now. I hurried up the hill towards the cathedral, determined to speak to the priest.

CHAPTER 24

And What Message Is That, Constable?

'A great evil has been done, my son, but from what you have told me, you are not involved in any way. Murder is a terrible crime. A life has been taken and nobody has the right to take a life except God the Creator. Those who carried out this ghastly deed will have to explain their actions before God on Judgement Day, and, if during their lifetime they are apprehended by the police, then the legal system will deal with them. That is God's law, and the natural law, Richard, here on earth.'

'But, Father, Uncle Jimmy told me that it's not a sin to kill somebody if you're fighting against them in a war.'

I was in Father Mooney's Confession box again and there was a whole bunch of big people waiting to go in. They had let me go to the front of the queue when I told them that my dinner was nearly ready. I wasn't telling a lie. Father Mooney went quiet for a wee while when I said that to him about Uncle Jimmy.

'Is your uncle a moral theologian, my son?' asked Father Mooney. I didn't know what he was talking about and I think Father Mooney knew that I didn't know what he was talking about. 'Is he an expert on God's laws, my son?'

'I don't know, Father, but he reads a lot of books and sometimes he gives me some.'

'Oh, my dear Richard,' whispered Father Mooney, 'I think maybe it's time we brought this to a close and you went on home. And, Richard, remember, you are not to blame for any of this mess.'

As I left the chapel, I was wondering how Father Mooney knew about everything. It was probably because he had read far more books than Uncle Jimmy. And as well as that, he talked to God every day, so he was bound to know everything.

On the way up the hill to my house, it was pitch black, except for the odd light from the moon when it wasn't behind a cloud. I heard heavy footsteps behind me and then a voice. I didn't turn round.

'Well, well, well, look who we have here – the blackout boy.' I just walked on, a wee bit faster. I recognised Big Burnside's voice. A fear came over me. 'And do you know something, Constable?'

'And what's that, Sergeant Burnside?'

'The blackout boy thinks the Germans are going to come and get rid of the likes of us.' Billy must have told him I'd said that. 'And do you know something else, Constable?'

'And what's that, Sergeant Burnside?'

'A wee birdie told me this very day that the big brave boys in the IRA will come and get me if I annoy that McCauley crowd again.'

'And what did you say to that, Sergeant Burnside?'

'Oh, I told the wee birdie I was scared stiff.' I heard the other cop laughing. 'And another thing, Constable,' said Burnside. 'Do you see that blackout boy up ahead of us?'

'I do surely, Sergeant.'

'Well, he can see in the dark.'

'Can he now, Sergeant? Isn't that a great thing?'

'Oh, yes. He has very sharp eyes, that boy, and so has young Kelly from the Bogside – at least one sharp eye he has. You know that crowd, too, Constable, the famous Kellys from the Bogside?'

'I do that, Sergeant. Sure who doesn't know the Kellys?'

I heard the two of them laughing all the time. It made me feel really scared. I felt sick in my stomach as well. I walked faster to get rid of them, but it didn't make any difference. I could still hear their big boots on the footpath.

'Richard?' I instinctively turned round at the shout. They were just ten yards behind me. 'Can you see us, Richard?' I could, because the moon was out. But I didn't answer. I could see the two of them, Burnside's silhouette and the silhouette of another cop that I had never seen before. But I'd know him again. I turned back and walked on.

'Do ye see that, Constable? He can see us. And do you know what that means? It means that him and young Kelly saw who did the shooting in the plots.'

'And it means something else, too,' shouted the other cop.

'And what would that be, Constable?' said Burnside.

'It means, Sergeant, that that young bucko up ahead of us, who can see in the dark, can give his two IRA friends a message.'

'Do you mean his sisters' boyfriends, Constable?'

'Aye, I do that.'

'And what message is that, Constable?'

'That we're coming to get them, and then we're going to hang them,' laughed the constable. 'Would that be right, Sergeant?'

'It would, Constable. You'd be right, there.'

Even with all the fear that I felt when the cops were behind me, I found it hard to understand why they were laughing, especially when it was their friend Mr Colhoun who was lying dead in a coffin just a couple of hundred yards up the hill. But I said nothing and ran on home.

I could smell the dinner cooking as soon as I opened the glass door. It must have been put on late. I was glad because I was starving with hunger and I'd been thinking on the way up that it would be burnt by now. My ma was standing beside the cooker in the kitchen. She didn't see me in the hall. The front sitting-room door was open a wee bit. The lock was still broken. The light was off, the bulb must have fused, but I could see a candle burning in a saucer and I could hear giggling. I opened the door a wee bit wider, quiet like.

I saw Kate on the couch with Peter. She was kissing him and his arms were around her. Laura was sitting on Joey's knee in the armchair. They were kissing as well. It was yucky and stupid. They wouldn't be doing that if they knew what I knew, that the cops were looking for Peter and Joey this very minute, and that our Liam was probably sitting in the other room, just staring down at the floor and saying nothing, and going more mental by the minute. Naw, the twins couldn't know about Liam yet or they wouldn't be doing what they're doing. I went into the kitchen.

My ma was stirring the stew and looked up with a smile. 'Hello, Dickie.'

'Hello, Ma. Do the twins know about Liam yet, about him being sick?'

'Naw, not yet, Dickie. Sure they only came in about twenty minutes ago and went straight into the sitting room. I didn't want to say anything yet, what with Peter and Joey being with them and all, and them being in such good form. Let them be for another while yet. Why don't you go into the living room? Your da's in there with Liam. I'll bring youse in your dinner in five minutes. Youse can have it on your knee.'

I couldn't tell my ma about Burnside and the other cop. She would go mental and start screaming all over the place. But I had to tell somebody. I opened the living-room door. My da was sitting in his armchair listening to the radio. It was turned down very low. Liam was on the couch, not doing anything, just staring at the floor.

'Da,' I said, rushing over to him, 'I have to tell you about—' Before I could say anything else, he shushed me.

'But, Da, it's about Burnside—'

My da shushed me again, this time putting his two fingers to his lips. He turned the wireless up. The newsreader was saying something about the war, something about the Germans invading somewhere in Russia.

'They'll be coming here soon to get the British out as well,' he laughed, 'and shifting the likes of Burnside. And talking of Burnside, Son, I heard ye made a great job of him the other night in the sitting room. Young Charlie's da was telling us all about ye. Wee Charlie told him how ye handled him. And that other wee lad, too, young Kevin, and ye wouldn't think butter would melt in his mouth, with his Rosary beads and all, and his big glasses, and him telling Burnside that young Charlie was deaf and dumb, and that the devil took his eye—'

'But, Da,' I interrupted, almost shouting, 'that's who I wanted to tell ye about. Big Burnside, Da. He knows about Peter and Joey shooting Mr Colhoun over in the plots.' There it was. I'd got it out. My da stared at me. He switched off the wireless.

'What did ye say there, Dickie?'

'I said, Da, that Burnside and another cop saw me on Creggan Hill tonight, just a wee while ago when I was coming up from the chapel, and they told me that they knew all about Peter and Joey shooting Mr Colhoun in the plots and that they were going to get them and hang them—'

Just then, my ma came into the living room with two plates of stew in her hands. She dropped them when she heard what I was saying. 'Christ Almighty!' she shouted as the plates fell to the floor, breaking, and making a mess all over the place. The shock of it made me jump, but I noticed that our Liam just stayed the same, staring at the floor.

'It's true, Ma!' I shouted to her. 'That's what Burnside and the other cop were shouting at me.'

'Barney, quick!' shouted my ma. 'Get Joey and Peter out of here this minute! And you, Dickie, take Liam upstairs to the bedroom till I call ye down. Now, Dickie, go now!'

As I was pushing Liam out of the living room and up the stairs, even with all the panic that was going on, I was thinking how hungry I was and that this was the third night this week that I wasn't going to get any dinner, and me starving. As we turned at the top of the stairs, I could see my da pushing Peter and Joey out of the sitting room and towards the kitchen, Laura and Kate following. I knew they were heading for the back way out, up the laneway and then to some other house that was safer than ours.

I was glad when Peter and Joey left. I didn't like them being in the house with us, knowing that they were murderers. And when I looked down from the landing, I could see my ma, too. She was looking up and down the street, watching out to see if any cops were coming.

I now knew a whole lot more about everything – not maybe as much as Bap Kelly, but a lot more than my da thought I knew, or my ma, or the twins, or Uncle Jimmy or even Big Burnside. And even if there was another raid tonight, Burnside would still learn nothing from me. No matter how much I knew, I would never blab.

None of it was my fault anyway. The whole mess had nothing to do with me. That's what Father Mooney had told me, and I knew he was right. And I knew, too, that big people could look after themselves, but they didn't always look after the likes of our Liam and me. But come what may, I would look after Liam. And with everything that was happening now with Peter and Joey, I knew that my ma or my da still hadn't told Kate and Laura about our Liam being sick. But I knew that when they did find out, and when they saw the state our Liam was in, they would go raging mad.

I always tried to think of good things when bad things were happening, but it's hard sometimes to do that. Especially when things were really bad, like right now. And as well as that, I'm not stupid enough to think that bad things will go away as if they had never really happened. But there were so many things going on in my head and all of them were so bad that I couldn't think of anything good. I mean, here I was in the house, all by myself. Well, not really all by myself. Liam was with me, up here in the bedroom, but he may as well not be because of the way his brain had stopped working right. A bit like the man in the next street who had shell-shock from the big war, but not the same. Shell-shock was for ever and our Liam was going to get better when he finished his medicine. But he might not.

And I'm thinking as well that, bad and all as our Liam was, it's a lot worse for Mrs Colhoun and Cecil. They're probably sitting beside the coffin, by themselves, looking in now and again at Mr Colhoun dressed in his B-man's outfit. I wouldn't like it if my da was dead and people were coming in to see him lying in a coffin and saying how sorry they were. That would be rotten.

I asked Liam if he was hungry. I knew he wouldn't say anything but I asked him anyway, just for the sake of talking to him, as if things were normal. But I wasn't stupid. And things weren't normal. The whole house was quiet with nobody in it but us.

'I'll make ye a piece, Liam, if ye want it, and a drink of milk.'

I looked into his blank eyes and I saw nothing. He was still like somebody who was dead with his eyes open, and I felt safe crying, because Liam's dead eyes couldn't see my red, wet eyes.

I went down the stairs and made four pieces of bread and jam and filled two cups with milk. I carried them upstairs to the bedroom. Liam was sitting there where I'd left him on the edge of the bed. I put the two pieces on his knee and told him to eat up. I put the cup to his lips and tried to pour some milk into his mouth, but it just dribbled down his front.

I felt sick and I felt bad and I felt lonely. I was beaten. I had no solution to any of this. There seemed no way out for me or for our Liam. And that was bad. It was the first time in my life that I knew that things were as bad as they could ever be: much worse than the worst days with Philson. Much worse than the day we were caught with no clothes on at the reservoir. Much worse than last night when Burnside and his bastards broke into our house and wrecked the place. And very much worse than the night in the chapel that I had to vomit on Billy and Cecil's trousers.

Nothing could be worse than how things were now. Our Liam could be mental, full time, and nobody was really bothering about him. They were too caught up seeing about other people who were not in our family. I couldn't understand it.

Again I pushed a bit of bread and jam into Liam's mouth, hoping he would eat it. It didn't stay in. It just dribbled out like before, with whatever milk was still in there, wee bits sticking to his lips. I knew that if he didn't eat and drink soon he would die.

'Dear God Almighty, what's happening here?'

I hadn't heard anybody coming up the stairs. But I knew Uncle Jimmy's voice. He hadn't listened to my ma about going over the border, either. I turned round when he came into the room with my da. And at the same time, I tried to clean up Liam's dribble with my hand, but it was too late.

'In under God, Barney, what's happened to the wain? Ye told me about the raid and about the place being wrecked and about Liam being a bit shocked, but ye didn't tell me about this.'

'He'll be all right, Jimmy, when he finishes the medicine. Our wee Liam'll be as right as rain. That's what the doctor said, Jimmy. It was that bastard Burnside, Jimmy, that shocked him like this, but when he finishes the medicine, he'll be okay.'

It was first time I had seen Uncle Jimmy crying. He stared at Liam and then at me and then back to Liam. And when he saw his dead eyes, he rushed forward to both of us and put his arms around us. I felt his tears on my cheek and saw him looking at Liam again, and I saw his body. Shivering it was, like somebody who was freezing cold. After about a minute or so, the shivering stopped and it was now *my* eyes he was looking at and not Liam's. 'Dickie,' he whispered, and he made me feel afraid, the way he spoke to me.

'Aye, Uncle Jimmy?'

'Now, what's this, Dickie, about Sergeant Burnside? Just tell me what ye told your da a wee while ago.'

So that's why he had really come back. For information. His voice was the same as the time that he told my ma that I shouldn't play with Billy Burnside. Sort of bossy. I didn't like it.

I told him everything I could remember about what Burnside and the other cop had said to me on Creggan Hill. And before I knew it, I was telling Uncle Jimmy the whole story as well about the night in the Wee Green, and about how dark it was except for the couple of minutes when the moon came out that night. And about the silhouettes of Joey and Peter that Bap and me saw running away after the shots were fired. But we didn't really know it was shots until the next day when we heard that Mr Colhoun was dead. And that we were the only two that knew, because the rest of the gang were leaving the Green and had their backs to us.

I had it all out before I knew it. But I was glad I told him, especially about the silhouettes, because if I hadn't, he would have known that I was holding things back from him.

I think now he was just testing me, for it wasn't long before I found out from him that Bap Kelly had gone through the same grilling as myself. Probably from his own da, who then told Uncle Jimmy to question me and to find out what I knew.

So when my da told Uncle Jimmy what I had said to him a while ago, he already knew the whole story, except for the part about what the cops had said to me on Creggan Hill. And I was thinking now that blabbing about this wasn't really blabbing. It was warning people. Real blabbing was giving things away, secrets I mean, that shouldn't be told.

But I wasn't a blabber and neither was Bap Kelly. Bap Kelly was just warning people as well. But it was murderers we were warning. That's what was now going through my mind. Warning murderers. And that didn't make sense at all. Not one bit. It might even be a mortal sin.

'Look,' whispered Uncle Jimmy when I'd finished speaking. 'Look, Dickie, youse know nothing, Son, you or young Kelly. Youse know nothing at all. That's what you've got to remember – youse know nothing. Youse saw some flashes when youse were playing in the Wee Green. Then youse heard some bangs. That's when youse got scared. And that's when youse all ran, okay? Youse heard somebody running, behind youse, mind you, but youse didn't look back. It was pitch black anyway and youse wouldn't have seen them because it was too dark. All this about silhouettes is nonsense. And stupid, because you can't see silhouettes in the dark. Isn't that right, Dickie? Isn't that the way it was? And isn't that what young Kelly told his da? And if that's all *he* knows, then that's all *you* could know, too, Dickie. Burnside's just trying to confuse you, Son, with his threats, trying to tie you up in knots about what you saw and heard. Don't heed the likes of that boyo. Sure look what he did to wee Liam and look what he did in this house. And if he asks ye again, Dickie, about any of this, just tell him ye saw nothing. And anyway, silhouettes aren't people – they're just silhouettes. Do ye hear me, Dickie? That's what young Kelly is going to say as well – that he saw nothing. Do you know what I mean, Dickie? Burnside's just trying to confuse ye. Do you hear me, Dickie?'

I heard him, all right. But I knew that it was Uncle Jimmy that was trying to confuse me, talking the way he was, about Bap Kelly telling his da that he saw nothing. For I knew that Bap would have told his da the truth about what we saw in the plots and his da would have told him as well that he couldn't have recognised anybody because it was too dark.

But Bap and me would never have told anybody else about what we saw. We wouldn't have blabbed. But this wasn't blabbing, telling our das and Uncle Jimmy, it was just telling them so that they would be warned. We trusted our das but they didn't trust us. And all this made me feel bad as well, especially the way Uncle Jimmy was bossing me. And now my da was talking the

210

same way. And I still couldn't get it out of my head that I was protecting murderers.

'He's right, Dickie. After what that bastard Burnside done, sure it's no surprise that he's trying to get you to say that you saw things when you didn't. He's just trying to turn the screw more, Dickie, after wrecking the house here and shocking wee Liam into the way he is now.'

They were making me feel worse, the two of them, the way they were talking down to me as if I were one of the Stupids, as if I didn't know what was going on, as if I had forgotten about the gun under the floorboards – the same gun that my da made me touch, the gun he swore me to secrecy about – and as if I didn't know now that it was the same gun that Peter and Joey had used to kill Mr Colhoun.

But even if it was my da and Uncle Jimmy, and not strangers who were talking to me like this, I had enough in my head anyhow without having to listen to them anymore. The tune would have to be changed. And I'd be the one to change it before I went mad altogether.

Change the tune I would. And quickly. Somehow. Some way. My brain began to work on a plan. And I was still thinking at the same time that even though loads of bad things were still crowding in on me at this minute, a lot more bad things were going to happen later. I knew that wherever my ma and the twins had gone with Peter and Joey, she was bound to have told the girls by now about how sick our Liam was. And I knew they would go mad when they heard, and more especially, when they came back to the house and saw the state he was in. They would blow their tops. That was the way the twins were. Always ready to explode.

But first things first. I mightn't be able yet to sort out what was to come later, but getting rid of Uncle Jimmy and my da right now would be a good start in clearing that part of my brain. The plan was coming. It began with shuddering sobs that soon produced tears down my cheeks. Hard dry sobs at first to get their attention. Then heavy, quick breathing with the eyes closed so as to give nothing away. I didn't bother about any snotters because I was sensing that the plan was working. I could see through the slits in my eyes that my da and Uncle Jimmy were backing off as well.

'Look, Barney,' whispered Jimmy, 'I have to go now. I think them two lads need a lot of looking after and I'm thinking, too, that young Dickie here won't say a word to anybody about what happened in the plots. I mightn't see youse for a while, till things blow over. Here, take this – it's for clothes and shoes for the wains here, and for food in case youse run short, and for medicine for wee Liam.'

Through the slits, I saw Uncle Jimmy handing two big, white £5 notes to my da. It was a fortune. I had never seen that much money before.

'Don't forget, Barney, this is for the house and the wains.'

'Right, Jimmy. Thanks for your help; and you've nothing to worry about on that score. I'll personally go down the town myself and get them what's needed.'

Before Uncle Jimmy left the room, I saw him taking one last look at Liam and me. And I didn't feel sorry that he was going or that it might be years before I saw him again. But two things were certain. One, I didn't want the cops to get him, and two, I'd have to make sure that the two £5 notes he'd given my da wouldn't be spent on Guinness. I might not be able to do anything about the first thing, but there'd be no problem, I was thinking, that the money would be in my mother's purse before too long. And I wouldn't have to blab on my da, I'd just make it happen, in my own time, in my own way.

Before my da and Uncle Jimmy were even at the bottom of the stairs, I was already in the bathroom washing the sweat and tears off my face. It had all been worth the effort. I was now ready for round two and I knew it wouldn't be long in coming.

Uncle Jimmy had hardly closed the glass door behind him when I heard my ma and the twins coming back into the house. The noise of them running up the stairs was like thunder. I heard my ma shouting for them to go easy and my da coming out of the living room at the same time and shouting the same thing after them. I hurried back into the bedroom to be with Liam.

CHAPTER 25

A Bit Of A Domestic Problem

'Oh, Sweet Jesus, what has the bastard done to our Liam?' That's the first thing I heard Kate saying. She was standing at the bedroom door with her fingers stretched across her mouth and her eyes staring at us.

'Dear God Almighty,' said Laura, 'look at our wee Liam, the wee darling. Dear God Almighty, Dickie, we only heard a wee while ago from Ma.'

They tip-toed across the room. Now they were kneeling down in front of Liam, looking at his face and trying to get him to talk to them. They were holding his hands and touching his cheeks and then hugging him, the two of them, but it didn't do any good. Liam's dead eyes still stared at the floor. I could have told them all about him, but they didn't ask me. They had to find out the truth for themselves.

'Oh, dear Jesus,' Kate said, her sobs getting louder and her whole body beginning to shake. I had seen Kate shaking before when she was annoyed about something, but never like this. The more she fussed around Liam the worse she got. Now her body was shaking with anger and rage. And I could see her sobbing face changing to a very angry face as she got up off her knees, letting go of Liam's hand. There was a mad look in her eyes, too, as she roared out of her, 'Right, right, this is it! He's not getting off with this. That bastard's going to pay for this. Are ye coming with me, Laura? To Burnside's?'

Laura didn't say anything, but her eyes were red with crying as she followed Kate out of the room. The noise of them squealing and shouting now as they rushed down the stairs was worse than when they had come up. It was even louder than thunder. The whole street must have heard them. I ran to the landing and looked over the banister rail. Then I went down the stairs a bit to see more. My da was standing at the glass door, his two arms stretched out, blocking it. The twins were still squealing as they tried to get past him. I could see my ma watching all this from the kitchen door. Her eyes were red with crying and she looked afraid.

'Now, now, now,' said my da, 'settle down now, girls. This isn't the way to go about things.'

But the girls squealed even louder, shouting at my da to let them past. But he wouldn't give in.

'He's going to pay for this!' roared Kate. 'That bastard's not getting off with this! Let us past, Da.'

They began to pull at him, trying to drag him out of the way. If it had been me trying to get out, I would have headed for the back door. But the girls mustn't have been thinking straight at that time.

'Ssssh, ssssh, ssssh,' whispered my da at them as he tried to calm them down. 'This isn't the answer. Not this way, girls. We'll see to Burnside later.'

'We'll see to the bastard now!' shouted Kate. 'Right now!'

And that's when it must have struck them that there was another way out of the house. Still screaming and roaring, they both turned, pushed past my ma and ran through the kitchen and out the back door. My da went down on his knees in the hall, his head in his hands. I heard him moaning something. I saw my ma turning to go after the twins. I didn't think she would be able to stop them. I had never seen such a scared look on her face. Not even when she was sick.

I had to see what was going on. I felt excited but very afraid at the same time. Bad things were happening again. And there was nothing I could do about it. This was a very serious time for the McCauleys, and I was stumped. Everything seemed to be out of my control – again. It made me feel useless.

Before running down the stairs and out to the front street to see what was happening, I went back into the bedroom to check on Liam. After I tidied around his mouth and cleaned up the mess of bread and jam on the floor, I whispered to him that I'd be back in a few minutes. He didn't bat an eyelid as I worked around him. Nearly everything was dead about Liam. But my da was right – the way the girls wanted to get back at Burnside for what he had done to Liam wasn't the right way. It could only make things worse. And probably would, the mood the girls were in. But what was the right way? Even *I* didn't know.

By the time I reached the street, the twins were banging on Burnside's door and shouting. My da was out there, too, watching. My ma followed me out and stood beside my da in the middle of the road.

Burnside opened the door. He still had his cop uniform on. The girls rushed at him, screaming and hitting out at him. Before he fully realised what was happening, they had scraped his face. You could see blood running down his cheeks. He'd put his hand up to save himself, but it was too late. They'd sunk their nails into him.

My da was shouting at the girls to stop. It was all happening in seconds. He rushed forward and tried to pull the twins away from Burnside, but he fell back onto the road. People were coming out of their houses to watch what was happening. Some of them laughed when they saw my da falling. But it wasn't funny – not to me anyhow. I didn't feel excited any more, just sick to my stomach. I was embarrassed as well, and very, very fearful. The twins could be arrested and put in jail for attacking a cop.

Burnside had now got his wits about him, even though Kate

and Laura were still punching out at him. He pulled out his baton and started to hit the twins. They fell back a bit, putting their hands up to save themselves, but Burnside kept swinging his baton at them. They kept screaming and shouting at him that he was nothing but a black bastard. I could see some blood on them.

'British bastard!' somebody shouted from the crowd that had gathered. 'Leave them girls alone!'

That's when my ma ran to help them but she only got in the way and he hit her, too. Her head was cut, the blood running into her eyes. She fell back and landed beside my da, on the roadway. She was screaming. I looked around at the crowd. I knew most of them. I saw Kevin with his ma. He had his Rosary beads out and his face was dead white. Danny was there, too, with Mrs Lardo. I saw him shouting and calling Burnside a bastard. I'd remember that.

Now everybody seemed to be shouting, just as Burnside was beating my ma and the twins away from him, but out of the side of my eye, I saw my da rising up from the road, roaring like a bull. The crowd hushed as we all stared at him rushing towards the cop with his head down. Before Burnside had time to do anything, my da had head-butted him in the stomach. The two of them went crashing onto the porch floor, and as my da kept beating him with his fists, the crowd began to cheer.

I didn't know then if I should feel scared for my da or proud of him. I think at that moment, I felt both. I felt proud of the way he'd got up off the ground and tackled Burnside when he saw what the cop was doing to my ma and the twins. But I felt a bit scared about what might happen after this, because you could get into very bad trouble if you fight with cops. He was still punching Burnside's face when their glass door opened. Mrs Burnside and Billy appeared from the hallway. When she saw what was happening, she looked very frightened. She put her hand up to her mouth, shocked, seeing her husband being beaten by my da. Billy started to cry.

That's when Mrs Burnside shouted, 'Stop, stop, the two of youse! What's this all about anyway? Have youse no respect at all? Do youse not know there's a man lying dead next door? In under God, what's got into youse?'

'Get into the house, woman!' Burnside squealed at her.

She backed into the hallway, pulling Billy after her. She didn't close the glass door. She just stood and watched as my da began to slowly rise off Burnside. He still held the cop's throat with one of his hands. Aye, I felt proud of him the way he had beaten the bastard and the way everybody in the street had seen him doing it. Even my ma and the twins were standing there watching everything and you could see that they were proud of him as well.

As my da began to release Burnside from the grip he had on him, I moved closer to them, because the two of them were saying things to each other. It was more like muttering than talking. Nobody else could have heard them. But I did. From my da it was like a sharp hiss out of the side of his mouth. Spittles were falling from his lips as he spoke and his face was covered with sweat.

'If our Liam doesn't come out of this, ye bastard, the state youse have left him in, I swear to God that I'll kill ye with my bare hands.' He was breathing very heavy, but I heard every word and I couldn't believe he was threatening a cop. This was bad, but there was a lot more to come. Burnside lay there gasping for breath, but he was still able to say something. It was now the cop's turn to hiss.

'Ye haven't heard the last of this, McCauley. Your day's coming. Aye, and the rest of your bunch, too. And it's coming sooner than ye think.'

I saw my da's fingers tighten again around Burnside's throat. Now I felt really scared. If he strangled the cop, they would hang him. 'Da,' I whispered, 'Da, we have to go home. Liam's waiting on us.' I don't know why I said that, or how it came to me, but it did the trick.

218

My da loosened his grip on Burnside's neck and half-turned to me. I could smell the sweat from him and I could see Burnside's eyes bulging with fear. He turned back to the cop. Burnside had no choice but to listen. My da still had him half-pinned down and he hissed some more.

'If that's a threat, Burnside, I hear ye, but let me make ye two promises. The first is that if there's one arrest after this night's carry-on, there'll be another funeral from this street within the week. The second is that I won't tell your good wife after your funeral what a lying, cheating, thieving bastard ye are. The docks police have ye well sussed out, with your whoring and paying for your pleasures with confiscated goods. It's only a matter of time, Burnside, before you're nabbed.'

I looked at the cop's face, the face of a beaten man in more ways than one. I had never seen anybody so shocked and scared in all my life, not even at Cnoc na Ros when we were electrocuting Marlborough boys. I didn't fully understand what my da had said to Burnside except for the part about him being a lying, cheating, thieving bastard. I knew what all those words meant because I had used them all myself at different times.

As my da got up off Burnside and was dusting himself down, another fear gripped me as everybody's heads turned to the sound of heavy running boots coming from the top of the street. A whole bunch of cops was coming towards us with batons in their hands. The crowd hushed and moved back, waiting to see what would happen next.

This is it, I thought. *The McCauley family are all going to be arrested – all except Liam and me – arrested and thrown into jail.* I could see it now: my ma and my da being taken in handcuffs and the twins being dragged away screaming, and Mrs Lardo coming and ordering us about in the house for a million years, the same way as she orders Danny. This is it. The end of the world for me. But that's not the way it worked out. My da's threat to Burnside saved the day.

'What's up, Sergeant Burnside? Are ye having some trouble here? We had a phone call to the barracks.' It was the cop who had been with Burnside earlier when they threatened me on Creggan Hill. I recognised him.

'Naw, I'm fine, Constable. It's just a bit of a domestic problem here. It's all been settled. Just get this crowd back to their homes. Everything's under control.'

And that was it. As simple as that. The crowd moved away. Doors banged closed. The cops moved back to the barracks and Burnside turned quietly into his own house and closed his front door behind him. But not before I saw the hateful look he gave my da, and not before I saw the bruises and scrapes on his face, and his bloody nose.

And for the rest of my life I knew that I had missed out on doing something that I should have thought of at the time: when my da had Burnside pinned to his porch floor with a stranglehold around his neck, I should have gathered the makings of two spits from the back of my throat, and when Burnside was least expecting an attack, make two direct hits, one to each eye, like a red-hot poker. It would always have reminded the big bastard that if he ever felt like threatening me again, he should think twice, and then forget about it.

I followed my ma and da and the twins into the house. Everybody was very quiet. Nobody asked me if I wanted anything to eat, so I just went up the stairs to see to Liam and put him to bed. Then I went to bed myself. I'd give my ma the two £5 notes tomorrow. I'd tell her that they dropped out of my da's pocket when he was fighting with Burnside. The truth was that it had been a good opportunity for me to take the two fivers out of his pocket when he had more serious things to be doing.

Before I fell asleep, I was thinking that this must have been one of the worst days of my short life so far, even if I had been to Confession twice.

CHAPTER 26

Cops Aren't Afraid – They've Got Guns

It was Saturday morning, and not one of our adult neighbours was in the street. They were all probably peeking out their windows at what was going on. But Danny and Kevin and me were out and we watched everything. It was brilliant.

Four men dressed in black suits and top hats carried the coffin out of the Colhoun house. Mrs Colhoun and Cecil came next. They were dressed in black, too. Mrs Colhoun's face was red with crying and she kept wiping her eyes with a hankie. Cecil held her hand. A whole bunch of people followed them out of the house. They were probably relatives, I had never seen them about before.

About twenty B-men in uniforms lined each side of the road and saluted as the coffin was pushed into the hearse. One of the horses did a dung and Danny sniggered. There were four horses altogether: two for the hearse and two for the passenger coach. They were all shiny black and had plumes on their heads. Cecil and his ma began to get into the coach. A man helped Mrs Colhoun and then lifted Cecil up and through the door. He banged it shut behind them.

The street was packed with strangers who must have been friends of Mr Colhoun. They were all dressed in black and some of them wore bowler hats. The rest just had ordinary hats or caps. Danny whispered that the boys with the bowler hats were Orangemen. I shushed him in case anybody would hear him, but I knew he was right. They didn't have the orange sashes on now that they wore every year in July and August when they marched down the hill from the B-man's hut. Then they always marched in rows of six across the road and followed the band that was playing Protestant music.

They were called Orangemen after King William of Orange, who was a Dutch king. I read that in a book Uncle Jimmy gave me. King William beat King James at the Battle of the Boyne in July 1690. The Boyne is a river in County Meath in Ireland. King William was a Protestant and King James was a Catholic, so it was the Protestants who won, even though it was the Pope who asked King William to fight King James. When I asked my da about this, he just laughed and said it was one of the great inglorious mysteries. I didn't know what he meant, so I just forgot about it. Until now.

We followed the funeral down the hill. It turned right at the crossroads next to the cathedral and Jack McDaid's shop and headed slowly over the Lone Moor Road past Ramsay's post office to the cemetery. Big Burnside was standing at the junction, directing traffic. He saluted when the hearse was passing him. He had red marks on his face. Barney McCauley marks, and scratch marks from the twins.

Kevin had his beads out. He was whispering the Rosary to himself.

'What are you doing, Doherty? You don't say the Rosary for Protestants,' said Danny.

'You do so.'

'You don't. Protestants don't do the Rosary.'

'He's dead,' said Kevin. 'He's not a Protestant anymore.'

'Protestants are British. They fight Catholics,' said Danny.

'RUC men aren't British, they're Irish,' Kevin replied, still muttering his prayers at the same time.

'They're not.'

'They are. They were born in Ireland. That makes them Irish.'

'What're Billy and Cecil?' I asked.

'Billy and Cecil are Irish,' said Danny. 'They'll just become British when they grow up.'

'That's stupid,' I hissed. 'Now shut up.' He didn't.

'It was the British who broke into your house the other night. They wrecked it looking for stuff.'

'What do you mean looking for stuff?' I said angrily.

'Guns and things. My ma said your da's in the IRA,' sneered Danny.

'He is not!'

'That's what my ma said.'

'Your ma has a big, fat head and she's thick all over as well.'

'My ma said that Big Burnside'll be back. They'll wreck your place again.'

'They won't.'

'They will. Your da beat him up and he'll get revenge.'

'He won't. My da told me that Burnside's going to be sorted out. He'll be afraid to come back.'

'Cops aren't afraid,' said Danny. 'They've got guns.'

I was thinking then that Danny might be right. 'Burnside's a bastard,' I said.

'I know,' replied Danny. 'My ma said that, too, and she said that your Liam could be mental for good because of Burnside.'

'Shut up,' I said. 'Our Liam's not mental. He's sick, and my da said he'll be better soon when he finishes the medicine.'

By this time, the funeral was nearly out of sight, so we turned and began walking up the hill again. Kevin asked us to join him in a decade of the Rosary for our Liam, to make him better. I said okay.

'In the name of the Father and of the Son and of the Holy Ghost,' Kevin began.

'Amen,' we said.

'Thou, O Lord, wilt open my lips.'

'And my tongue shall announce Thy praise.'

That's when Danny farted. Two accidental farts. Fat people fart when they can't help it. Danny and me laughed. Kevin didn't. That's when the praying stopped, and when we just kept quiet. We knew we were in the wrong. It was bad timing, Danny blurting off like that.

'It's a sin,' shouted Kevin, 'laughing at somebody farting, especially when you're in the middle of the Rosary and somebody's getting buried!'

It was then I started thinking about what Kevin was saying. He was right, it wasn't nice to be laughing when Cecil's da was dead and was this very minute being taken to the cemetery, and probably by the time we got home, he would be buried in a hole in the ground. Naw, it wasn't right, and it wasn't fair, either, that our Liam could be mental for life and my ma's new baby was dead. And it wasn't fair that Bap Kelly had only one eye. And it wasn't fair that Danny Doherty's da had been killed by a cow in the slaughterhouse.

When we were heading home up the hill, nothing seemed to be fair to me, especially when none of it was my fault. Danny and Kevin must have been thinking sad things as well, because they were very quiet, too, the rest of the way home.

Chapter 27

I'd Have To Buy My Own Comics Now

It was early on Sunday evening and things were very much quieter and calmer in our house after everything that had happened over the past few days. Me and my da were in the living room.

'You didn't tell me about the letter from the school, Dickie, about the scholarship examination next year,' said my da as he turned the music down on the wireless.

'I forgot, Da. It's in my bag. I'll go and get it.'

'Young Charlie Kelly's da was telling me about it. He said there's only about six or seven of youse going in for it.'

Kate and Laura sniggered.

'Smarty-pants,' said Kate.

'Brain-box,' said Laura.

I wasn't sure how to react to the twins after the beating up of Burnside and their part in it. And them being the girlfriends of murderers. I didn't reply to them. I didn't even heed them. I walked out of the living room to go upstairs. Liam was standing in the kitchen beside my ma. She was washing the dinner dishes. He wasn't speaking or anything. I said a prayer into myself that Liam would get better. I hated to think he would go mental for good.

'Hello, Ma!' I shouted. 'Hello, Liam!'

She turned around. 'Dickie, would you take Liam upstairs and get him ready for bed? I know it's early, but he needs the rest. That's what the doctor said.'

'I will, Ma, but I have to get something for my da first.'

'Just take him now, Dickie. Your da can wait.'

She looked very tired and very pale as she was speaking and she turned Liam around and pushed him towards me. He didn't speak as I guided him into the hallway and up the stairs. He was still stiff as if he didn't want to go anywhere. I kept talking to him all the time, but he said nothing. His eyes were still dead in his head.

'Right, Liam, sit down there,' I whispered as I pushed him towards the bed. 'I'll get ye ready in a wee while.'

Something was up. Something else was wrong. Something very bad. I knew it by the look on my ma's face and the way she spoke to me. Whatever it was, my da or the twins didn't know about it yet, but I had a feeling that before the night was over, everybody would know. I left Liam sitting on the bed, and before closing the door behind me, I told him that I'd be back soon to see about him and to tuck him in. I took the scholarship letter from my schoolbag. It was a good excuse to go downstairs again.

My ma was still in the kitchen, finishing the dishes. She didn't hear me as I walked towards her. I wanted to try to find out what was wrong.

'We were at the funeral yesterday, Ma, me and Danny and Kevin. Mr Colhoun's funeral, well, just down as far as the cathedral.' As I spoke, she jumped, turning to me in a frightened sort of way. She looked terrible.

'God save us and bless us, Dickie, you scared the wits out of me, there. Did you put our Liam to bed?'

'Yes, Ma,' I lied. She turned back to the jaw-box. 'We just went as far as the Lone Moor Road, Ma. Cecil and his ma rode in a carriage. It was like a stagecoach, Ma, only swankier. And there was a whole bunch of Orangemen there but they had no orange sashes on them like they do at the Twelfth, and there wasn't a band or anything.'

I was talking stupid stuff. It was coming out of my mouth before my brain had it properly sorted. But I wasn't finished yet and I couldn't seem to help myself. It was as if I didn't want my ma to say anything about what was worrying her.

'Will Mrs Colhoun get the Gwyns now for Cecil?'

'What?'

'The Gwyns, Ma. Will Cecil get the Gwyns?' My ma stared at me. Her blank eyes were a wee bit like Liam's. She didn't answer.

The Gwyns was charity money you got if your da was dead and if you had no money to buy food or coal or clothes or shoes. You got it off Gwyn's Institute down in Brooke Park. There was a museum in it as well with stuffed birds and animals in glass cages. It was scary, sometimes, looking at them.

'What Gwyns?' my ma said. 'What are ye talking about, Son?' Her eyes were still blank and she was still very scared looking, so I just shut up about the Gwyns.

'When will Liam get better, Ma?'

Her blank eyes were still staring at me, but this time she spoke: 'Soon, Dickie, soon. When he finishes his medicine. Maybe next week.'

'Will Big Burnside come back, Ma?'

'Naw, Dickie, he won't. Your da sorted all that out.'

'Danny Doherty's ma said he'd come back, Ma, and he'd wreck the house again.'

'Danny's ma has a big mouth, just like the rest of her,' laughed my da as he came up behind me in the kitchen. I hadn't heard him, but he tickled me under the arms as he spoke, and that made me laugh. But I didn't want to laugh, I just wanted to find out what was up with my ma. And now I couldn't because of my da. I think she would have told me if he hadn't come into the kitchen and spoiled everything. But maybe it was my own fault, blabbing away about Mr Colhoun's funeral and about our Liam and about Big Burnside and about the Gwyns. Maybe if I'd just come down the stairs and asked my ma straight out what was wrong, she might have told me. I mightn't be such a brain-box after all; mightn't even be a smarty-pants. I might be a Ballybunkumskite, a nincompoop, or as near as there is to the Stupids.

'Here, Da. Here's Mr Philson's letter about the scholarship.'

'Right, Son – just what we were talking about in there, the twins and me. Just you do that wee exam and let me and them and your ma worry about where the money'll come from for books and things. Just you concentrate on your schoolwork and leave the rest to us.'

You could smell Guinness off him as he spoke. That's when I put my hand into my pocket and produced the two £5 notes. He stared at them, eyes wide open. 'Talking about money, Da,' I said, 'these two fivers fell out of your pocket on Friday when you were fighting with Burnside. I forgot to give them to you because of all the hullabaloo. Better late than never, Da.'

He stared at the fivers in disbelief. He must have been wondering all this time what had happened to them. Without a word, my ma reached forward, took the notes from me and put them into her apron pocket. My da said nothing but he looked embarrassed. Just then, the noise of a lorry in the street and loud voices coming from beyond the glass door distracted us. I turned and ran outside. My da followed, but only as far as the front door.

A crowd had gathered. There was a large furniture van outside Big Burnside's. Two men were carrying stuff from the house. They put it into the van and went back into the house again for more. Danny and Kevin and Cecil and Billy were standing there watching. I moved closer to them. Big Burnside came to the front door and looked up and down the street. He had his cop's uniform on, gun and all. Up close, his cuts and bruises looked a lot worse. He turned and went back into the house. It was Danny who asked the questions that I wanted to ask.

'What's happening, Billy?'

'We're moving house.'

'Why?'

'I don't know.' Billy's face looked sad.

'When are ye going?'

'Today.'

'Where are ye going to live?'

'I don't know.'

'Will ye be going to the same school?'

'I don't know – they didn't tell me.'

'Will ye be able to come up and see us some time, after ye move?'

'I don't know. It might be too far away. If I can.'

Billy began to cry, quiet like, to himself. We didn't say anything else to him. He moved up to his front door without saying anything else to us, either. Maybe it was better that way, after everything that had happened with his da and my da and the twins, and my ma as well, and our Liam, and even with me. But I knew in my heart, and I felt sad about it, that my best friend, Billy Burnside, couldn't help having a big bastard for a father. And I felt sad for his ma as well, because she was a nice woman.

It seemed to take hours for the men to load the van, but as soon as they did, they banged the back doors closed and drove off. Within a couple of minutes, a police car pulled up beside Burnside's house and parked where the van had been, and within another minute, Mrs Burnside and Billy got into the back seat. We were standing close by, but even though she saw us, she didn't smile at us as she normally would. Big Burnside got into the front passenger seat and as the car moved off, Billy started to wave at us, but his ma pulled his arm down.

'Will we ever see him again?' whispered Kevin.

Danny and me didn't say anything because we didn't know whether we would or not. What I *did* know was that I'd definitely have to buy my own comics now. And I had a lump in my throat, too.

The crowd began to move away as the car turned the corner and headed down the hill. Danny's ma and Kevin's ma were standing near Burnside's house, looking up the street as the police car disappeared. They spotted us. Danny's ma's big, fat arms were folded as she spoke. 'Right, Danny, be in before dark.'

'And you, too, Kevin,' said the other Mrs Doherty. 'Youse can play for another hour.'

I didn't feel like playing with anybody. I turned to go home, but I was near enough to Mrs Fatso Lardo to hear what else she was saying.

'Imagine everything happening like that the way it did. Ye could hardly imagine it, could ye, the B-man getting buried yesterday, and Burnside having to leave the street today because of Barney McCauley, and—'

'Aye,' interrupted Kevin's ma, 'and then them two poor souls getting shot dead last night out at Killea, them two friends of the twin McCauleys.'

I felt sick and weak as I listened. I couldn't believe what I was hearing.

'Aye, just about fifty yards from the border they were, on the tar road. The B-men were waiting for them in the ditch. Riddled them, they did. Mrs Kelly from the Bogside came up this afternoon to tell Kitty McCauley. She heard the whole story.'

'Aye, sure I was talking to Mrs Kelly when she left McCauley's house. It must have been a terrible shock for Kitty and then her having to tell the twins and all. And Mrs Kelly was telling me, too, that if them two young fellas had reached the border, there was a van there waiting to drive them safely away, God rest their souls.'

As I was walking back to the house my head was spinning with the thought of Peter and Joey lying dead in pools of blood, and if they were now in Hell or if they had confessed their sins before leaving Derry. I said a quick silent prayer that they were not in Hell.

'Well, what's happening?' said my da when I reached our front door. He must have been standing there all the time. I hardly heard him. My head was spinning.

'What?'

'What happened up there?'

'Up where, Da?'

'Where do you think, Son?'

'They're away, Da.'

'I know they're away. But where are they away to?'

They're away to Timbuktu, you big, fat, Guinness-smelly slob. They're away to live next door to the Kellys in the Bogside. They're away to live in a tree house in Killea. They're away to Gwyn's Institute to sleep in the museum with the stuffed animals for the rest of their lives. You know nothing, Da. You know nothing about anything. All you're good at is drinking Guinness and annoying my ma. You're not even fit to be told by my ma that Peter and Joey are dead. No wonder she's standing out there in the kitchen washing the same dishes all day the day.

He had a bottle of Guinness in his hand and he began singing *Kevin Barry*. I walked past him into the house and straight out to the kitchen. My ma was sitting at the table drinking a cup of tea. Her face was still white and her eyes were red from crying. I could hear the twins in the living room, singing along with the music on the wireless.

'You'll have to tell them, Ma. You'll have to tell them about Peter and Joey.'

She put her two arms out and reached for me and pulled me to her in a tight hug. I could smell snuff from her. I didn't know she snuffed. She must have got some from Danny's ma or Kevin's ma. She sobbed as she spoke.

'I will, Dickie, I will. I'll tell them in a wee minute. Just give me another wee minute.' She didn't ask me how I'd heard, but

I wanted to be there for her when she told them, so I went into the living room and closed the door behind me.

'Here comes the wee genius,' laughed Kate.

I said nothing. The music was still playing on the wireless.

'So you've seen the Burnsides off, have ye, Dickie?'

I just nodded.

'Furniture and all?' asked Laura.

I nodded again.

'Well, it won't be long before there's another cop in there,' sneered Kate.

'They wouldn't do that,' laughed Laura. 'Not after what happened.'

'Mark my words,' said Kate, 'that's a police house, so they're bound to put another cop into it. Them bastards never give up.'

'Well, anyway,' Laura went on, 'Burnside's a goner. We'll not be seeing *his* big face in the street any more.'

'Burnside's not dead yet,' snarled Kate, 'but his day's coming, just like the B-man's.'

I felt sick listening to them. If only they knew about Peter and Joey lying dead on the Killea Road, riddled with bullets and the blood flowing out of them. The same as the blood flowing out of Mr Colhoun in the plots. If only they knew at this minute what my ma knew and what Danny's ma and Kevin's ma knew and the Kellys knew and, more than likely, what Uncle Jimmy knew, because it was probably his van that was on the other side of the border. If only they knew, they wouldn't be talking the way they are now. They would be crying and sobbing and squealing the same way that Mrs Colhoun did the other day when she was told that Mr Colhoun had lain dead all night in the plots.

Aye, the whole thing was a mess. And I had no way of clearing it up. And even if I could clear it up, would I want to? It wasn't my mess. That's what Father Mooney had told me. None of this mess was my fault.

But the crying and the sobbing and the squealing started earlier than I thought, because the music on the wireless had stopped for the news, and after talking about what was happening in the war in Europe and a few other things, the newsreader revealed it all to the twins:

'And now to Northern Ireland, from where we've received reports that two IRA men were shot dead late yesterday evening by police auxiliaries near the border between Londonderry and Donegal. According to a police statement, the two men in question, Peter Clifford and Joseph McCarroll, were wanted for questioning for the recent murder of Special Constable Colhoun. When challenged to halt, only yards from the border, they each pulled a gun from their pockets and began firing at the special constables. The two men died instantly from a hail of bullets from the defence forces.'

Before we even heard another item of news, Kate and Laura turned to each other, shock on their faces. The two of them had gone pure white.

'Ah, naw, God, it couldn't be!' cried Kate. 'Naw, not Peter and Joey, surely to God not. Not our Peter and Joey!' Kate's cry now changed to a squeal. 'Dear God Almighty, it can't be them! Not my Peter.'

'Oh, Dear Jesus!' squealed Laura. 'Dear Jesus Almighty! Joey.'

At that minute, my ma came into the living room. The music was back on the wireless, but you could hardly hear it because the squeals of the twins got louder and louder.

'Ah, naw, naw, naw!' screeched Kate as she sank to the floor on her knees.

I stood there gaping as Laura knelt down beside Kate and threw her arms around her. I felt useless again, not able to do anything or say anything. I was lost for words. I must have been a sight standing there watching my two sisters. And as usual, I got the blame. Everything was my fault. Everybody's mess was my fault. I was the villain again. I was useless. I was the stupid nincompoop. At least that's the way my ma saw me as she clipped me round the ear with one hand and switched the wireless off with the other.

'Get up them stairs, Dickie McCauley, and don't come down till I tell ye! Can ye do nothing right?' she shouted, her eyes blazing at me.

'But, Ma—'

'Don't talk to me! Get out of this room now, and let me see to the twins!'

She was blaming me again for something I hadn't done. But she'd be the sorry one when they told her they'd heard it on the wireless and not from me. There were so many angry thoughts, bad thoughts, spitting thoughts, going through my mind as she nearly took the hand off me when she slammed the living-room door after pushing me roughly into the hall. That's the way I felt but I wouldn't really have done or said anything bad to my ma. I had spat on my ma only once in my life and I'd sworn then I'd never do it again.

Before going back up the stairs to Liam, I thought I might go out to the porch to tell my da the bad news about Joey and Peter, but when I saw his silhouette through the glass door, and him drinking the Guinness from the bottle, and his hoarse voice still singing *Kevin Barry*, I turned instead and walked slowly up the stairs. From behind the door in the living room, the loud moans of my mother and the screeching of the twins still reached me, even as far as the upstairs landing. To shut it all out, I closed the bedroom door behind me with the intention of quietly getting Liam ready for bed.

But Liam was already in bed. His shoes and socks and clothes were lying all over the floor. Instead of being annoyed with him, I was delighted. And excited. I could hear my heart thumping. Liam had got himself ready and he was now in there with the blankets pulled around him. Normal like. His eyes were closed, not staring like they had been. I felt like crying and I felt like laughing and I felt like running downstairs to tell everybody the good news, but I didn't. It wasn't the right time to do that. Instead, I walked across to the bedroom window and looked out.

It was still daylight, but it would be dark in less than an hour. I could see the men over the wall, in Brooke Park, doing something with the big ropes attached to one of the barrage balloons. I couldn't imagine Hitler's aeroplanes smashing into those barrage balloons. It would be stupid for everybody: the pilots getting themselves killed and then the planes crashing down on the houses in Rosemount and the bombs exploding as well, killing hundreds of us. Naw, that would be silly.

And down the street a bit, I could see Danny and Kevin leaning against the air-raid-shelter wall, probably talking about silly things. The workmen had finished the job yesterday when they put on the cement roof. It had been brilliant watching them pouring the wet concrete into the wooden frame. It would harden in two days. That's what they said. And everybody agreed it would make a great hideout for the gang. But it would take weeks for the inside to dry out. That's what they told us as well.

Kevin said he'd get candles, because it would be dark in there, day or night. Danny said we could capture some Marlborough boys, weaken them with shocks at the electric wire at Cnoc na Ros, and then torture them again, by candlelight. I told him to shut up.

None of them knew that I might be doing the scholarship exam for the College next year along with two of the Marlborough boys. And one of them, Harley, had told me he was glad that we took the corrugated iron from the Wee Green, because the cops had called at his house and told his da that the tunnels were dangerous and would have to be filled in. Harley had asked me as well about our Liam, and when I told him how sick he was, he said he would light a candle for him. How could I torture a boy like that again?

A big furniture van passed slowly beneath my window. It wasn't the same one that had taken Big Burnside's stuff away, but it looked as if it was pulling in at Burnside's house. I had to open the window to get a closer look. I was right. It stopped outside Burnside's.

By the time the two men got out of the van and opened the back doors, a big, black car pulled up behind it. A cop got out of it, and a woman. She must have been his wife. Two wains got out of the car as well – a girl about the same age as me and a boy the size of our Liam. Our Kate was right. It wasn't long at all before another cop was in the house. He opened the front door. His wife went in first, then the girl and boy, and then the cop himself. My da must have been watching what was happening as well, because as soon as the cop closed the front door behind him, he started singing *Kevin Barry* again, this time loud enough for the whole street to hear him.

I closed the bedroom window in case the noise from my da would waken Liam, but, instead, it was the noise of the window slamming down that wakened him. And I was glad, because he began to speak for the first time since the raid. I stayed at the window, with my back to him. I didn't want to rush at him and hug him in case he went blank again. I felt excited hearing him but I had to stay calm.

'Dickie,' said Liam, 'can I join your gang?'

My eyes filled with tears. My whole body began to sob, the way a baby's does. It seemed ages before I could reply. It was as if it were a dream, not really happening. It was as if somebody else should be there in the room, some big person who could take charge, right now, right this second, and say all the right things to Liam, to make sure that everything would be okay. I felt a bit scared.

Just as I was answering Liam, I noticed that Danny and Kevin had moved away from the air-raid shelter. They stood across the street from Burnside's, watching the two men carrying furniture into the house.

'Aye, Liam, you can join the gang. How would you like to be in it right now, right this minute?'

I turned around as I spoke. Liam was half-sitting up in bed, leaning back on his elbows. His face was lit up with a big smile. The dead eyes were gone. Our Liam was better.

'Honest, Dickie?'

'Aye, honest, Liam. You're in the gang from now on.'

Liam flung the bedclothes off him, shouting his thanks as he rushed across the room. He nearly knocked me down with the hugs he gave me. Then he pushed himself off me and looked at my face.

'Were you crying, Dickie?'

'Naw, Liam,' I lied. 'I was laughing a wee minute ago. The tears were running out of me laughing at Danny and Kevin. They were down at the air-raid shelter talking away, but when they saw the wee girl belonging to the new cop, they soon moved up to get a closer look. That's what I was laughing at, Liam. Danny and Kevin looking at a girl.'

He laughed at first, then his face got serious again. 'What new cop, Dickie?'

I watched his face as I replied, praying into myself that his good humour would stay and that he was better for good.

'The new cop that took over from Big Burnside. Big Burnside's away, Liam. They sent him somewhere else. Somewhere away from our street.' For a few seconds, Liam stared straight into my eyes. My heart sank.

'I'm glad he's away, Dickie. I didn't like Big Burnside. He's a bad man.'

My heart rose again. Our Liam was back on the right track. He was talking sense. Big Burnside *was* a bad man.

'And, Dickie?'

'Aye, Liam?'

'Can I go with all youse to swim in the Killea Reservoir next year?'

'Ye can, Liam.'

I was looking out of the window again because I didn't want Liam to see my red eyes and the tears in them, but a million things were happening in my mind that I would have to sort out. And the first thing was the gang.

'And will youse take me to see the man with no legs that lives in the tree house?'

'We will, Liam.'

Billy was definitely out of the gang, and maybe Cecil, too. Bap Kelly was the boy to fill Billy's shoes. I'd tell him tomorrow.

'And, Dickie?'

'Aye, Liam?'

'Can we jump from the tar road at Killea onto the stony road in Donegal? The thing ye told me about?'

'We'll do that, too, Liam.'

It was nearly dark outside, but it was still light enough to see Danny and Kevin leaning against the barracks wall, watching the new cop's daughter kicking a tube and cover against the air-raid shelter. And she looked nice, too. Her fair hair was bobbing up and down each time she kicked the ball, and not once did she miss it. She was good. Maybe better than Billy Burnside. And definitely better looking. That's when I decided that she'd be in the gang, too, even though the rule was that it was only boys who could join. But it was me who made up the rules, and anyway, there was nobody else around to take Cecil's place if he didn't come back. And even if he did, the girl was still in the gang. What I say goes.

'And, Dickie?'

'Aye, Liam?'

'When I'm old enough, can I go a run with you in Uncle Jimmy's van?'

'When the war's over, Liam. After the war.'

'Fuck the Germans,' said Liam.

I laughed when he said that, because that wasn't the war I was thinking about. And I wondered once more if it was a sin to laugh when somebody said 'fuck'. I'd have to remember again to ask Father Mooney about that, at next week's Confession. And I'd write it down tomorrow on my new sin list in case I forgot.

But there were a few other things I knew I had to do before I went to bed, just some of the million things that were still on my mind. And because the squealing and the moaning noises and the sound of my da singing *Kevin Barry* had all stopped downstairs, I thought it might be a good idea first if I brought Liam down to the front hall to play a game of some sort. Somebody in the house was bound to hear us sooner or later. And when they did, it would mean more tears. But this time they would be good tears.

That's part of what I was thinking anyhow. And I was never too far wrong. It was a brilliant plan – the best yet.

'Right, Liam,' I said. 'Bring the Tiddlywinks downstairs to the hall, and when I'm setting them up, you can swing on the glass door.'